St. Clair drew Grabowski to a quieter place near the wall, but she hit her hip against the desk and lost her balance. Sleep deprivation was hitting hard tonight, she thought, or maybe it was that ridiculous red drink. She took a step backward to steady herself, but instead caught her leg on something, then completely lost her balance and fell over backward.

At that moment, a loud crack like a pistol shot echoed through the crowded room. Someone screamed.

St. Clair scrambled to her feet and looked around wildly to figure out where the sound had come from. For an instant she couldn't see where everyone was looking. Then she did. High in the vaulted ceiling, the wire tying the giant wooden-chair mobile to the beam had snapped. Freed from its bond, the huge unbalanced sculpture started to fall. The chairs seemed to drop in slow motion, like a huge, brightly painted snowflake. Slowly, quietly, the sculpture fell toward the black piano and the sculptor still sitting with his hand on the keyboard.

"Look out!" St. Clair screamed. All over the room others were shouting, "Look out!"

But the chairs dropped faster and faster, collapsing with a splintering crash on the piano and on Soren Berendorf, master sculptor.

Also by Janet McGiffin
Published by Fawcett Books:

EMERGENCY MURDER

PRESCRIPTION FOR DEATH

Janet McGiffin

FAWCETT GOLD MEDAL • NEW YORK

A Fawcett Gold Medal Book
Published by Ballantine Books
Copyright © 1993 by Janet McGiffin

Library of Congress Catalog Card Number: 93-90536

ISBN 0-449-14881-5

Manufactured in the United States of America

First Edition: December 1993

CHAPTER

1

MAXENE ST. CLAIR was sitting in the red plastic armchair in the supply room behind the ER nurse's station at St. Agnes Hospital. She was wearing her usual summer work clothes—cotton print skirt and blouse topped by a lab coat—and her short red hair was unruly from the high humidity. She was staring moodily at her bloated feet propped on the third shelf where the blue toweling wrapped in sterile paper provided a comfortable ankle rest. Maybe stronger support hose might reduce the swelling, she thought. Elevating them wasn't helping.

"Something happens to the body after forty," she commented to Shirley, the overweight nurse who ran St. Agnes' ER from three to midnight. "Systems break down, starting with the veins."

In her case, the circulation problem was increased by potato chips, a Reuben sandwich from Tony's Café, ninety-degree heat and humidity, and eight straight hours on her feet in the ER. All had conspired to balloon out her legs and her fingers, although without the wedding ring, it was hard to tell.

She had only worn the ring two years, and it had been off nearly a year now, but the finger still seemed naked without it. It wasn't the man she missed, it was the security of the partnership. For once in her life, there was a back-up income, a shoulder to lean on, someone to face the world with. For two short years she had stopped wondering what she would do if she were in a car accident or seriously ill,

1

and without those worldly pressures, she concentrated fully on her academic research at Marquette University. The concentration had paid off with a series of well-accepted papers and a renewed research grant. Not that she had been a worrier before she was married, but single women thought about things like darkened doorways or disability insurance—things her married women friends did not.

Her marriage had been neither satisfactory nor long—double doctor alliances rarely lasted—but her glimpse of the solid marital base was hard to forget. She had left the marriage and the research position at Marquette at about the same time, to take a breather as ER physician at St. Agnes, but now when she saw a wedding ring on a woman's finger, she felt a twinge of longing. Maxene St. Clair's brief marriage hadn't soured her on the institution. Rather, the experience had reaffirmed her conviction that humans were born to live in pairs.

"Two more hours and you can put your feet up and keep 'em there," said Shirley, stretching her heavy black arms and straining the fabric of her white nurse's uniform dangerously across the back. "And lay off the potato chips if you're going to drink beer like you do. Look at those legs, honey. Didn't they teach you in medical school what happens to people who eat too much salt?"

Maxene St. Clair frowned at her swollen ankles and puffy feet. "I promised Dr. Hochstedder that I'd go to his wife's art exhibition tonight after work."

"With those legs? Are you crazy?"

"What can I do? Dr. Zelazak said his wife has some artwork there, too. All the doctors are going. It's at a gallery that's run by some doctors' wives."

"You mean a bunch of doctors will be sitting around telling each other how great they are."

"Don't start, Shirley. Some doctors don't care about money and power."

"Easy not to care when you've got it."

Shirley dragged a gray metal folding chair into the doorway of the supply room, positioning it to view the outside doors to the emergency room. The ER was empty now, but emergency rooms in Milwaukee's inner city didn't stay quiet long. Shirley lowered her large posterior into the chair and took a harsh look at her own legs. Their swollen appearance was more related to obesity than to salt intake. Her rolled stockings creased the heavy flesh above her knees.

The pneumatic doors to the ER hissed. Shirley looked up and scowled.

"It's that pimp, Rolondo. You stay put while I see which poor girl got beat up working for him tonight."

St. Clair put her head back, closed her eyes, and ran her fingers through her rebellious red hair. Her whole body longed for bed. Even though tonight had been a slow Saturday, the rest of the week had been heavy. The usual shootings and stabbings had increased to an appalling rate; then yesterday's thunderstorm had overflowed the storm drains and the subsequent street flooding caused a rash of car accidents. One was fatal. None of the ER staff had had a chance to sit down yesterday, and last night St. Clair had been too tired to sleep well. She woke groggy and sluggish, a condition that worsened as the day went on. Even the frigid blast of St. Agnes' air-conditioning hadn't perked her up. Shirley worked the same hours but didn't seem fatigued. What was her secret, St. Clair wondered, dozing off. Maybe it was a decent sex life. Shirley was always bragging about her husband, Roy.

The scrape of Shirley's folding chair woke her with a start. It wasn't Shirley, however. It was Rolondo, the pimp, who had reversed the chair in the doorway and was straddling it, facing her.

"Hi, Doc," he said, flashing a gold front tooth.

Rolondo was the best-dressed and best-paid pimp in the inner city, according to him. His higher-priced prostitutes worked out of apartments; the rest worked the streets. Tonight Rolondo was wearing a pale blue linen suit with black shirt and black tie. His tight curls had been recently trimmed, and his black face gleamed with after-shave.

St. Clair didn't return the smile. "Can't you protect your girls at all?" she snapped. "Why do they keep getting beat up?"

Rolondo adjusted the break of his trousers and straightened his tie. His calm expression did not waver.

"You're tired," he said. "The slavery my people knew wasn't nothing compared to what sister Rosalie puts you through. But that's no reason to take it out on me, now is it?"

St. Clair closed her eyes and counted to ten. When she opened them again, Rolondo was still gazing calmly at her. She sighed.

"I apologize," she said. "In fact, it's considerate of you to drive your injured workers down here instead of making them take the bus. You're a real humanitarian, Rolondo."

"Thank you."

"Which poor girl is with you tonight?"

Shirley stuck her head in the door. "Ain't no girl here," she snapped, glaring at the pimp. "This dude just dropped in for a chat. And he can drop out again. Get your ass out of my supply room, pimp. These chairs are for people who work."

Rolondo ignored her. His calm gaze shifted to St. Clair's puffy feet, still propped comfortably on the third shelf. "You should take better care of them legs, Doc. Ain't nobody gonna look twice at a woman with legs of an elephant."

St. Clair lowered her swollen feet to the floor and slipped them into her sturdy brown leather sandals. She adjusted the cotton print skirt to cover her knees. "Thanks for the tip. Is that what you came in to tell me?"

Rolondo smiled, approving. "Perking right up. I like that. 'Cause I got a favor to ask."

Joella Rodriguez, the receptionist, appeared behind Rolondo in the doorway, her blue eye shadow fluorescent. She was wearing a pink leather miniskirt, purple tights that matched her silk blouse, and pink sandals with four-inch heels. A white lab coat topped the ensemble. She was holding two cups of coffee, one of which she handed to St. Clair. The other went to Rolondo.

"What's up, dude?" she asked, giving him the high sign.

"One of my ladies is sick."

"I didn't see you with no lady."

"She's at home. Needs a doctor to look at her."

Shirley choked. "You're asking Dr. St. Clair to make a house call on a prostitute?"

"My lady is a person like anybody else."

"Of course she is." Maxene frowned at Shirley.

Rolondo pushed harder. "Lady's real sick. Won't sit up. Can't even talk straight."

"How long has this been going on?" St. Clair took a sip of the coffee and grimaced at the bitter taste.

"Late this afternoon, is what I heard."

"Did you call the public health nurse?" It was a half-hearted attempt to stave off the request. Milwaukee Health Department nurses visited homes in the inner city every day carrying stacks of hospital and clinic referrals. Sometimes they brought sick or injured people to the ER in their own cars; then, after the patient had been discharged, they made a home visit and sent St. Clair a follow-up report.

In the last few years, though, public health nursing salaries had dropped in relation to other nursing jobs in Milwaukee, and drug-related crime had made the inner city dangerous even for the blue-uniformed nurses who traditionally were left in peace. Now twenty-four nursing positions were open, and many inner-city schools rarely saw a public health nurse sitting in their nurse's room.

"A nurse came by. Said take her to the hospital. But lady won't get out of bed," said Rolondo.

"Call an ambulance."

"She wants you."

St. Clair groaned. After nearly a year of working in the ER, she had met many of Rolondo's prostitutes. They came to St. Agnes ER when they were beat up or sick, even for pregnancy and post-abortion checks. She hated to think of a girl lying ill in one of Rolondo's apartments. Rolondo made his prostitutes work no matter how sick they were.

"Can you wait an hour and a half?"

"I'll be back." He rose elegantly, picked a caramel from the box of chocolates on Joella's desk, and disappeared from view. The outer doors hissed.

Shirley sat down in the metal chair and looked sternly at St. Clair. "That girl probably lives in the worst part of the city, and you're going there at night?"

St. Clair already regretted her decision. Violence in the inner city had escalated over the last few years, and cross fire from random shooting was a serious hazard day or night.

"How could I say no?" she argued, trying to convince herself. "The girl is one of Rolondo's victims. Do I have to make her the victim of a medical system, too?"

Shirley tightened her lips. "Have it your way, but I'm coming with you. Else I might have to break in a new doctor."

Joella propped a trim hip against the doorjamb and began applying mascara to already heavily encrusted lashes. "That's new for Rolondo. I've never seen him worried about any sick hooker."

Shirley scowled. "Don't you be thinking he's a nice guy. Profits are down, that's all."

Joella left to answer the phone. "For you, Doc," she smiled. "It's that cute detective of yours, Joseph Grabowski."

St. Clair's late-night fatigue vanished. She hadn't seen Grabowski in weeks. They had met in the ER one night about six months before when he had appeared with a gunshot wound in his upper arm.

The professional relationship had relaxed into a personal one, especially after Shirley and Joella noticed that St. Clair's post-divorce blues evaporated whenever Grabowski was around. Joella made a few phone calls, unknown to Maxene, and Grabowski had started dropping into the ER. He said he came to make sure the violence outside hadn't blasted through the white hospital doors, but he always managed to arrive near shift's end, when a quiet after-work drink soothed them both.

They went out to dinner a few times; then St. Clair got caught up in one of Grabowski's investigations. The relationship had pulled her completely out of her post-divorce doldrums. But then Grabowski's work schedule changed: he was working when she was free, and vice versa. She missed him more than she wanted to admit.

"Grabowski! Are you coming by?"

"I'm stuck on a stupid security assignment." He paused. "I'm actually calling to find out if a friend of mine got hurt and showed up in your ER. His name is Wyoming Syzinski."

"His real name?" She laughed.

"His mother has a great sense of humor. We grew up together on the south side of Milwaukee, then he went to art school in San Francisco and settled in Arizona. Last spring he wrote he was coming home for a while. He was only back two weeks when the idiot disappeared. Even his sister doesn't know where he is." Grabowski's voice sounded weary and worried.

"How long has he been gone?"

"More than a week. He stayed with me a couple days; then he said he found a great place with the right rooms for a studio. I haven't seen him since."

"Maybe he got busy."

"We were supposed to meet here tonight and he didn't show. I called headquarters to find out if he got mugged or was in an accident, but all they said was that he's collected twenty-five parking tickets. They're about to issue a warrant."

St. Clair thought over the patients she'd seen in the last week. "He hasn't been here on my shift; Wyoming isn't a name I'd forget. Joella can go through last week's records in case he came in on another shift, and she can call Admitting to see if he was admitted any way besides the ER."

"I appreciate it, Max. He's a nice guy but not sensible. Artists—they live in another world."

St. Clair hung up slowly.

"Did he ask you out?" Joella was examining her purple lipsticked mouth in a small mirror.

"He's working."

"That's what happens when you fall in love with a cop." Joella went back to work on her eyelashes.

"I'm not in love," St. Clair said, without conviction.

A wave of discouragement washed over her. Most of it was the fatigue that came near the end of a nine-hour shift, she knew, but at this hour it was hard to separate tiredness of the spirit from tiredness of the body. During her shift she concentrated on not allowing herself to admit she was tired. Denial was the trick to her life over the last year, too. Discouragement and other feelings could be ignored until they changed, she kept hoping, like people believed they would get well if they simply ignored their illness.

She realized suddenly she hadn't mentioned to Grabowski that she was going to visit one of Rolondo's prostitutes tonight. She felt guilty about the omission, but Grabowski already didn't like her working in an inner-city ER and was likely to send a squad car to go with her. St. Clair didn't want police protection. She would be with Shirley and Rolondo. Inside his own territory, Rolondo was king.

An ambulance pulled up, the doors hissed, and Dr. St. Clair went back to work.

Rolondo appeared when her shift ended at midnight. He let his white Cadillac idle by the emergency room doors while Maxene tossed a blood-pressure cuff, stethoscope, percussion hammer, and respirator mouthpiece into her purse. She and Shirley walked out to the dark parking lot and got into Maxene's yellow Nissan Sentra. The car was still oven-hot from the day, and as they drove deeper into the inner city, the car grew hotter. The air conditioner had broken the week before, and St. Clair had been too tired to take it in for a shot of Freon. Now the fan only blasted hot air. Shirley cursed under her breath and hung a heavy arm out the window.

The scorching heat of the city streets had cooled, though, and traffic had expanded. Stretch limos, Cadillacs, and red Porsches with black leather seats cruised the streets. St. Clair followed Rolondo's white Cadillac as it drifted in and out of traffic going north on Twenty-fourth Street toward Center Street. The heat in her car was intense, and as she turned onto Center Street, she noticed a red light on her control panel. The engine-temperature arrow had moved all the way to "H."

Shirley was fanning herself with a parking ticket she had picked off the dash. She pointed at the red light. "How come a well-paid doctor like you can't buy a new car?" she complained. "Ain't it enough your air conditioner is busted? Your engine got to overheat, too?"

St. Clair eyed the warning light. "Aren't you supposed to turn on the heater when your engine overheats? Cools the motor or something."

"Do that and I'm getting out," said Shirley. "I don't want no heat stroke."

"Maybe the radiator needs water. Is there anywhere to stop?" The warning light seemed to be getting redder, if that was possible.

Shirley snorted. "In this part of town? You'd lose your purse and worse in five minutes. I don't know what you're doing down here, honey. That hooker can get herself to a hospital. Welfare pays for ambulances."

St. Clair too had lost faith in her decision to make a house call in the heart of the city after midnight, especially since Rolondo's taillights were receding faster than she could keep up. She listened for the sound of her engine, but the boom boxes on the sidewalk and the radios in passing cars drowned the noise. She stepped on the accelerator but got no response. The car had died. She coasted it over to the curb by a fire hydrant.

"First the door handle, then the air conditioner, now the engine," she muttered, trying to start it again.

"Be glad I'm with you, honey," Shirley said ominously. "Ain't safe here for no white person this time of night, especially no woman. Put your purse under your arm tight and take hold of me. We'll find a phone and call Roy to come get us, if he ain't out drinking someplace."

A cab drove by. St. Clair jumped out of her car and waved her arms. The cab accelerated. "Hell," she said, and slammed the car door.

Shirley was waiting on the sidewalk, a frown on her normally impassive face. They stood looking at the open doors of the string of taverns down North Avenue, hoping for a phone booth. As they waited, a trio of young men came up behind them, one carrying a boom box turned up full volume. The noise made the air vibrate. Maxene felt her purse move under her arm. She tightened her elbow and moved closer to Shirley.

"Is there going to be a problem?" she murmured, annoyed to hear her voice tremble.

Shirley glanced over her heavy shoulder at the trio. Her deep voice rose easily above the boom box. "You gonna snatch my bag, you snatch it good," she warned them, "because if you grab and miss, I'm going to kick your ass all the way to Twenty-fourth Street."

Resignation sank over St. Clair. She could almost feel the knife blade in her ribs.

"Must we die over a handbag?" she murmured, closing her eyes. "Let's give them our purses and buy new ones."

Shirley's thick arm shook with laughter. "Open your eyes, honey. We gonna live."

A white Cadillac had pulled up in front of them smooth as silk, and the window rolled down, revealing the calm features of Rolondo. The lock on the back door popped up, and St. Clair let Shirley and herself in.

Rolondo accelerated smoothly into traffic. "That beater of yours finally die? You want me to have it stripped so's you can get the insurance?"

St. Clair leaned back into the soft leather. Cool, aftershave scented, air-conditioned air wafted over her, and a sense of well-being replaced the panic. She smiled. "Why not?"

Rolondo's sick employee lived in a three-story brick apartment building half a block from Isaac Coggs Community Health Center and down the street from the 5th District Police Station. The building had been beautiful decades before, when German immigrants built the neighborhood north of the downtown. The brick front steps were laid in an intricate pattern, and brick planters flanked the entry. But now rough cement patched the cracks in the brick steps, and broken vodka bottles littered the planters.

An oval piece of heavy beveled glass in the front door showed a spacious front hall with a ceiling high enough for a chandelier. A bare light bulb hung there now, and the cove molding was heavy with dirty cobwebs. The mosaic tile floor was chipped, and decades of grime had rounded the corners of the foyer. The heavy front door was unlocked.

Maxene and Shirley followed Rolondo's Italian leather shoes up the dingy wooden steps to the third floor. Like the other landings, this one was illuminated by a bare bulb hanging from a frayed wire. There were two apartments, one on each side of the landing. A curtain of black beads shrouded the door on the right. The beads rattled as Rolondo pushed open the door.

The apartment was dark and cooled to refrigeration temperature. The carpet was deep and red, muting the heavy jazz that bubbled from the stereo system in the front hall. A faint red glow came from the living room where the color of the red leather couches was made even more intense by heavy rose-colored shades on the two brass table lamps. Black, sequined pom-poms dangled from the closed curtains. The air was heavy with incense and boiling chitlins. St. Clair choked, then covered it by clearing her voice.

Shirley inhaled appreciatively. "Somebody here knows how to cook."

Rolondo led the way down the hall past a tidy kitchen

and a bathroom redolent of perfume, to a small room that had probably been a linen closet when the building housed families that used linens. The light from the hall showed that the room held only a cot. The air reeked of vomit.

Shirley flicked on the light switch, but the overhead bulb didn't go on. After St. Clair's eyes got used to the gloom, she could see a young black woman lying very still on the bed.

"Can you find me a flashlight?" St. Clair asked Rolondo.

He went into the kitchen and came back with a candle and some matches, then disappeared down the hall. Shirley lit the candle and held it over the bed. Behind her gathered three women, anxiously peering into the room.

"What did the public health nurse tell you?" St. Clair asked the group of women. She sat gingerly on the edge of the cot.

"She came about four-thirty," said one. "Said Latoya needed a doctor bad."

"Anybody else sick here?"

"Somebody always be sick, but not like this." The woman dropped her voice to a whisper. "Latoya was seeing things. Lights, colors, drawings on the walls."

Shirley groaned. "What was she on? The truth, now."

"I never saw her take nothin'."

St. Clair felt for the woman's arm under the sheet. The skin was cold and damp with perspiration. The woman was quiet. St. Clair felt a sudden dread shoot through her. She fumbled for the pulse on the woman's wrist.

"Hold the candle over here," she told Shirley. She tilted the woman's chin back and felt for the carotid pulse. She grabbed the stethoscope from her purse and hurriedly put it on the woman's chest. She waited, holding her breath, concentrating for the sound. Candle wax dripped on the sheets. She finally picked up a faint heartbeat. The woman was barely breathing. She rolled her onto her back and lifted an eyelid, but the room was too dark to tell whether the pupils were dilated. She took the percussion hammer and tapped gently on the girl's wrist. No reflex. She stripped back the sheet and tapped on her knee. The lower leg didn't jump forward as it should.

"She doesn't look good," said Shirley.

St. Clair shoved the stethoscope and hammer back into her purse. "Let's call an ambulance."

At the kitchen table Rolondo was having a beer and a plate of chitlins. St. Clair picked up the wall phone and dialed 911.

Rolondo stopped chewing. He sat, fork in midair. "What's wrong with her?"

"I don't know." St. Clair spoke briefly into the phone, explained the situation to the ambulance dispatcher, then dialed St. Agnes and asked to speak to Dr. Malech, her ER replacement.

"The ambulance will bring her to St. Agnes," she told Malech. "She's completely unresponsive, and her vital signs are minimal. It could be rat poison that got into the food; it could be a virus. The women here say that she's the only sick one, but the population in this apartment changes hourly."

She hung up and started back toward the sick woman's room. The squeal of brakes stopped her. On the street outside the window, something was happening. There was another squeal of tires and something else that sounded like a car backfiring. Only it wasn't a car, not backfiring that many times. It was gunshots.

CHAPTER

2

OUTSIDE ON THE street in front of the building, the shots repeated, five, six times. Then the squeal of tires came again, along with the screams. Doors and windows started banging all over the building. People were shouting. Someone in the front room of Rolondo's apartment was yelling, "Rosa! Rosa!"

St. Clair ran to the front room window. Below and slightly to the side, two people were lying on the steps to the apartment building, half sprawled across each other. The woman's arm was stretched out toward the door, as if she had been trying to get inside and had fallen before she could get the door open. The man was lying sideways across the steps, as if he had turned to look at his attackers. A bag of groceries lay on the sidewalk, its cans and packages spilled across the dirty cement.

The man was white, and the woman was black. From the street lights, St. Clair could see that the man was wearing jeans and a white shirt. The woman was wearing a mini-skirt and cropped T-shirt. People were beginning to gather around the bodies, including Rolondo and Shirley. St. Clair ducked back in the window and ran for the stairs.

By the time she got outside, Shirley had unbuttoned the man's white shirt and was holding her handkerchief over a bullet hole that was bubbling blood just below and to the left of his rib cage.

St. Clair's face felt numb. Her breath was coming in short gasps, with not enough in each gasp to bring her brain

14

air. The ground was spinning. Her heart was pounding so hard that it sounded like guns, more guns, or maybe the gunshots were in her ears and she would hear them forever. Vomit stung the back of her throat. Someone was groaning. She crouched on her hands and knees on the steps, trying to get air inside her lungs, trying not to throw up. She felt someone shaking her arm, hard. It was Shirley.

"Pull yourself together!" Shirley snapped.

The groaning stopped. It had been her. Air started to come in larger breaths. The nausea subsided, and the pounding in her chest grew softer.

"How can this happen?" she whispered.

Shirley's lips were tight. "Just take a look at these two. If they're lucky, they might live."

Airway, breathing, cardiac. The ABCs of cardiopulmonary resuscitation were the first step of first aid. The man's airways were open, his nostrils flaring very slightly, and his chest rising faintly. The pulse on his neck and wrist was faint but steady.

She turned to examine the girl.

She had been shot in the back where nothing but her shirt had obstructed the bullets. Two holes were slowly oozing blood from her shoulder. She was breathing very slowly.

St. Clair fumbled in her own purse for a handkerchief and covered the wounds in the young black woman. She started looking for more bullet holes. As far as she could see in the dim light there were only two.

The wail of the siren appeared in the distance and came rapidly closer. It stopped with a wrench of brakes; the doors flew open, and two ambulance attendants lifted out a stretcher. They gently examined the young woman, then lifted her onto the stretcher and wheeled it toward the ambulance. "Anybody know this woman's name?" demanded the driver, gazing around the crowd.

Rolondo nodded, shortly. "Rosa." He watched without expression while the attendants lifted her into the van.

"And the man?" The driver was writing in his notebook. When no one answered, he carefully patted the man's jeans pockets and dug out a wallet. He flipped it open.

"Syzinski," he read. "First name, Wyoming. That's a new one."

St. Clair's jaw dropped. She stepped forward to get another look at the victim, already being lifted into the ambulance. "Wait!" she said. "I know this person. I mean I know who he is."

"You coming to the hospital?" the ambulance attendant demanded. "If you are, I won't take all the information now."

"I'm coming. I'm a doctor," she added, climbing into the ambulance after Syzinski.

"Stay out of the way," the medic ordered. "We're going to put the other victim in here, too. They called us for another one upstairs, some kind of poisoning. Although," he amended, looking at the white face of the wounded man, "I'm going to call another ambulance. These two can't wait."

The trip to St. Agnes took less than ten minutes. St. Clair stared at Wyoming Syzinski's ashen face and wondered what he had been doing that got him to a street where he would be gunned down in an aimless drive-by shooting. When the ambulance doors opened at St. Agnes, she found Dr. Malech ready with the crash cart, two interns, and the X-ray technicians.

"Portable X ray, stat," he ordered, "Type and cross-match blood. Start IVs."

St. Clair stepped out of the way and watched the medical team go to work. In only minutes the patients were X-rayed, hydrated, and dressed for surgery. The two gurneys swished through the doors.

St. Clair sat down in Joella's chair and picked up the phone with a shaking hand. She took two deep breaths and dialed police headquarters, a number she knew well from months of returning Grabowski's social calls. The switchboard operator said Grabowski was out on a case. St. Clair didn't want to leave a message.

"This is Maxene St. Clair. I need to talk to Grabowski."

The operator was apologetic. "I should have recognized your voice, Dr. St. Clair. Grabowski is downtown at an art gallery; he said he was waiting for a call from you."

St. Clair wasn't sure she heard right. "An art gallery?"

"He's overseeing a private security operation. It's a big party of some sort; and the gallery owner wanted a cop there besides her own guards."

"What's the name of the gallery?"

The operator laughed. "Rhinestones, if you can believe that. It's on the East Side, downtown."

"Rhinestones? That's where I'm supposed to go tonight!"

"Then you can find him in person." The operator sounded relieved. "I'll try to call him on his beeper, but he's been impossible to reach all evening. I don't think he can hear the beeper; the noise there must be incredible."

St. Clair hung up, then hunted through the phone book for the number of the gallery. The phone rang fifteen times. Finally someone picked up the receiver. St. Clair could hear party sounds, loud voices, someone playing the piano.

"Can you get me Detective Grabowski?"

"Who?"

"A police detective. Grabowski."

"Is he in uniform?"

"No."

"Then I can't help you, my dear. There are literally hundreds of people here, and there's no way I could find anyone." The phone went dead.

St. Clair slammed down the receiver. She flipped to the yellow pages for a taxi, then looked up to see Rolondo and Shirley leaning against the counter.

"I followed the ambulance," Rolondo said. "They got both my ladies here now."

He paused while they listened to the murmur of voices behind a curtained exam table. "You all be wanting a ride home?" he continued. "Your car being stolen and all. I'm driving Shirley."

St. Clair smiled slightly. "I do," she admitted, "but I'm not going home. I'm going downtown to find Grabowski to tell him about his friend being shot. He's at an art gallery named Rhinestones."

The white Cadillac was parked in the loading zone in front of the hospital, motor running. St. Clair sat in front, the air-conditioned breeze aimed at her throat.

"Rhinestones is downtown on the East Side," she said to Rolondo.

"I know where it is," he said testily. "Nice gallery, if you like that kind of stuff."

St. Clair raised an eyebrow. "You into art?"

"Not all people of color think naked women on black velvet is art. Besides, ain't much about Milwaukee I don't know."

St. Clair felt embarrassed. "What else do you know about Rhinestones?"

"It's run by a couple of white women. They started out a few years ago with some home-painted junk. Now they have better."

Rhinestones was located on a narrow side street in the gentrified East side of downtown Milwaukee. Carefully understated shops with tasteful antique-lettered signs were tucked among galleries, boutiques, and restaurants. All were dark except for the brightly lit Rhinestones.

A group of people were standing on the sidewalk, smoking. The women were wearing black cocktail dresses, the men in summer suits, their jackets slung over their shoulders. They stopped talking and watched St. Clair climb out of the Cadillac.

"Maxene?" one of the women asked tentatively as the Cadillac slipped into the night. She was smaller than St. Clair, with short, curly, dark hair and heavy shoulders. She was wearing a black sheath with spaghetti straps that emphasized the heaviness of her shoulders.

St. Clair peered at her through the darkness. The woman

looked familiar although not like any doctor Maxene knew. She probably wasn't a patient either, since St. Clair's patients tended to come from the inner city and didn't wear understated black cocktail dresses. Possibly she was from Marquette University where St. Clair had spent six years as a professor, doing research. Then she recognized the woman. She was Dr. Hockstedder's wife, one of the artists St. Clair had come to see.

"Lillian?" St. Clair guessed.

The woman nodded. Her eyes slid over the wrinkled, bloodstained cotton dress. "Was that your chauffeur?"

"Hardly. Lillian, there's an emergency," she said. "I'm looking for a police detective who's working here tonight. Got any idea where he is?"

"There's a detective here?"

"Never mind. I'll look inside." She hurried to the door.

The air-conditioning and voices hit her with a blast. Masses of well-dressed people jostled white-jacketed waiters. Someone shoved a gallery brochure at her and she put it into the pocket of her dress. The noise made her head ache. Maxene pushed through the people until a space opened, and she found herself standing next to a black lacquer grand piano.

The piano squatted in the center of the gallery where the ceiling was two stories high. An open balcony ran around the second floor. A huge sculpture hung directly over the piano, suspended by a wire that ran upward through a large metal hook in the central cross beam. Then the wire ran across the ceiling over the crowd, through another hook on the ceiling by the front wall of the gallery, then down the wall to end behind a gleaming ebony reception table.

The sculpture hanging from the wire was made of about twenty-five wooden chairs painted bright primary colors and nailed together at odd angles. The entire sculpture was nearly fifteen feet square and swayed slightly like a giant mobile in the breeze from the air conditioner.

Underneath it a thin man sat at the piano, playing idly

with the keys. He was wearing a black shirt and black jeans and the melody he played rose faintly above the crowd.

The man's hands caught Maxene's attention. They seemed too big for his arms, and his head seemed too big for his short body. As he played with the keys he chatted with a blond woman wearing a red dress with fringe on the hem. She was leaning against the piano, intent on the man, oblivious to the crowd. Her black high-heeled sandals had gold chains instead of leather straps, and she wore a heavy gold chain around one ankle. She rubbed one foot against the other as if she were scratching mosquito bites. The man laughed.

"That's the sculptor himself at the piano," said a voice at St. Clair's elbow. "Soren Berendorf. And that's Kitty Zelazak with him, Dr. Zelazak's wife. She does watercolors."

St. Clair turned with relief. It was Louie, who rented the downstairs flat in the Milwaukee duplex bungalow where St. Clair had moved the year before. Louie owned the antique shop next to Rhinestones. He was an unabashed art groupie and spent as many evenings as possible at art gatherings, dressed to the teeth.

Tonight Louie's black satin trousers gleamed like his black opera pumps, his chartreuse silk shirt was open to the third button, and a large, flowered, silk scarf was knotted loosely about his throat. The scarf was anchored to his collar by a gold scarab pin with glittering emerald eyes. Louie was biting his nails.

"Have you seen Detective Grabowski?" Maxene demanded. "I have to find him. It's urgent."

"Is Grabowski that good-looking Polish cop you go out with? Lots of dark hair and a mustache, teensy bit thick around the middle? He's here somewhere." Louie waved his hand vaguely.

St. Clair stood on her tiptoes to see through the crowd. There were too many people to locate anyone specific. She found herself watching the sculptor who was now holding the hands of the woman in red. The woman was trying to pull away.

Louie held up two fingers touching. "Soren and I are like this," he said, beaming. "He let me help put up his exhibit. Every sculpture had to sit in exactly the right place. And hanging the big one up there, let me tell you, it was a doozy."

He handed her his cup of red punch. "Taste it," he commanded. "I call it Sailor's Delight. My own brew."

"I can't," St. Clair protested feebly, looking at the vivid red liquid. "I'm hunting for Grabowski."

"Trust me. You'll love it."

St. Clair took a cautious sip. It was sticky sweet and loaded with vodka. "Sailors Take Warning is more like it." She coughed.

Louie beamed and modestly changed the subject. "Isn't the tension just fabulous in that big wooden piece over the piano? The off-symmetry, the clash of color and imbalance, the attraction and repulsion of gravity and weight. And the title—'Disappearing Art'—perfect! It's never the same from moment to moment, the way each chair moves separately and individually."

St. Clair frowned. The swinging movement of the chairs was making her queasy.

"I don't like it," she confessed. "It's not symmetrical. But I'm here for Grabowski. One of his friends was shot tonight."

Louie looked interested. "Try the upstairs galleries or the basement. It's a big exhibit and he could be anywhere. They had a few threats."

"Threats?" St. Clair craned her neck, searching the crowd.

"Some group sent letters saying they hate Soren's exhibit and want to burn it up. So Rosalyn, the gallery director, hired private security guards. Your policeman is supposed to make sure they're doing their job."

St. Clair couldn't see Grabowski. Her watch said nearly one A.M. On the balcony, someone tossed a handful of glitter over the railing, then more handfuls. The glitter caught the bright lights and turned the air into a million sparkles that swirled in the breeze from the air conditioner. The sparkles drifted over the sculpture, gilding the bright primary colors. A drift of sparkles floated upward and clung to the nearly invisible taut wire that held the sculpture high over the lacquer piano. The wire became a silvery line that appeared suddenly, as if unmasked, a cobweb over the crowd. Some glitter drifted downward onto the piano like a coat of silvery snow and became sequins on the black shirt of the sculptor at the keyboard and on the red dress of the woman leaning over him.

The noise of the crowd stilled as the sequins descended. It was the biggest crowd Maxene had seen in an art gallery. Even the balcony was jammed with people chatting, drinking, and staring at the huge sculpture that dangled just out of their reach. She decided to look upstairs for Grabowski, as Louie had suggested.

When she started pushing through the crowd toward the spiral steps, however, someone gripped her arm. It was Dr. Hochstedder. His yellow tie was loose, and his navy blue sports jacket hung crookedly. His normally pale face was shiny red, and beads of sweat stood out on his upper lip. His thin graying hair poked upward.

"Maxene St. Clair," he leered at her. "Whatever are you doing here?"

"You invited me. I came to see your wife's exhibit."

She disengaged her elbow from his fingers and kept looking through the crowd for Grabowski. Hochstedder leaned close; his breath reeked of wine.

"Lillian's got a little exhibit upstairs that she's pretty proud of. I don't understand it." Hochstedder swayed and tossed off the rest of his red wine.

"You don't understand why she's proud of it?" St. Clair edged away.

"I mean I don't understand 'em. They watch you at night like cats. Their eyes glitter."

A waiter walked by with a tray of filled wineglasses.

Hochstedder studiously selected one and placed his empty glass in the same spot. He leaned forward and put his lips next to her ear.

"They could be real."

"Quite an illusion," St. Clair said. "You'll have to excuse me. I'm looking for a friend of mine. One of his friends was shot tonight."

"Who?" Hochstedder hung on to her upper arm to steady himself.

Maxene pried off his fingers and answered, just to make him let go of her arm. "The person I'm looking for is Detective Grabowski, and the person who was shot was Wyoming Syzinski."

"Wyoming?" Hochstedder fumbled his wineglass and splashed red wine over her sleeve. "That's a funny name."

Again St. Clair firmly removed his hand from her arm, then started up the steps to the galleries.

People were sitting on the open winding steps, eating hors d'oeuvres off pink plates. The circular balcony on the second floor was scalloped, making shallow alcoves over the main floor. Groups of people clustered in the alcoves to look down at the black lacquer piano, the sculptor, and the woman in the red dress.

Off the balcony were four small galleries. St. Clair pushed through the crowds and scanned the first three rooms quickly, without paying much attention to the art exhibits. Joseph Grabowski was nowhere.

One room remained. Because of the crowd St. Clair couldn't see into the room at all until she had edged through the people blocking the doorway. When the last man stepped aside, she gasped.

The exhibit was all busts sitting on pedestals, stylized and nonhuman but still more starkly real than any she had ever seen. They even had skin tones—some white, some black, some dark brown. Their eyes glittered like glass. They seemed to be spectators at their own personal exhibition, visitors watching the crowd with secret and distant expressions.

Some were women and some were men. All were human scale, but they seemed larger, or smaller, Maxene couldn't decide which. Maybe it was because they sat so detached—no bodies, just a faint semblance of shoulders under a neck. They carried a silence with them that made the noise of the crowd drop away.

One sculpture was of an Asian woman, or possibly a Native American, Maxene decided, forgetting about Grabowski in her amazement. She crossed the room to take a closer look. The bust was of a woman young enough to have soft flesh around her mouth but old enough for lines at her eyes and suggestions of ropy tendons at her neck. Her hair was sculpted of clay. Across the room it had looked real, but up close Maxene could see it was clay with lines etched to suggest long hair pulled into a bun at the nape of the neck.

A man with bushy gray hair and distinctly protruding ears was staring at it closely.

"They're just the size of real heads, aren't they?" he said. "Amazing technique."

St. Clair nodded, wondering if he were a sculptor. She was about to ask when Louie came up behind her.

"Like heads on stakes," he said.

St. Clair jumped, startled. Louie stood next to the sculpture facing St. Clair, and made his face blank, like the expression on the face of the sculpture. St. Clair shuddered.

"It's almost as if there's someone in there trying to say something," she said.

But Louie's attention had been caught by someone behind St. Clair. He waved energetically.

A tall woman with helmet-smooth black hair was standing in the doorway. She was so thin that her shoulder blades showed through her white sheath and white lace jacket. Her cheekbones stood out like wings on her narrow face, and her mouth was a thin red line. She threaded through the people in the room, smiling a tight smile, nodding at a few people, touching others on the back or arm.

When she reached Louie, however, her pleasant expression vanished.

"Where's that detective?" she snapped.

"He's around somewhere. What's the problem?"

"He's supposed to be keeping an eye on things, and I haven't seen him for hours. Find him and tell him I want him."

Her cold eyes roved the room, rested on Maxene, flicked downward to take in her stained cotton dress, support hose, sturdy sandals. She turned and walked away.

"Who was that?" St. Clair demanded.

"Rosalyn Mueller. She runs the gallery. One tough lady. Normally she's not that abrupt, but she's under a strain tonight. The threats, you know."

"She seemed to know Grabowski."

"Well, he's on the police force," Louie said evasively, not meeting her eyes.

St. Clair took a meditative sip of her drink. Why should she care how well Grabowski knew this predatory reptile? Grabowski was a grown man, free to know anyone he wanted. All she wanted now was to find him, give him the bad news, and go home. She turned toward the door.

"Lillian Hochstedder does these busts," chattered Louie, waving at the sculptures. "She was outside when you came in. She just started sculpting a few years ago, and already she's fabulous." He began collecting empty plates and glasses from people who had finished eating.

Maxene realized suddenly how tired she was and how much her feet hurt. She walked to the top of the spiral stairs to scan the well-dressed people sipping wine. Lillian Hochstedder was coming up the crowded steps, trying to step carefully between the legs and scattered plates, but she stumbled and tipped over a glass. A waitress wearing a black dress with a white apron and cap quickly began to mop up the spill.

Kitty Zelazak was no longer standing at the piano talking to Soren Berendorf. He was alone at the grand piano now, head leaning forward against the piano. As St. Clair watched, Louie hurried over to talk to him, but the sculptor ignored him and kept fiddling with the keys.

All at once she saw Grabowski's thick dark hair and mustache. He was wearing his blue seersucker suit with a burgundy tie, and he was standing at the receptionist's ebony desk by the front door, talking on the phone.

"Grabowski!" she yelled out, then realized he couldn't hear her over the noise. She hurried down the steps, pushed through the people, and sidled behind the side of the desk, hugging the wall. She caught up to him as he was turning to go into the office, and grabbed his arm.

His face lit up. "Maxene!"

"I've found Wyoming!"

"What?" he said, "It's so loud in here, I can't hear. You found Wyoming? Where is he?"

St. Clair drew him to a quieter place near the wall, but she hit her hip against the desk and lost her balance. Sleep deprivation was hitting hard tonight, she thought, or maybe it was that ridiculous red drink. She took a step backward to steady herself, but instead caught her leg on something. She grabbed at the wall, then completely lost her balance and fell over backward.

A loud crack like a pistol shot shattered through the crowded room. The sound bounced off the walls, echoing from everywhere. Someone screamed.

St. Clair scrambled to her feet and looked wildly around to figure out where the sound had come from. For an instant she couldn't see where everyone was looking. Then she saw. High in the vaulted ceiling, the wire tying the giant wooden chair mobile to the beam had snapped. Freed from its bond, the huge unbalanced sculpture was falling. The chairs seemed to drop in slow motion, like a huge brightly painted snowflake. Slowly, quietly, the sculpture fell toward the black piano and the sculptor still sitting with his hand on the keyboard.

"Look out!" St. Clair screamed. All over the room, others were shouting, "Look out!"

But the chairs dropped faster and faster, then collapsed with a splintering crash on the piano and on Soren Berendorf, master sculptor.

CHAPTER

3

"GET THE WOOD off him!" Grabowski ordered. "Call an ambulance!"

Security guards pushed the crowd aside, dragging bits of timber off Berendorf and the piano. In a few minutes a space was cleared around the sculptor, who was lying partially beneath the piano. The piano bench had broken, but the piano itself was standing, although it tilted under the weight of the broken chairs.

"Careful!" Grabowski snapped savagely at the two security guards who were lifting part of the sculpture off the piano. Maxene leaned over Berendorf until she could feel his breath on her cheek. A massive blow on the head could sometimes stop respiration. She felt for a pulse. It was faint and slow. The man's face was pale, and there was a nasty red patch above his ear.

"Soren!" she said loudly. "Can you hear me?"

No response. St. Clair examined his head closely without moving it, for fear of spinal damage. A lump was forming on his temple with a small amount of blood. St. Clair touched it gingerly. It was soft and swelling rapidly under her fingers.

Careful not to move Berendorf, St. Clair felt for pulses in his arms and legs. All were present but faint. The pulse in one foot was hard to find. She felt his ribs and shoulders to check for broken bones. All she could tell was that the circulation was adequate and that no bones were severely broken. She sat back on her heels with her fingers on his wrist pulse to monitor his heartbeat and respirations until the ambulance arrived.

Rosalyn Mueller, the gallery owner, knelt by St. Clair. Her face was ashen, and beads of perspiration clung to her forehead. "Is he going to be all right?" she whispered.

"I don't know. He's had some terrible blows on the body and head, but his breathing is all right and his pulse is regular. He needs to get to a hospital right away. Can you find a blanket?"

Rosalyn barked an order. A blanket appeared; the crowd moved back.

Under St. Clair's fingers, Berendorf's pulse began to flutter. The faint breaths stopped. She reached into her shoulder purse and pulled out the respirator mouthpiece. With this she could breathe air into his lungs without getting any secretions from the man's mouth into her own.

Cupping the sculptor's chin in one hand and pinching his nose with the other, she put her mouth over the mouthpiece and began to breathe. The man's chest raised slightly as the air expanded his lungs.

St. Clair drew a deep breath and continued breathing air into the lungs, trying to calculate twelve breaths a minute. Out of the corner of her eye, she watched the man's chest rise and lower. During his exhalations she moved two fingers to the carotid pulse on the side of his neck. It was slow and unsteady, but still beating. Sweat began trickling down her forehead, and she felt dizzy from hyperventilating—getting fresh air into her own lungs before breathing it into the mouthpiece.

An ambulance siren wailed outside, and the door to the gallery burst open. Two medics wheeled a stretcher up to her and dropped it down to floor level. One technician tapped her on the shoulder. He put a rubber face mask attached to some hand bellows over the sculptor's face and squeezed the bellows gently. The chest raised. The other technician started an IV.

St. Clair sat on the floor watching them and waiting for her dizziness to pass. A hand took her elbow, helping her up. It was Grabowski. He started to say something, but he was interrupted by Louie, in tears.

"I can't believe it actually fell!" he wept. "Such an artist! Such talent."

Before she could respond, a medic with a clipboard stepped up. "Are you a doctor?" he asked.

"Dr. St. Clair. I work at St. Agnes ER."

"How long were you doing respirations?"

"Two minutes maybe."

"Anything else you want to report?"

"Pulse was uneven. I can't tell if anything is broken. He was hit hard on the head."

The medic's eyes roved over the mass of wreckage piled on and around the piano. "That stuff just fell on him?"

"Out of the blue!" Louie sobbed.

The medic took a portable phone from his belt and spoke into it at length. Finally, he put the phone away. "Doctor ordered X rays," he told St. Clair and the other medic. "We're supposed to apply a neck splint, back splint, and transfer him as fast as possible. I'll get the portable X-ray machine."

St. Clair nodded; the doctor at the other end of the line was doing a good job. "Which hospital are you taking him to?" she asked.

"St. Agnes'. Dr. Malech."

Grabowski and two uniformed policemen were pushing the crowd away from the piano. "Split 'em into three groups," Grabowski was saying. "If anybody saw or heard anything about why this thing fell, I want their names, addresses, and where they can be reached."

Louie kept clinging to St. Clair's arm. "One minute he was playing the piano, and the next minute . . ." His voice trailed off into a sob. He put his hands over his mouth.

St. Clair put her arm around him. "Let's sit down. There's nothing we can do."

She was exhausted. Breathing for someone else used every muscle in her chest and back. She led Louie toward the reception table and lowered him into a chair, dragging up a chair for herself.

Rosalyn Mueller was sitting behind the reception table, her sleek head pillowed on her arms. "How could this happen?" she sobbed. "I'm toast. His lawyers will have me for breakfast."

"Surely he won't sue?" St. Clair was surprised. "It was an accident."

"He sued the parents of a little girl who drove her tricycle into his Mercedes. And if he dies, his relatives will sue for sure, once the lawyers get through with them. I can't believe the damned sculpture fell. My insurance will go through the roof, if the police don't shut me down first."

"He looked all right to me," said St. Clair, not certain if she was offering comfort. "He's hurt badly, but he's not dead."

Just then, Kitty Zelazak, the woman in the red dress who had been chatting with Berendorf at the piano, hurried up to them. She bumped against the table; then her knees gave way and she slid to the floor. Dr. Zelazak hurried to her side and patted her cheeks. St. Clair pulled herself to her feet and went into the gallery office to look for a blanket.

A loosely woven white afghan was artistically draped over the white leather sofa. When St. Clair picked it up, the breeze from her action toppled a pile of papers from the desk onto the floor. On top were some sketches: casual, free-hand drawings of the chair sculptures. In one of the sketches a skull had been drawn inside a sculpture. The skull was grinning.

Maxene carried the shawl out of the office. "There's a couch in here," she reported.

Dr. Zelazak picked his wife up under the arms and half dragged her into the office and onto the couch. St. Clair lifted her legs onto the white leather and spread the shawl over her. The woman lay limp with her eyes closed. Maxene automatically took her pulse. Normal, strong seventy-two. Zelazak shook his wife's arm.

"Kitty! Can you hear me?"

Kitty moaned. "My head! I have such a headache."

"It's that damned punch," muttered Dr. Zelazak. "It's got vodka and Kahlúa and God knows what else mixed in there."

"Something wrong here?" The medic was standing behind her.

"A faint." St. Clair went back to her chair beside the reception table. The medic followed her.

"Who was the man under the pile of kindling?"

"Soren Berendorf," said the gallery director. She put her head back down on the table and started to cry again.

"He's the sculptor who did all this work," Louie said, waving his arm at the gallery.

"Does he have any relatives?"

"Not here," Louie answered. "He's from New York."

"What about a job?"

"I told you. He's a sculptor."

The medic raised an eyebrow. "And do sculptors have health insurance?"

No one answered. The medic made a few notes on his chart, then hurried to the sculptor, now resting on a stretcher. St. Clair walked over to look down at him. The medics had removed the face mask and he was breathing for himself, but he was still unconscious. The medics wheeled the stretcher to the door, past Grabowski and a uniformed policeman.

St. Clair went back to the reception table and stared at the frayed piece of snapped wire hanging from the eyehook screwed low into the wall behind it. A police officer elbowed her out of the way and began snapping photos of the wire. She sank into a chair, legs stretched out in front of her. Her watch said 2:00.

By now the room was nearly empty; only two people were still being questioned by a uniformed policeman. Grabowski patted St. Clair's shoulder.

"Time to go," he said. "I'll walk you to your car."

"My car died. I caught a ride here with a friend," said St.

Clair, with a sudden vision of her dead car by the fire hydrant.

"Then I'll give you a ride home. You can tell me about Wyoming on the way."

"Grabowski," she put a hand on his arm. "Do you know how that sculpture fell?" The thought that had been creeping into her head since the sculpture fell could no longer be avoided.

"The wire broke."

"Out of the middle of nowhere, a wire broke?"

Grabowski sighed. "The crime lab may be able to tell us if it was defective or old."

"There's another possibility," said St. Clair, carefully. "Somebody tripped over the wire and caused it to break."

"What do you mean?"

"Me. I stepped backward and tripped over something." She pointed at the police technician unwrapping the frayed wire from around the hook. "It looks to me like the wire broke near the hook, right where I fell over it. In fact, the minute I tripped over it, I heard a sound like a pistol shot. Then the sculpture fell."

Louie had come up while they were talking and had overheard. He took her arm. "No, no, dear, impossible. Tripping over that wire wouldn't make it break. I hung that piece myself, and I can assure you definitely that there was nothing wrong with that wire."

Grabowski had his notebook out. "You hung the sculpture yourself?"

"Well, there was me, and Rosalyn, and Soren himself, of course. He supervised. Had his fingers in everything." He giggled.

Grabowski scowled. "How do you know there was nothing wrong with the wire?"

"It was new wire, straight off the coil. The rest is in the basement if you want to see for yourself."

"We'll do that right now," Grabowski ordered.

Louie took a long minute to retie his silk scarf around his neck and anchor it with the scarab pin. Grabowski looked sideways at St. Clair, who smiled. She liked Louie, although his eccentricities wore on her occasionally. He was a genuine phony, a self-acknowledged hysteric who enjoyed emotional turmoil. His apartment was filled with mismatched dishes, antique furniture, and piles of unpaid bills. Louie's sense of self dropped off the horizon occasionally, and he looked the other way.

The door to the basement storage area was in the gallery office. Rosalyn Mueller had left the reception table and moved to her executive chair behind the massive desk. Kitty Zelazak was still lying on the sofa, a damp washcloth draped over her forehead. Ronald Zelazak was sitting on a chair beside the couch, holding a plastic cup of water and looking irritated.

"Let's get going, Kitty," he urged. "It's a hell of a lot more comfortable in our house than in this place." He gave an annoyed look at the trio as they trooped past.

Louie wiggled his fingers at Kitty. "How's the girl? Don't you worry about a thing, dear. Maxene says Soren is doing all right."

"Where are you going?" Rosalyn demanded.

"Storage," Louie said. "The detective wants to see the rest of the coil that wire came from. Okay if I show him?"

"I can get a search warrant," Grabowski said casually.

"No need," Rosalyn said. "I'll show you myself."

The basement extended beyond the walls of the gallery. A steel door the size of a small van was on the outside wall with a lighted digital control panel mounted on the wall.

"Rosalyn and I share the basement," Louie explained, waving at the expanse. "Since we use the same entrance for loading and unloading, we split the expense of putting in an electric security door. Of course only Rosalyn and I know the combination."

Wooden crates and loose shredded packing materials were piled on the Rhinestones's side of the basement, and five or six antique wooden chests on Louie's. A series of lockers, each with a padlock, ran along the back wall. Paintings were stacked inside. Louie rummaged through the litter of shredded packing materials on the floor and pulled out a half-empty spool of wire.

"Exhibit A: the wire," he said. "As you can see, the price tag is still on it. I bought it myself at the hardware store on Oakland Avenue." He handed it to Grabowski with a flourish.

Grabowski stuck the spool in his jacket pocket and wandered around the basement, his loafers echoing on the cement. At the far end, he flipped on a light, and St. Clair could see a matching set of stairs. Grabowski wandered back. "Smells funny down here."

"That's varnish remover," Louie said quickly.

"Or paint thinner," Rosalyn suggested. "I repair damaged paintings. If we open the big door to the outside, there's plenty of ventilation." She waited to see if Grabowski had any more questions, then led the way upstairs.

Kitty Zelazak and her husband had disappeared, and the gallery was empty except for a lone policeman standing guard at the front door. The sculpture in the middle of the room seemed pathetic, just a pile of mismatched, painted kindling.

Rosalyn looked pointedly at her watch. "Can I go home?"

"We can all go." Grabowski nodded to the cop, then turned to Rosalyn.

"Lock up while I'm here," he ordered. "I want the place to stay the same until I've had a chance to go over all the reports."

"And when will that be?" she asked pointedly.

"Depends on how fast I decide to read."

Maxene and Louie waited on the sidewalk while Grabowski accompanied Rosalyn back to the office to get her purse and keys, then watched her triple-lock the heavy glass door. She pulled down a metal-barred shutter and secured that with a padlock.

The night had cooled, and the stars were bright. A comfortable sweet-smelling breeze blew off the lake. Grabowski waited until Rosalyn and Louie were safely in their cars and pulling away from the curb before he took Maxene's elbow and steered her across the street to his dented green Plymouth. He put his arms around her and held her tight.

"Nice job taking care of that poor guy in there," he said into her hair. "I haven't seen you in action since I brought that guy I shot into St. Agnes."

"That poor sculptor," she shuddered. "He didn't even have a chance to get away."

Grabowski opened the car door and deposited her into the passenger seat, then got into the driver's seat.

"Tell me about Wyoming."

St. Clair drew a deep breath. "I think he's going to be all right," she said. "I found him by accident when I was visiting a patient after work tonight."

"Address?"

"Corner of Fifth and Center."

"I beg your pardon? You went there after work?"

St. Clair continued without answering. "And while I was in the apartment of my patient, there was a drive-by shooting outside. Wyoming was one of the people who was shot."

Grabowski said nothing. He leaned his head against the headrest and closed his eyes. "Why can't we do anything to stop these shootings? It's getting worse."

St. Clair waited without speaking.

Finally, Grabowski lifted his head. "You say Wyoming is going to be all right?"

"He was only shot once, in the spleen area. I went with him and the other victim to the hospital, but I didn't stay for the surgery because I wanted to tell you."

"What was he doing on Fifth and Center?"

"He was coming up the steps of the apartment building carrying a bag of groceries. We could ask Rolondo."

"The pimp? Why ask him?"

"Wyoming was with one of Rolondo's girls."

Grabowski drove, thin-lipped and silent, up the quiet streets of the north shore neighborhoods, elbow on the window ledge, hand clenched in his heavy dark hair. St. Clair opened her window to combat the icy blast of the air conditioner and watched the bugs collect on the windshield.

North Stowell Street was dark, the big maples shading the street lamps. As Maxene put her key into her front door, Louie's lights went off. In the kitchen, she pulled out a chair for Grabowski and took two beers from the refrigerator. Then she called the hospital.

"He's still unconscious, but his body systems are stable," she reported, hanging up. "They think he might need blood and they've put out a call for donors. He's O-positive, if you know a healthy donor."

"I'm O-positive. I'll go now." He polished off his beer.

"Do you want me to come?"

"Go to bed. I have to go back to the office afterward, anyway."

At the top of the stairs, he kissed her on the cheek, then hurried out. She stood listening to his footsteps click down the sidewalk and then to the slam of his car door. After the motor died away in the distance, she called the hospital again, had a long talk with the surgery resident, then went to bed.

CHAPTER

4

THE PHONE WOKE Maxene St. Clair the next morning. Birds were splashing in the backyard birdbath, and the faint smell of bacon drifted in through the open window. She rolled over to look at her clock. The motion made her head ache. Seven A.M. Grabowski was on the phone, sounding tired.

"I saw Wyoming last night. He just lies there, won't wake up."

"Did you call the hospital this morning?"

"Every hour. Still won't wake up. Why not, Max?"

She tried to clear her foggy brain. "Could be shock, could be blood loss, could be dregs of the anesthesia. I had a long talk with the surgical resident last night after you left. He said the surgery was clean, no complications, and they got the bullet out without problems. Wyoming should be just fine. He's healthy, in good condition, the bullet didn't hit any major organs, and his vital signs were never far from normal. He should pull out of it just fine."

St. Clair stopped. Actually, there was room for worry: infection, allergies to drug therapy, reaction against the blood transfusion, a bullet the X ray missed. Better not to talk about these complications unless they became real.

"The nurse keeps telling me he's all right," Grabowski said.

"Did she also tell you how the girl he was with is doing?"

"I can't keep track of every gunshot victim in the city."

"Of course not, Grabowski." He was pushed to the edge.

St. Clair waited to let him regroup. "You were up all night?"

"And feeling every minute of it. About six in the morning, I finished reading the interviews with the people at the gallery. It amazes me how witnesses at the same event can see entirely different things. From these reports, you'd think people were in different galleries."

"So what happened? Did the wire just snap?" Her voice quavered.

There was a pause. "Are you still worried that it was your tripping over the line that made it break?"

"It's awful to think I might have caused that sculpture to fall. Grabowski, the man was a sitting duck—he couldn't even get out of the way."

"The crime lab is checking out the wire," Grabowski said. "They say maybe it was cut."

"What do you mean, cut?"

"It was new wire, thick as my thumb, and the hooks were still screwed tight enough into the wall to hold the sculpture up there for years. It's unlikely the wire snapped. While the lab works on that end, I'm looking for whoever might want that sculpture to come crashing down—like that group who threatened to burn it up."

"Could there be a professional jealousy angle?" St. Clair asked. "The sculptor himself could tell you when he's well enough to talk."

"Max. I thought you knew. Berendorf died."

St. Clair lay absorbing this. One part of her brain didn't want to accept it even though the physician side of her wasn't completely surprised. The sculptor's injuries had been severe, and his condition was critical. He had stopped breathing at the gallery and needed resuscitation.

On the other hand, she couldn't believe the accident had even happened. It was so dramatic, it seemed staged. She could still hear the crash of the huge mobile of chairs hitting the piano, the banging wood colliding with piano keys and strings. She had never been at the scene of a serious accident before, and last night she had seen two—the drive-by shooting and the sculpture falling—and they had jumbled together during her sleep.

She shuddered. The movement made her head hurt. Lack of sleep plus the violence of the night's events had left her with a tension headache that resembled a migraine. She probably had been grinding her teeth when she slept, too; her jaw muscles felt tight.

"Did Berendorf ever regain consciousness?" she asked.

"No. They started CPR again in the ambulance but gave up shortly after he got to the ER. Shock induced by injuries, is what the people at St. Agnes told me. You can find out more this afternoon when you get to work."

St. Clair rubbed her forehead, trying to remember the sequence of events the night before. "Shock induced by head injury? He had multiple scalp contusions."

"Don't know."

"Are they doing an autopsy?"

"I haven't requested one. It's a simple injury case, at least that's what was on the chart when I was down there giving blood for Wyoming."

St. Clair nodded, forgetting he couldn't see her. She felt anxious and uncertain. Would Berendorf have survived if she had taken better care of him at the gallery? Dozens of physicians were there, but no one had offered to help; emergency medicine was her specialty, after all, not theirs.

"Max?" Grabowski's voice broke into her thoughts.

"I should have ridden in the ambulance, Grabowski. Emergency medical technicians are good, but they're only trained to handle common problems. They wouldn't know how to handle a multiple injury case like that. If I had stayed with him, he would have lived."

"You're not God, Maxene. A lot of doctors have a God complex, but you've avoided it so far."

"And a lot of doctors do what they can, then wash their hands and forget about it. I can't do that." She let the anger out.

"Be realistic, Max." Grabowski was patient. "How could you have saved him if you had gone in the ambulance? He was badly hurt. He stopped breathing once, remember? Besides, you aren't employed by the ambulance company. Even if the medics had let you ride in the back, they wouldn't have let you touch him. When Berendorf left the gallery in the ambulance, he was stable. Isn't that what you said? How were you to know he would go into shock?"

"I'm a doctor. I should know." Her voice wavered.

"This isn't like you, Maxene. Is something wrong?"

"Yes, Grabowski. I tripped over the wire that held up the sculpture; then I didn't make sure he got to the hospital safely." And, a voice inside her said, you let a black girl drop into a coma because you didn't get there soon enough. You could have left the ER for fifteen minutes—long enough to convince her to come to the hospital.

She started to cry.

"Maxene, I'm coming over. You're sick or you're too tired. I'm sorry I called so early. Calm down, I'll be there in twenty minutes."

St. Clair swallowed her tears and drew a long breath. "I'm all right. It was a shock, hearing that he died. What else happened last night that I should know about?"

"Nothing. I have no leads, only a pile of reports. Go back to sleep; I'll call you later."

St. Clair rolled over. Her head ached. She tried to reconstruct the events of the night before, but all she could feel was persistent dread. Inside her was a pool of darkness the color of the street when she had looked down at the two bodies. Is this what people felt after earthquakes or bombings, she wondered. She had read that jurors forced to hear about grisly crimes cried easily, had trouble concentrating. Did that happen to people who witnessed a shooting or saw someone killed in an accident? She wondered how the other people at the gallery were coping. But they hadn't tripped over the wire; they hadn't done inadequate first aid; they hadn't failed to get the victim safely to the hospital. The ache in her head subsided when she closed her eyes. She dropped back to sleep.

Four hours later, she was pulled from slumber by tapping

on her kitchen door. The door clicked open, and Louie called her name. In a moment he was standing in her bedroom.

Louie was wearing purple cotton drawstring trousers and a lavender T-shirt that was too small. His stomach bulged over the drawstring. Maxene checked to make sure her nightshirt wasn't rolled up under her armpits and sat up.

Louie settled on the end of the bed with his feet tucked under him like an elf. His mustache drooped.

"I don't suppose you could write me one little prescription," he said, scratching his throat delicately, fingers arched like claws. "Hives. It's nerves, of course. I know it, you know it, but what can I do? I woke up with my skin on fire. Take a look here behind my ears, down my neck."

Maxene peered foggily at his arched neck. Her eyes were so tired they wouldn't focus.

"I'll write you a prescription for cortisone cream and antihistamines," she said. Then she added, gently, "Did you hear about Soren?"

Louie nodded. He tucked his feet tighter under him. A tear rolled down his cheek. "I just called St. Agnes emergency room. The nurse remembered my little accident with the sleeping pills last year, and she didn't want to tell me, but when I said I was your neighbor, she took pity on me and broke the news. Then she told me to come talk to you."

"Did you know Soren well?" St. Clair passed him a box of tissues. He blew his nose delicately.

"I thought we had something going once, but the relationship died before it lived. Soren was straight as an arrow, but solitary. Geniuses have to work alone." His shoulders shook.

St. Clair patted his shoulder. "You were a big help to him, Louie, passing out drinks and gathering up the plates. I'm sure he appreciated it. You helped hang that big sculpture, too, isn't that what you said?"

Louie sat up straight and began biting his nails. "That's right, and now I'm in trouble for it. That detective of yours is coming down to the shop this morning to ask about

Soren and me. Some nasty individual, and I could name names, told him last night that I was fiddling with the wire just before the sculpture fell." A sob escaped from Louie's throat.

St. Clair suppressed a smile and patted his hand. "Relax, Louie. One of your so-called friends is jealous of your gallery connections and is being nasty. Grabowski doesn't make haphazard arrests. He's looking for information, and you're first on his list because you know people in the art world." She tried not to think about Grabowski's stories of the mistaken arrests he had personally masterminded.

"But he already talked to me last night!" Louie wailed.

"Maybe he thought up more questions."

Louie scratched his wrists. "The honest truth is that Soren and I had our differences. The man was a puffed-up ego masquerading as a human being, a complete waste of skin. He had very few friends, the way I define friends. Certainly I wouldn't count myself as one of them."

"I thought you were close."

"Not close enough to be invited to all his little soirées. You'd be surprised at who practically lived at his house, like our charming hostesses last evening. My relationship with Soren was a close business one, if you know what I mean."

"Not really."

"I did some wood finishing for him—and you don't need to mention that to your detective friend. I do the same for lots of artists, and they don't want it spread around. Artists pretend they do all their own dirty work, but they're plain lazy, if you want my honest opinion. Soren wasn't above accepting help and giving no thanks for it."

The phone rang. Maxene glared at the machine. During her residency, when she had been enslaved to the phone, she had come to hate phone calls, especially at home. Half the time she turned off the ringer since most of her friends called her at work. It was Grabowski again.

"Do me a favor?" he asked. "I was just chatting with your strange friend from downstairs. What else do you know about him besides he makes the worst punch I've ever tasted?"

"He's sitting on the end of my bed."

"He's what?"

"Put your imagination on a leash. We were discussing the art world."

"Well, watch what you say. This isn't the time to explain, considering you're in bed together, but find out about his relationship with Soren Berendorf."

"What are you telling me?"

"Just find out if he and Berendorf had any serious differences. I'll call you after our little chat at his shop." He hung up.

Louie was clawing the backs of his hands, leaving long red welts. "That was Detective Grabowski, wasn't it? What did he want?"

"He wanted to know how well you knew Soren Berendorf. It's not serious enough to claw yourself until you bleed. Look, I'll write the prescription, you fill it, then go down to your shop and make a list of everything you know about Soren Berendorf—his friends, his nonfriends, people who might crash his sculptures."

Louie put his face in his hands. "The police are going to arrest me! I'll be interrogated under hot lights in a nasty green cement cell!"

"Take it easy, Louie, everything will be all right. Now will you get off my bed so I can get dressed?"

St. Clair followed Louie through the kitchen to the back hall stairs and locked the door behind him, hoping he would stay out long enough to let her shower and dress. Then she called Grabowski back. He picked up the phone on the tenth ring, chewing something crunchy.

"You sounded more cheerful on the phone just now," she said. "Is Wyoming better?"

"Yes. He's still unconscious but better, whatever that means. I hope the nurse isn't saying that so I'll stop calling every half hour." He took another bite.

"Can you hear me through your chewing? Or shall I call back after you've had your moment of nutrition?"

"Be happy your public servant is working through meals. Did you find anything out from that peculiar neighbor of yours?" Grabowski demanded.

St. Clair organized her approach. Grabowski's attitude toward the Milwaukee gay community was barely neutral, and he was apt to lean on Louie out of reflex.

"Why are you giving Louie fits by making him think he's a criminal? What do you know that I don't?" she asked.

"I'm just fishing for information. A few people said they saw Louie fiddle with the wire just before the sculpture fell, but they aren't reliable witnesses, frankly, light-in-the-loafers, artsy-fartsy crowd—probably pure nastiness. The opinion down here is that the sculpture fell by accident."

"So why are you working on the case?"

Grabowski sighed. "Nearly every bigwig in the city was at the gallery last night, and none liked being detained for questioning. They want their names cleared, the faster the better. Have you seen the front-page photos? The art critic—one of Louie's pals—was snapping celebrities and got terrific shots of the crash, including the body. I'm surprised he didn't throw up all over his camera."

St. Clair was silent.

"Are you there?" he asked, after a moment.

"What about that wire?" she asked. "Was it cut, or did it break when I tripped over it?"

"The lab doesn't know yet, Maxene. We may have to figure out another way to find out what happened. I had hoped one of the hundreds of people there saw something, but so far no one reliable did."

"Including me. I even fell over the wire, and I didn't see anyone carrying wire clippers. It was very crowded."

"Which is why I'm looking for someone nosy enough to be watching other people." Again he bit into something crunchy.

"Like Louie."

"He knows the gallery people involved, and he's into gossip. I don't know if he had anything to do with it, but I want a chance to find out everything he knows."

"But he doesn't know anything," Maxene protested.

Grabowski sighed.

St. Clair persisted. "After Louie, where will you go? Will you talk to everyone there last night?"

"No, there are too many. I'll start with the gallery people—owners, receptionists. If the wire really was cut on purpose, they might know the motive."

"It was such a strange accident, Grabowski," she mused. "A new cable snaps in the middle of a crowded reception and only one person gets hurt."

"Agreed, Max. I don't believe in accidents, which makes me more certain your tripping over the wire didn't break it. It's too bizarre." His voice trailed off.

"Listen, Grabowski, I've got three hours before I start work. Let me tag along with you."

"You want to make sure you didn't kill him? Forget it, Max. The last time you stuck your charming nose into one of my investigations, you ended up as a patient in your own hospital, and I got gray hairs."

"That's because we were dealing with the medical world. This is the art world—less dangerous."

"Not true. I hear jealousy is more cruel among artists than among doctors."

St. Clair hung up slowly. She took a carton of cherry yogurt out of the refrigerator and stood eating it while she looked out the window at the back garden. Ruby, her cat, was stalking sparrows fluttering in the birdbath. Her orange body glided through the English daisies without moving a single stalk. The sparrows flew away.

Why had the sculptor died? He had been all right when he was placed in the ambulance. What had happened in the ER? Al Malech was in charge—an immensely capable doctor despite his macabre sense of humor. But St. Agnes ER could be chaotic. When it was crowded, fights broke out; once she had even called the police. She needed more in-

formation. This afternoon at the hospital, she could look
through the medical record and the nurse's night shift report.

Louie's car pulled out of the driveway, and his tires
squealed toward downtown. Soon Grabowski would be at
Louie's antique shop carefully dragging Louie over the
coals. In the meantime, she had a logistical problem—how
to get around without a car.

CHAPTER

5

GRABOWSKI HUNG UP the phone and pulled the yellow pages of the Milwaukee phone book toward him. He started making a list of all the art galleries in town, cross-checking them against the names and business addresses of the people at the gallery opening. All the galleries and museums in town had been represented by directors or owners. He wondered what draw Rhinestones had. Wasn't it just another store for paintings? Or did Rosalyn Mueller have more power than she seemed? She had persuaded Soren Berendorf to hold an opening there, and Berendorf was supposed to be a big name in the art world, according to the bits of conversation he had overheard last night.

He stared across the big gray metal desks lined up three deep on either side of a central aisle. Each desk was tidy or nearly bare—the opposite of detectives' desks on television. Paperwork had to be completed, or the captain of detectives was down their throats. That didn't mean that cases were solved; it just meant appearances were more important than reality, a philosophy promoted by Milwaukee city officials who termed the bulldozing of slum housing "urban cleanup," ignoring the fact that the slum dwellers were now homeless.

The blinds were partially closed over the long window that ran the length of the room. Sunday mornings were quiet, only a few detectives on duty. Today's group had gray hair and beer bellies, testimony to seniority as the determining factor for who worked the day shift.

The 250 Milwaukee police detectives considered themselves the elite of the police force, an attitude that annoyed coppers on a beat. Thanks to the increase in crime, cops on a beat now handled the burglaries and robberies that used to be the realm of detectives. It was nothing to see a street copper do a robbery start to finish. Detectives did homicides, or important burglaries such as the governor's house. Among detectives, there was a hierarchy, too, with jockeying for positions on an interesting task force or for special squads. Only the vice squad cops seemed content, drinking their way through bars to bust prostitutes.

Two detectives were drinking coffee, sitting on the raised platform at the front of the room that served as a lineup for suspect identification. With the overhead lights off, the black curtains pulled over the long windows, and the footlights on full, witnesses could safely review the lineup from the front row of desks. The interrogation rooms down the hall were empty this morning and, in the holding pens behind the lineup stage, only a single man paced the maze of barred cells.

Technically, Grabowski didn't need to be here at all. Detectives worked shifts like regular coppers, and his shift was four to midnight. But the accident at the gallery had been so bizarre, and so many "important people" had been there, that his captain had told him to stay on it until he knew what happened, or figured out how to sweep it under the rug.

Grabowski's eyes burned from lack of sleep. The drone of voices soothed like a lullaby, and the stage and its occupants blurred. He put his head down on his desk and fell asleep.

Fifteen minutes later someone tapped him on the shoulder. At first he couldn't remember where he was, then a carefully typed report fluttered onto the desk. It was from the crime lab.

Grabowski read through the report, then stared out the window. A vision of the falling sculpture formed in front of his eyes. He'd never seen anything like it; the noise of all that wood hitting the grand piano still rang in his imagination. He called the lab.

"What kind of cutters did the job—wire cutters, machete, acid?" He hung up on the language in his ear, picked his jacket off the back of the chair, and set off to interrogate Louie.

On Sunday mornings the downtown East Side streets were normally deserted except for a few restaurants open for brunch. This morning, a cool breeze was blowing off Lake Michigan two blocks away, and a few bicyclers were cruising toward McKinley Beach. The sidewalks were already heating up, though—today would be another sultry scorcher.

Louie's shop, "Certified Antiques & Watercolours" sat cheek by jowl with Rhinestones Art Gallery. The gray wood sign with red letters creaked gently in the breeze, and a smaller version graced the door above the brass knocker. Blue-and-white-striped awnings sheltered a healthy crop of red geraniums.

Grabowski pushed on the door. Still locked. He peered through the shop window, but white lace curtains obscured the view. While he was debating whether to cross the street for an overpriced cup of coffee in the tea room, Louie came hurrying up the sidewalk. He dropped his keys twice while fumbling at the lock.

"Sorry I'm late, Detective. If I'd known you were the superprompt type, I'd have waited to run to the drugstore for the prescription your friend Maxene was kind enough to write me."

Louie dropped a small paper sack and a tube of ointment fell out. The door opened with the tinkle of chimes, and they were in the shop.

"Iced cappuccino?" queried Louie. "Cold herbal tea?"

What Grabowski really wanted was a beer. "Coffee," he conceded. Louie disappeared into the back.

The shop was tightly packed with antique furniture and smelled sweetly of cinnamon, flowers, and furniture polish. Air-conditioning blew a cool breeze across Grabowski's sweaty neck. A calico cat was curled up in a rocker, her presence a carefully chosen artifact to give the shop an old-fashioned feel. She eyed the detective and jumped off the chair. Grabowski took her place. The air conditioner whirred, the rocker rocked, he fell asleep.

When he awoke, a tall glass of milky iced coffee was sitting on a small table next to his elbow, a paper doily protecting the flowered saucer. Grabowski took a suspicious sip, accustomed only to black coffee in a chipped mug. It was surprisingly good. He drained half the contents and stood up to look around.

The maze of polished tables and chairs was made hazardous by a clutter of needlepoint footstools and children's antique toys. On the walls hung paintings softly lit by track lights. Grabowski was staring at a small abstract painting done in strong colors when Louie came out of the back. Louie had rolled up his sleeves and looked the part of the casual but efficient antique dealer. He was squeezing a small amount of ointment onto the back of one hand. He began rubbing it in.

"Watercolors fit with antiques, which is why I carry them." He fussed, straightening the painting a trifle. "Everybody's great-grandmother dabbled in watercolor flowers. Besides, color on the walls keeps the shop from looking like a nursing home for aged furniture. It's an art to making antiques look valuable, Detective. You can't imagine."

Grabowski was getting annoyed watching Louie rub ointment into the back of his hand. "Nerves?" he inquired. "Something under your skin?"

"Whatever do you mean?" Louie's fingernails dug into the back of his hand.

"You're a nervous kind of guy, aren't you, Louie? Things get to you."

Louie straightened his shoulders and tightened his lips. "Life hits me harder than it does other people, if that's what you mean. I have always longed for a temperament like yours, so quiet and calm."

Grabowski cut him off. "Yesterday a few people mentioned you worked on this show for Soren Berendorf. Why? Did you have a personal interest in Berendorf?"

Louie sat down on a trunk and passed a hand over his forehead. "It's common rumor that Soren and I were once a twosome. Not true. Soren was straight, although he had fun dressing like he played both ends of the field. Unhappily, I was never more to Soren than a business associate."

"You mean a groupie."

"No need to insult me, Detective. You really should control your prejudices. I am a contributing member of this community, whether or not you like my life-style."

Grabowski felt a twinge of shame. Maybe he was getting too old to stay up all night reading reports, then work straight through the next day. Fatigue was affecting his objectivity. On the other hand, provoking people into honesty by insulting them was a time-honored police interrogation method.

"So you hang watercolors around just to keep the place from looking decrepit?" he asked.

"Watercolors also bring some added income to what I make selling or refinishing antiques. Someone who will drop a couple hundred for an oak side table won't flinch at another fifty for a watercolor to hang over it. I handle talented local amateurs as well as professionals—not that there's much difference here in the back woods of the art world. Rhinestones is a case in point."

"Meaning what?" Grabowski took out his notebook.

Louie frowned at the notebook. "I hope I'm not harming anyone at Rhinestones by passing this on. Rhinestones was started by rank amateurs; worse, dilettantes. The gallery was the brainstorm of several doctors' wives who had taken so many art classes that they had stacks of canvases in their attics. It was never supposed to be more than a tax write-off for their husbands."

Grabowski sat down in the rocker again and propped his notebook on his crossed knee. "That's an expensive write-off, even on paper, if they had to cover rent and expenses by selling amateur paintings."

Louie waved off the objection. "Granted, they sold only a few initially, but their expenses were minimal. The first Rhinestones was in the basement of a building a few blocks from here that one of their husbands owned as a bonafide tax break. The girls staffed the gallery themselves, although Rosalyn had a ghastly time scheduling because of tennis tournaments or ski vacations." Louie rolled his eyes.

"Mrs. Mueller is also an artist?"

"Ms. She's divorced. No, Ros is the brains of the outfit. She was bookkeeper for her husband's practice before he got rich and turned it over to a bookkeeping service. She thought up the idea for a gallery and ran it from the basement for about a year. Then she got a divorce and used her settlement to move next door here. That was when Rhinestones became a real gallery—real artists, real commissions."

"What happened to the doctors' wives?"

"The original organizers still show their work there since their contract was written on flypaper by a medical lawyer who specialized in keeping medical groups together. Rosalyn puts the doctors' wives' stuff in an upstairs gallery."

"So now Ms. Mueller makes money?"

Louie shrugged. "The space looks terrific and has plenty of foot traffic, but rent is high and making a profit on art isn't easy. Still, if anybody can do it, Ros can. Look what she does for opening nights."

Grabowski changed directions. "Do you make the punch for all her openings?"

"I scratch her back; she scratches mine. Our front doors are side by side, and when either of us does well, the other gets pulled along. If Ros needs help putting an exhibit or an event together, I'm delighted to help and vise versa."

"Let's get back to last night. Did you help set up the exhibit?"

"Several of us did, since Ros won't hire extra labor, the little penny pincher. Let me think." Louie put his fist under his chin and raised his eyes toward the ceiling for inspiration. "There was Rosalyn and Soren, of course, and Lillian and me. And Kitty. Afterward we came here for cappuccinos."

"Did you all hang the big one over the piano?"

"Of course. Lillian, Kitty, and I lifted it while Ros and Soren pulled on the wire. They anchored it to the wall."

"So you knew how heavy it was." Grabowski was scribbling notes.

"I was surprised. I had expected balsa wood or bamboo, but the chairs were oak and the thing weighed a ton. Well, you saw it fall." Louie shuddered.

"Kitty who?"

"Zelazak." He spelled it. "She did the seagull mobile and the watercolors. She's earnest, but strictly amateur. She's part owner."

"And Lillian who?"

"Hochstedder. Another part owner. She did the clay busts. Quite striking. Did you see them?"

Grabowski shook his head. "What do you think about this arson threat? Could those people have tried to sabotage the sculpture?"

Louie leaned forward and lowered his voice. "I'll let you in on a little secret, Detective. The arson bit was strictly PR just to get press. Ros got great press coverage, what with police protection and all. But wait, are you telling me the sculpture didn't fall by accident?"

The door chimes broke into Grabowski's response. Rosalyn Mueller walked into the room.

Her black hair was still a smooth cap, but she had dark smudges under her eyes and her mouth drooped. She was wearing black silk slacks and a white silk blouse that clung to the bones in her shoulders. Louie hurried over to pull up a chair for her. She smiled faintly at him.

"I came over for one of your iced cappuccinos, Louie. I couldn't sleep last night, and now I can't bear to look at Soren's things in the gallery." She dabbed at her eyes with her handkerchief.

Louie patted her arm. "Wait right here, pet, I'll fix you

one of Louie's specials." He picked up Grabowski's empty glass and turned toward the kitchen.

Rosalyn stared at Grabowski feverishly. "What have you found out about the accident? Do you know how it happened?"

"The crime lab thinks the wire was cut."

At the kitchen door, Louie dropped the glass and covered his mouth with his hands.

Rosalyn jumped. Her face turned even more pale. "You mean somebody wanted that sculpture to fall on Soren?"

Grabowski ignored the crash. "Or just to fall and damage the sculpture. According to the lab, several strands of wire had been clipped, so only a few were left holding the sculpture. They could have snapped at any time."

"It could have hit anyone, not just Soren," called Louie, who was picking up pieces of broken glass. "The room was packed."

Grabowski waited for Rosalyn Mueller to speak, but she sat looking ahead of her. The planes of her face seemed flattened, and her jaw and nose sharpened. The corner of her upper lip twitched. Grabowski broke the silence.

"Who might want to sabotage the sculpture?"

She shook her head, still staring ahead. A tear rolled down her cheek.

Grabowski waited to let her compose herself. "Can you think of anyone who might want to damage this gallery by staging a serious accident here?"

Louie hurried into the kitchen and came back with a glass of iced coffee. He patted Rosalyn's shoulder and glared at Grabowski.

"Don't strain yourself, dear. We're simply trying to figure out what happened. I'll go with you next door. No need to handle that by yourself."

"But that's all there is, doing things by yourself," she murmured. "In the end, nobody else will do it. That's what Soren used to say." She sipped her coffee. "Let's go next door and get this over with."

Rhinestones Gallery smelled like spilled wine and

spoiled cucumber sandwiches. Louie pulled a plastic garbage sack with cups and paper plates over to the front door, then went into the kitchen and began washing dishes.

Grabowski stood with Rosalyn looking over the sculpture of chairs, now only brightly painted kindling mounded next to the piano. Nothing had been moved except the wire and the few pieces of wood that had been cleared from around the body. The gallery was dead quiet. Grabowski could hear Rosalyn breathing.

"Ros, oh Ros." Louie's voice rang out. "Could you help me a teensy bit with these dishes? Unless of course you mind the smell."

Rosalyn grimaced. "He's trying to cheer me up by keeping me busy. Besides, there's no way I can get the caterers to come back. They bolted as soon as the police let them go."

Grabowski watched her walk into the office. Despite her pale face and shaking hands, if she were in shock from the accident, she didn't show it. Her shoulders were straight and the edge in her voice clearly audible over the clatter of dishes.

Grabowski sat down on the bottom step of the stairs and contemplated the mess. Plastic champagne cups and paper plates littered the stairs and corners of the room. It was hard to see the sculpture in the clutter.

Art was foreign territory to him, mysterious objects with no apparent value that sold for enormous sums. Last night's crowd had been doctors, lawyers, investment types. Money was the draw, he supposed, and status. It was outside his value system. The only thing he knew about art was the painting of the Virgin Mary in Father Dominic's study.

He wished Wyoming were here to guide him through this territory. Wyoming had come from the same South Side Milwaukee neighborhood as Grabowski, but Wyoming had seen something in his surroundings that Grabowski never could. Wyoming was always drawing on walls, or sculpting mud into the spitting images of detested teachers. Who would have guessed that a kid who could steal the hubcaps off a car at a red light would turn into a sculptor?

Grabowski became aware that someone had come down the stairs and was standing next to him. She was wearing jeans and a T-shirt with "Chanel" across the chest. It was Kitty Zelazak, the woman in the red dress.

"Isn't it amazing how the life in something disappears when it changes shape?" she said in a subdued voice, looking at the wreckage. "All the bits are there, but it's not a sculpture anymore."

Grabowski nodded. "Like anything that dies."

She didn't seem to hear. "When we opened this gallery, I thought everyone's paintings were as valuable as anyone else's. But after Ros got real artists, my own stuff looked awful."

Her voice seemed as frail as her body, which looked as if a shadow had fallen over her. Grabowski wondered if she remembered who he was. He was about to introduce himself when she laughed a shaky laugh.

"I'm embarrassed to hear myself saying 'real artist.' A group of us who took painting classes together opened this gallery to get rid of our stuff—a joke, really. Then Ros started promoting the place, pretending it was real art." She shrugged.

"Wasn't it real art?"

"When I started painting, I thought that what separated hobbyists from real artists was that hobbyists couldn't sell their work. But that just showed how much I didn't know about art."

Rosalyn came out of her office then, trailed by Louie. She looked more energetic and directed. Hands on hips, she stood facing the demolished sculpture.

"How soon can we tidy this up, Detective?" she demanded.

Grabowski leaned his tired head on his hands to think. The police photographer had taken ample photos; there was no need to dust it for fingerprints—everybody in the gallery had their hands on it at one moment or another—and besides, what would fingerprints show? What he needed was a pair of sharp wire cutters.

"Clear it away," he conceded.

Rosalyn and Louie began arguing about how to best sort out the rubble. Grabowski wandered into the kitchen.

The tiny kitchen doubled as a repair shop with a miniscule sink, coffee maker, two-ring burner, small microwave, and a below-the-counter refrigerator on one side. On the opposite wall, an impressive array of tools hung beneath a layer of cabinets. There were three types of wire cutters, a rack of screwdrivers and hammers, plastic sacks of picture wire, and small jars of white paint the same color as the walls.

Grabowski started opening drawers. One was filled with jars of chemicals marked with their use, most for cleaning or repairing painted objects. He jotted their names in his notebook. On the other side of the kitchen, the drawers held coffees, teas, and packages of cookies.

Kitty Zelazak stood in the doorway. "Why the search?"

Grabowski watched her out of the corner of his eye. "There's a chance the wire was cut, that the sculpture didn't fall by accident."

She swayed slightly, then steadied herself on the doorjamb.

He kept looking through cupboards. "Did you know the deceased well?" he asked.

Tears began flowing down her cheeks. "You'll find out sooner or later," she said. "Soren and I were lovers."

Grabowski stopped his search. "How long ago?"

She looked startled; the tears stopped. "Well, a little while. It wasn't really broken off, we just stopped."

"You angry about that?"

"Angry enough to cut the wire? There were people with better motives than me, Detective, and you won't have to look far. Soren's relationship with me was broken off as a mutual decision. He said my work wasn't improving. He felt a mentor should have more of an effect. Frankly, I think he was bored with me."

Grabowski was trying to figure out what this all meant when Rosalyn Mueller pushed past Kitty into the kitchen. Her face was flushed, and she was holding her left hand by the wrist. Blood was running down her fingernails. She opened the cupboard with cans containing paint and chemicals and dug some Band-Aids out of the back, then ripped one open with her teeth and fumbled with it. Grabowski smelled expensive perfume. He took the Band-Aid from her and covered the scrape. Rosalyn Mueller looked more alert now, and he needed information.

"Aren't you worried that your cookies and your lethal chemicals might mix?" he asked.

"They're not even close to each other. Besides, when I serve real food, I hire caterers."

"I have a couple more questions," he said. "Could we sit in your office?"

Rosalyn became even more self-assured when she was sitting behind her designer desk. She relaxed in her leather chair and drummed her nails on the arm.

Grabowski took his time flipping open his notebook. "I need to know who might want to have that sculpture fall. Got any ideas?"

She shrugged. "When I moved into this location, I cut into the business of the galleries around here. Milwaukee isn't Chicago; there are only so many art buyers to go around."

"How about the letters threatening arson? Could those people have cut the wire?"

Rosalyn looked him straight in the eye. "Possibly, but I have no idea who they are. They may be the invention of gallery owners around here whose businesses suffered because of my contacts in upper-class Milwaukee society."

Grabowski wrote down the names of the galleries Rosalyn Mueller felt were most affected by her business and also made a note to himself to check with the caterers. They may have noticed something while they were moving among the crowd last night.

He left the gallery uncertain about what he had accomplished. The only thing he knew for sure was that Lillian Hochstedder, Kitty Zelazak, and Rosalyn Mueller were a lot more complicated than they first appeared.

CHAPTER

6

SURVIVING WITHOUT A car couldn't be difficult in a city as obsessed with public transportation as Milwaukee, St. Clair thought, sitting at her kitchen table and flipping through the phone book for the Milwaukee City Transit information number. The streets were full of buses. She could avoid buying a car for a while, she thought, cheering up. Her work at St. Agnes started punctually at three and ended at midnight. She could take a city bus there and a taxi back. No more running out of gas, no more flat tires, no more scraping inches of ice off both sides of the windshield, no more insurance.

Not owning a car appealed ecologically, too: no more contributing to the greenhouse effect. A friend in Madison had gone years without a car, finding taxis cheaper. Of course that was Madison, where bicycles were a major transportation method and waiting outside at night for taxis was still safe.

In fact, it was a good thing her car had broken down, no, been stolen. She better get that straight in her head so she didn't make any slips with Grabowski. Eventually, he may figure out that she had left it for scavengers in the inner city. Her car had barely started the last time she gave him a ride, and they had joked about how many people dumped their beaters in the Milwaukee River to collect the insurance. The inner city was another dumping ground.

The Transit Information lady came on the phone. Maxene needed to take two buses, with a transfer on North Avenue. St. Clair put down the phone, less optimistic about being without wheels. She suppressed the feeling and picked up the phone again and dialed St. Agnes. She asked for Intensive Care.

"A gunshot victim came in last night," she began.

The floor secretary cut her off. "Tell Detective Grabowski that his friend is stable."

"I'm calling about the other gunshot victim. A woman."

"Just a moment." Muzak, Henry Mancini style, came over the phone. After a brief wait, a nurse replaced Mancini. Her voice was tense.

"Who's calling?"

"Dr. St. Clair."

A note of relief entered the woman's voice. "The police told me to get the name of anyone asking about the other gunshot victim. The woman is doing fine. She was transferred to the floor."

"And the other black woman who was brought in last night? First name Latoya. Came in about the same time. Very sick. Unconscious."

"Just a minute."

More Mancini. St. Clair took a carton of yogurt out of the refrigerator and spooned some into her mouth. So the woman was better. That meant the police would be asking her if she knew who was in the drive-by car. The nurse came back on the line.

"According to the computer report, a Latoya Thompson was admitted to the ER, but she died. No stated cause of death."

St. Clair said nothing.

The fact sat there in front of her, almost a physical thing. It wasn't as if patients didn't die in the ER. Staff helped each other through the ensuing depression, but there was no one to help St. Clair on this one. The girl asked for her, then died in the ER while St. Clair and Rolondo were driving down to the gallery. Would she have died if St. Clair had got there earlier?

"Dr. St. Clair?"

"I'm still here. Will there be an autopsy?"

"Yes. The chart went to Pathology."

That meant the attending physician couldn't figure out what to write on the death certificate. Autopsies weren't as common as they used to be, now that so many diagnostic tests were done while the patient was still alive. Autopsies now focused on specific organs. She wondered what organs Aaron Simonson, the pathologist, would start with.

"I'll be in the ER at three," she said. "Would you mind requesting that Pathology send her chart to the ER clerk?"

"Can't promise anything. You know Dr. Simonson."

St. Clair hung up. She sat at the kitchen table and thought about the girl who had died so young. She thought about the other women in the apartment who had worried about Latoya. She wanted to see them, to tell them how sorry she was about Latoya's death. Somehow it might ease her own feelings of sorrow and guilt. She flipped to the yellow pages and called for a taxi to come in half an hour, then stepped into the shower.

It was oven-hot on the corner of 5th and Center, and a bus blew grit into St. Clair's eyes. She paid the taxi driver, adding a healthy tip to allay his nervousness at being in a notoriously dangerous neighborhood. Rolondo's apartment building had been near this corner, but she wasn't sure exactly where. The dilapidated frame buildings with their boarded-up windows looked even more horrible during the day with aluminum cans, beer bottles, and dog excrement littering the sidewalk.

She spotted a loading zone that looked like the one where Rolondo had parked his car. The apartment had to be in the brick building in front.

The broken vodka bottle still sat among the others in the front hall when St. Clair pushed open the door. She climbed the three flights of steps and knocked on the black-beaded door. The black beads rattled. She waited, more nervous by the minute. Even though Milwaukee didn't have neighborhoods like Los Angeles where white people were ill-advised to go, a woman alone was still fair game for robbery or even rape. The door finally opened a few inches and the small black girl who had been at the apartment the night before looked out cautiously. Her eyes were swollen and red-rimmed.

"How are you doing?" St. Clair asked gently. The girl looked like a puff of breeze would blow her over.

"Okay." She opened the door and let Maxene into the front hall.

"Did you hear about Latoya?"

The girl nodded and sighed. "Rolondo told us. What did she die of?"

"I'll try to find out when I get to the hospital this afternoon. Is anyone else here sick?"

The girl shrugged. "Not so far as I know."

St. Clair hesitated. She couldn't think of anything more to say. The girl seemed completely used up, mentally, physically, emotionally.

"Can I look around Latoya's room?" St. Clair asked. "Maybe there's something that will help us figure out what happened."

A few articles of clothing were piled on the rumpled cot. St. Clair looked through them, hoping for a wrapper from a take-out store, but there was nothing. She shook out the sheet and folded it carefully as the girl stood watching in the doorway.

"There's something under the bed," the girl said.

St. Clair got down on her knees. There were several ashtrays overflowing with cigarette butts, and an open box of chocolates with a few pieces gone. "Do you know where she got the chocolates?"

The girl shrugged. "She practically lived on chocolate and cigarettes."

St. Clair tucked the box under her arm. "I heard Rosa is doing all right," she said, wanting to leave the tired girl with something besides bad news. "Her gunshot wound wasn't too serious, so they moved her out of Intensive Care. I'll see her this afternoon."

"That car just came out of nowhere; nobody knows

why." The girl paused. "Do you know how the man who was shot is doing?"

"Still unconscious."

"Poor dude. Moves in and gets shot, same week."

St. Clair's jaw dropped. "He lives in this building?"

The girl jerked her head at the door across the hall. "Rosa and Latoya knew him. Nice, they said. A real person."

"He wasn't visiting your, uh, establishment?"

"He never came here."

But why should she be surprised? Wyoming had been carrying groceries. Of course he lived here. St. Clair gestured behind her at the door across the hall. "I want to get in there and look around."

The girl shrugged, as if nothing surprised her anymore, or maybe her curiosity was all used up. She went into the kitchen and returned with a long butcher knife that she inserted between the doorjamb and the door. She forced the lock and pushed open the door.

"Lock it behind you," she said. "You never know."

The apartment was laid out the same as Rolondo's except that the rooms were nearly bare. No curtains hung over the big front windows that looked out over the street, no rugs lay on the worn hardwood floors, no stereo sat in the entry hall. Large boxes were piled in the hall and living room.

A white wicker chair and a small white couch covered with plastic were pushed into one corner. Sales tags from a furniture store were taped to the plastic.

St. Clair walked down the hall, peering into the rooms on either side. The kitchen had been partially tidied for living. The cupboards were empty, but dishes were neatly stacked in a wooden dish rack and a sugar bowl and salt and pepper shakers sat on a scrubbed oak table. The refrigerator, however, was well stocked: eggs, two-percent milk, fresh vegetables, cold Millers, and vanilla ice cream in the freezer.

In the bedroom, a narrow foam pad on the floor served as a bed. The yellow top sheet and striped Navaho blanket were folded neatly at the foot. Boxes stacked on their sides served as clothing cupboards.

St. Clair went back to the living room and stood looking at the boxes and wooden crates plastered with moving stickers that read, "Fragile" and "This side up." She crouched to check for identifying labels. "Syzinksi" was written on one. Proof. Or was that evidence?

She took a more careful look around. As an artist's studio, the flat was perfect. It had big rooms, tall ceilings, lots of light, and probably cheap rent. The flat had the feeling of the beginning of pleasant habitation. Syzinski had moved in; he just hadn't started work yet. There was no phone, however; she'd have to call Grabowski from Rolondo's kitchen phone, to tell him she'd found where Syzinski lived. As she started toward the door, however, the knob turned. She froze, wanting to run into the back of the apartment, or yell for help out the window. The door was opening. "Who is it!" she demanded loudly.

Four long black fingers wrapped themselves around the doorjamb, and Rolondo walked in.

Relief flooded over St. Clair, and she sank onto a packing crate, her knees trembling.

"This is the apartment of the man who was shot last night. He's a friend of Detective Grabowski's," she blurted. "I came by today to tell the women in your apartment how sorry I am about Latoya."

"Too bad you didn't get here soon enough to keep her alive."

St. Clair's temper flared, guilt mixed with anger. "And you shouldn't have let that girl get so sick before you called me."

Rolondo remained impassive. "I came to the ER at ten-thirty when she was still talking. You didn't leave to come here 'til midnight. Then your beater broke down. Is that my fault?"

St. Clair glared at him. "Why didn't you call me before ten-thirty?"

"She wasn't so sick then."

"You're telling me she got this sick, this fast?"

"Ask anybody here. What did she die of? Nothing any of the other ladies is going to get, is it?"

"Worried about profits?"

"You spending too much time with Shirley."

St. Clair drew a breath. "I don't know what she died of. They're doing an autopsy."

"What for?" Rolondo scowled.

"She can't be buried until a doctor writes on the death certificate what she died of. That's what the autopsy will tell. The coroner has to worry about communicable disease, or maybe that she didn't die of natural causes."

Rolondo was silent for a long moment. "What do you mean, natural causes?"

"Food poisoning, for example, is a natural cause. Poison of other kinds is not. Mind if I use your phone to call Grabowski?" St. Clair stood up.

"You telling me Latoya was poisoned in my house?" Rolondo demanded.

"No, I'm saying she wasn't under a doctor's care before she died."

"You was there."

"But I wasn't taking care of her. I saw her only briefly, and I didn't really examine her."

Instead of answering, Rolondo held up a warning hand and walked silently to the door. He yanked it open. Standing in the doorway was Grabowski.

"What the hell are you two doing here?" Grabowski snapped. Dark circles were etched under his bloodshot eyes.

"I was just about to call you," St. Clair said, astounded. "I was visiting across the hall, and the woman there told me Wyoming lived here. So I came over to make sure."

He scowled. "What were you doing across the hall?"

"I told you about it last night, remember? I came here after work to see an employee of Rolondo's who was sick. While I was here, your friend was shot."

Grabowski walked into the room and looked around him.

His shoulders were slumped, and his clothes looked like he had slept in them.

"Haven't you gone home yet?" St. Clair asked gingerly.

He shook his head, then sank down on a packing crate. "Is this really his place? Why didn't he tell me?" His voice sounded plaintive.

St. Clair wanted to put her arms around him, but Rolondo was watching. "Maybe he was waiting until it was fixed up."

"Why pick this dump?"

Rolondo frowned. "Some people call this their neighborhood."

"And some call it the Fifth Police Precinct," Grabowski snapped, "where there's the highest gun use in the city. Couldn't he have found a better place?"

St. Clair looked around again. Her previous opinion that it was a perfect artist's studio still held. She decided not to say so, at least until Grabowski got some sleep.

"The woman who was shot last night knew Wyoming," she said instead.

"She's a prostitute, for God's sake."

St. Clair decided the discussion could be continued later. She tucked her purse under her arm and moved toward the door.

"Where are you going?" Grabowski demanded.

"To St. Agnes. I thought I'd stop in on Wyoming before my shift starts."

Rolondo remained where he was, arms folded, leaning against the wall.

Grabowski glared at him. "You can leave, too."

"I ain't leaving until I look around. One of my girls was shot when she was with the dude from this apartment."

"It's not related," Grabowski said.

"She was related to me. She worked for me, she looked to me to take care of her, and she got shot."

"Since when have you cared what happened to the girls who work for you? And there's nothing here you can find out. I'm sealing this place until we have a chance to go over it. Figuring out what happened is my job, not yours. Stay out of it, and out of this apartment."

"Incidentally," he added, looking hard at St. Clair, "we found your car on Third and North Avenue, completely stripped."

"Really?" St. Clair looked at Rolondo.

"What do you mean, really?" Grabowski demanded. "Is this another coincidence?"

"My car broke down on the way over here last night, and I guess vandals stripped it before the tow truck could get there."

"Stripped it of what? Your car was nothing but a worn-out engine and four bald tires."

St. Clair eased out the door.

She lurked in the hallway until Rolondo had made his leisurely exit. "Any chance I could get a ride to the hospital?" she murmured, looking at her watch. "I'd call a cab, but it would take some time for one to get here, and I'd like to drop in on Rosa before I start work."

Rolondo had parked in the loading zone in front of the apartment and left the white Cadillac running, so it was nicely air-conditioned when St. Clair relaxed in the cool red leather of the front seat.

"You be wanting a new car when your insurance money comes in," Rolondo stated, driving slowly down Center. He pointed a warning finger at two prostitutes taking a breather in the shade on some apartment steps. They dragged themselves to their feet.

"I was hoping to get along without one for a while," St. Clair answered, watching the women. "I hate car shopping. That's why I always drive my cars into the ground."

"I can get you one, cheap."

St. Clair considered the idea. Driving a hot car held a certain antiestablishment appeal, but her middle-class mores would never go for it.

"I'd live in guilt, worrying about the poor person who came out to get his car and found it gone," she confessed.

"My brother owns a used-car lot on Burleigh."

St. Clair flushed. "Sorry," she said quickly. "I didn't mean to suggest it would be stolen."

Rolondo wasn't listening. "Latoya didn't die because of anything in my flat," he said, "but that cop friend of yours is going to make it seem that way. He's been looking to bust me for years."

St. Clair studied Rolondo's profile. Rolondo brought his prostitutes to the ER to get sewed up fairly regularly, and he had helped St. Clair get herself out of a sticky situation only a few months before. Rolondo never stated anything without a specific purpose.

"What are you saying?" she asked.

"I don't want to spend no time in jail for something I didn't do, and your friend the cop will make it his job to see that's exactly what I do."

St. Clair watched the boarded-up houses slide by. Grabowski wasn't on the vice squad, and he didn't care how prostitutes made their living, but he hated pimps. Especially, he hated Rolondo, who flaunted his illegal activities blatantly and made more money than any cop. "What do you want?" she asked.

"I want you to find out why Latoya died and make sure it didn't have nothing to do with me."

St. Clair considered the request. Aside from Rolondo's completely self-serving motives and the fact that he appeared to feel no sorrow over the girl's death, St. Clair saw an injustice coming, and it bothered her. The pimp's occupation made her sick, but it was part of life and would exist even if Rolondo did not. Prostitution was terrible, but it didn't have to lead to death. Some prostitutes tucked away money and eventually lived their own lives. Rolondo was a necessary evil who protected his women from worse fates. Besides, St. Clair too wanted to know why the girl died.

The drive-up entrance to St. Agnes was upon them.

"What if I find out that she did indeed die in your flat from something she ate there?" she asked.

"You ain't gonna 'cause nobody else is sick."

St. Clair was about to debate that when Rolondo's car

phone rang. He was deeply into a conversation in a language she vaguely recognized as English when he stopped the car in the turnaround and she let herself out.

CHAPTER

7

SHIRLEY WAS AT the nurse's station chatting with a group of nurses and orderlies when St. Clair slammed shut Rolondo's car door and came through the glass automatic doors of the ER.

"I was telling about our little adventure last night," Shirley greeted her, looking grim. "The shooting victims are okay, but the sick girl died."

St. Clair nodded. "I went over to Rolondo's flat to tell the other women."

"You had quite a night," said Joella, patting her on the shoulder.

"That was only half of it," said St. Clair, feeling depressed. "After the shooting, I went downtown to where Grabowski was doing security at an art gallery, to tell him about his friend being shot. When I was there, a sculpture fell out of the ceiling and crushed a man. He also died."

There was a long moment of silence.

"I'm going up to see Grabowski's friend before shift starts," St. Clair added, pulling on her lab coat.

"Say," said Shirley, "did you find out why Grabowski's friend was there last night? Aside from the obvious?"

"He actually lives there, in the flat across the hall from Rolondo's." She decided to omit the part about her breaking and entering the flat with Rolondo, at least until the rest of the hospital staff had left.

Wyoming Syzinski was still unconscious when St. Clair looked through the glass windows of the Intensive Care

Unit. Two bags of fluid were hanging over the bed, one with blood.

The nurse sitting at the monitors filled her in. "His hematocrit was falling, but it's better now. Do you know him personally?" She looked at St. Clair's white lab coat and name badge and jotted the name on the chart.

"I know a good friend of his. I feel like I should know him."

Syzinski's face was as pale as the sheets. His chest rose gently. St. Clair went through the glass cage and took Syzinski's motionless hand.

"You're going to be all right," she said to him. "You've had a bad accident, but you'll do fine. Grabowski is looking after you."

Rosa, the other gunshot victim, was down the hall in Progressive Care. St. Clair glanced at the chart before going in. Her eyes were open, but she was lying quite still. IVs were dripping into both arms.

"Remember me?" St. Clair asked, leaning on the bed rails. "I was there when you were shot last night."

The girl shook her head.

St. Clair headed toward the second-floor doctors' lounge to pick up a cleaner lab coat. As she came out of the elevator, she collided with Dr. Hochstedder and Dr. Simonson, the hospital pathologist.

"How's the head?" St. Clair asked Hochstedder. "At the gallery last night, you were really tying one on. You were telling me about your wife's sculptures. The glittering eyes?"

Hochstedder laughed, then winced in pain. He rubbed his head. "I don't remember anything except that awful sculpture falling." He looked at his watch.

"Excuse me, Maxene," said Dr. Simonson. "What's the story on the crush victim? Your name was on the ambulance report as the Good Samaritan. Police are requesting an autopsy. What'd you do to him?"

"Basic first aid," said St. Clair, evenly. "I didn't know about the autopsy. What's the problem?"

"Not a natural death, which is putting it mildly. I've got another Good Samaritan of yours from that night, a poison victim. You out drumming up business?" He chuckled.

St. Clair forced a smile. Simonson's humor was nauseating, but she wanted the results of both autopsies, and for this she had to stay on his good side.

"I'm glad you're doing the autopsy on the poison victim," she said sweetly. "I was afraid they'd send her to the county lab. She died so quickly after she became ill; I really want to know what happened."

Simonson flipped his candy wrapper in the direction of the receptacle by the elevator. "What were the symptoms?"

"When I saw her, she had been vomiting for only a couple of hours but she was already in a coma. Completely unresponsive. Respirations way down."

"What made you think it was poison?"

"The symptoms came on so fast, and her friend said she was seeing things—I think she meant hallucinating—so I wondered if she got into rat poison. The stuff is everywhere in those flats. When will you be done?"

"Don't rush me. Sister Rosalie moved a couple of stiffs ahead in line, people whose insurance will actually pay for autopsies. I could be through with them by ten tonight. Who was the crush victim, anyway?"

"A sculptor. One of his own sculptures fell on him." The elevator doors slid shut on Simonson's shriek of laughter.

In the doctor's lounge, Dr. Zelazak was lying on the couch, a medical journal spread over his narrow chest. He was snoring softly, his mouth a round circle, his thin brown hair poking upward. St. Clair carefully pulled a white coat from the cupboard, but her elbow caught a tangle of metal hangers, and they hit the ground with a clatter. Zelazak opened his eyes.

"Damned art gallery," he said, spotting her and struggling to a seated position. "I didn't get to sleep until three A.M., I'd still be up if I hadn't slipped some Valium into Kitty's hot chocolate."

"You drugged your wife's cocoa?" St. Clair stopped picking up the hangers.

"Do it all the time. She's nervous; can't sleep, drinks that herbal crap—ginseng tea, for God's sake, dandelion tea—and thinks it relaxes her. Really, it's the Valium."

St. Clair made a mental note to get the news to Kitty Zelazak as soon as possible, maybe through Louie. She barely knew Kitty, but this sort of deception was scary. What if the woman got behind the wheel of a car with a head full of Valium?

"Your wife looked very upset last night," she said. "I don't blame her for not being able to sleep."

"Exciting, wasn't it? Like a house falling down. Made me jump, I'll tell you, and I've got nerves of steel."

"I was referring to the man being killed."

"Oh him. Can you believe he was sitting there when it fell? How unlucky can you get?"

"Did Kitty know him well?" She slowly put on her lab coat.

"Can't think why she would, him being an artist."

"So is she."

Zelazak made a face. "Painting is her hobby; she's a dabbler, like her girlfriends. Keeps them busy."

"But the invitation said that her art work was in the show. That means she's good, doesn't it?"

"It means her canvases were piled all over the house, and I told her to get rid of them."

St. Clair felt herself becoming annoyed. "When do you stop being amateur and start being professional?"

"When you get rich." Zelazak dragged his feet off the couch and ran a hand through his thinning hair. He looked at his watch, then poked his beeper to make sure it was working.

St. Clair stood looking down at Zelazak, her hands in her pockets. "Did your wife ever work outside the home?"

"When I first went into practice, she helped out at the clinic as the receptionist and bookkeeper. She's a bright gal. Every once in a while I have her look over the bookkeeper's shoulder. Kitty caught a couple of misbillings last quarter that would have cost me fifteen thousand in Medicare payments. If you don't mail those things in on time, the bastards won't pay."

"She still works for you?"

"In an emergency. Office staff lasts a couple years, tops. It's boring waiting for patients to come in. That's why the receptionist I have now helps as a medical aide, and does my books, too."

"Doesn't your receptionist mind having Kitty look over her shoulder?"

"Oh, the girl before this one minded, but I didn't have trouble replacing her. The Medical Society has a list of front-office girls."

He rose to his feet and stretched. "Got to go. Surgery. Hope I can stay awake."

"Maybe a surgery nurse will pinch you," St. Clair forced a joke.

"Why not? They should get a chance, too."

St. Clair was scowling as she walked into the ER. Joella was putting on a coat of clear polish over the preexisting scarlet.

"Look who's in a crabby mood." Joella smiled.

"Do I have moods?" St. Clair leaned against the counter. "Do you people actually have to put up with my moods?"

"Don't take me so seriously." Joella blew on her nails. "Of all the doctors around here, you are the least moody. I only asked because you looked crabby, not because you are in a crabby mood, if you catch the difference."

"What do you know about Dr. Zelazak, the surgeon?" St. Clair asked.

"Last week in the cafeteria I saw him pat a little redhaired student nurse on the ass."

St. Clair was astounded. "What did she do?"

"She didn't dump her coffee on his you-know-what, like I would have. You white girls have a lot to learn about handling dudes. Some days I sit in that cafeteria and think, 'Joella, honey, you should put up a sign in the elevator:

Classes: Self-respect in the workplace.' Shirley and I could straighten this place out. That pimp Rolondo called for you," she added. "Here are his numbers. The first one is his car phone. Let it ring awhile so the scrambler can work."

Rolondo picked up the phone on the fourteenth ring.

"You be wanting a ride home?" he asked.

St. Clair was pleasantly surprised. She hung up with a smile. "He wanted to give me a ride home," she reported.

Joella frowned. "You watch your step, honey."

At 7:00 P.M., St. Clair took her dinner up on a tray and sat by Wyoming's bed. "Shirley told me that unconscious people know when a friendly soul is nearby," she said to him, munching on her carrot salad. In the quiet, she could swear that his attention was on her, that his unimpaired senses knew she was there and were recording it until his conscious mind woke up.

She was finishing her Jell-O and telling him about her day when Grabowski came in. He was wearing a rumpled khaki jacket and slacks with Polo shirt. He leaned on the bed rail across from her.

"Nice of you to look in on Wyoming," he said, rubbing his forehead. "The nurses said you were here before."

"I feel like I know him, maybe because I've been in his flat."

Grabowski looked down at Syzinski and spoke without lifting his eyes. "Sorry I yelled at you earlier today. I had spent a lot of time banging on doors trying to find his flat, and when I walked in and found you and that pimp already there, well, I lost my perspective."

"Hard to keep perspective when people get gunned down on the street for no reason."

"He only came back to get the Midwest into his bones again," Grabowski said. "He should have stayed in the desert where it was safe—just rattlesnakes and rednecks with rifles in their pickups." He took a couple of deep breaths and ran his fingers through his heavy black hair.

"We grew up together," he went on. "We got in the same trouble, liked the same girls. He's been gone fifteen years,

and we still call each other a couple times a year, write at
Christmas. I spend a week or two in Arizona with him every year. He's always got some woman trying to domesti-
cate him."

"You miss him," said St. Clair.

Grabowski nodded. "I don't understand him, but I miss
him. He's got some clue about life that I didn't catch. He's
alone painting or doing his sculpture all day, but he under-
stands people better than I do, and I'm with people all day
long."

St. Clair smiled.

Grabowski went on. "At Madison, during college, he always had weird types around, artists, musicians. Seems like
I know only cops and criminals."

"He's going to be all right, Grabowski."

Rolondo showed up at the ER at midnight and slouched
elegantly through the electric doors, his white Cadillac left
purring in the patient loading zone. Shirley, Joella, and
Maxene followed him out of the ER into the warm night.

"Watch your step, honey," Joella muttered as she got into
the black Oldsmobile her boyfriend was driving. Maxene
and Shirley got into the backseat of the Cadillac. Shirley
patted the red leather with affection.

"I sure do hope Roy is up when I get home," she said.
"He ain't going to believe the style I'm ridin' in."

St. Clair hoped her neighbors were asleep. They already
treated her as an eccentric to be tolerated at arm's length.
As a divorced woman who worked nights, drove a Japanese
car—or used to—rode a bicycle to do her grocery shopping, and lived amicably upstairs from a confessed member
of the gay community, St. Clair had few real backers
among her neighbors. She didn't need them to see her rid-
ing with a stylishly dressed pimp in his white Cadillac.

At Shirley's Lannon stone house in the middle-class
black neighborhood on the North Side, Shirley's husband
Roy was playing poker on the cool front porch. Rolondo
shook hands all around and accepted a beer and a cigar.

St. Clair smiled resignedly at the beer pressed into her hand and sat with Shirley on the porch steps, sipping it.

"Not a bad life," she said, after listening to Shirley mutter about Rolondo's popularity among the poker players. She looked at the stars and watched people pass around plates of something very fried. She felt as at home on this porch as she did sitting on Grabowski's front porch on the Polish South Side, or sitting in the faculty meetings at Marquette where she spent the ten years before she started working at St. Agnes'. Or sitting in Louie's antique store drinking one of his villainous concoctions.

She frowned, wondering what Louie was up to. He had a hysterical nature, given to extremes. After his "accident" with sleeping pills the year before when one of his relationships fell apart, she had kept an eye on him.

"Rolondo," she said. "This is nice, but I need to get home."

This time she sat in front with the air conditioner blowing on her legs. Rolondo was silent until they had crossed the river to the East Side.

"I talked to my lady who got shot today," he said. "She saw the car that drove by, but she didn't recognize it or anybody in it. But she said it wasn't no accident."

"What do you mean?"

"She said they was aiming at her. I mean to find out why. Maybe somebody moving in on my territory. Tell your cop friend to help me, and he'll find out quicker why his friend got shot."

"Help you, how?"

"Whatever your cop friend finds out, tell me. I'll do the same."

In front of St. Clair's Milwaukee bungalow, he parked behind a dented green Plymouth. "Your friend, the cop. Can't he drive a better car than that beater?"

"He had a new Ford Taurus Sho, but it was stolen a month ago. I'll talk to you about your proposal tomorrow."

Grabowski got slowly up from the porch swing when she crossed the grass. "I came to get you at the ER, but they said you left with Shirley and that pimp. Do you realize that cruising the city with a pimp at this hour is not the safest way home? What did he want?"

"He thinks his girl was shot on purpose to cut into his business."

"More reason you shouldn't be driving with him."

"He's planning to find out why, and he says if you tell him what you know, he'll reciprocate. He has sources you don't."

"I don't know a thing, and if I did, I wouldn't tell him." He followed her up the steps and into the kitchen and accepted a cold beer. "What happened was a random shooting. They're on dope, they have guns, they shoot them. Simple as that."

He put down his beer and put his arms around her. "Max, forget the pimp. I'm lonely. I don't want to go home alone anymore. You never know when life will suddenly end and you've missed something very big."

"You talking about what happened to Wyoming?" Her voice was muffled in his shirt.

"I don't know. . . . Go to bed; you look beat."

Why hadn't he stayed, St. Clair wondered, turning off the porch light and locking the door behind him. She was still wondering an hour later when she finally fell asleep.

CHAPTER

8

GRABOWSKI WOKE AT dawn the next morning thinking about Rosalyn Mueller. He had dreamed about her, an eerie dream where no one looked like themselves. Rosalyn had been talking in a throaty, emphatic voice, sounding excited or angry. He went out to the front porch to let the morning air dissipate an uneasy feeling.

The sun was a red ball rising over Lake Michigan. Grackles were poking their beaks into the dew-damp lawn and a low-flying seagull mixed his loud cries with two crows sitting on the neighbor's low fence. Grabowski went back in the kitchen to make coffee and his first ICU call of the day. The news was the same: no better, no worse. Dr. St. Clair had visited several times before midnight. He dragged a kitchen chair through the living room and out on the front porch and put his feet up on the railing while he waited for coffee to brew.

The porch railing was cracked and needed replacing, like many things in the bungalow. In fact, the whole porch needed replacing, as Wyoming had pointed out. Grabowski had bought the place for a song because it was falling down, thinking it would be fun to fix up, but he had yet to get enthusiastic about starting. For a studio, Wyoming had said, the bungalow lacked light, and the ceilings weren't high enough, but for a friendly place to come home to, it was perfect.

Wyoming's apartment off Center made a decent studio, except for the dangerous neighborhood, Grabowski had to admit. The rooms were full of daylight and were big enough to hold his easels and pedestals. Still, it didn't come close to Wyoming's house in Arizona.

In Arizona, Wyoming lived in a two-room adobe cottage at the end of a dusty street in a half-Mexican village north of the border crossing at Nogales. Mountains filled every window, and the wide veranda all around the house was shaded by a latticework of interwoven sticks that broke the blazing western sun into dappled shade. Grabowski spent a week there last summer, sleeping off his burnout in a hammock on the veranda. Every day he watched the sun march across the desert sky, and every night he listened to lizards rustling on the veranda roof.

The coffee smelled ready. The sand on the kitchen floor crunched under his bare feet while he tossed a couple of sweet rolls into the toaster oven. The cleaning lady had put a layer of aluminum foil in the bottom of the toaster oven, he noticed, probably tired of scraping out burned sugar. Grabowski was addicted to sweet rolls, coffee, and beer. The cigarette addiction had been broken fifteen years before.

He took his coffee and roll out to the porch, thinking about Rosalyn Mueller. She was unlike any woman he had known—elegant, educated, smart. And wealthy, he thought, although he wasn't sure. She was divorced from a surgeon, but how much she got from the divorce, or how much she earned personally, was hard to tell. He wondered how helpful the tax authorities would be, given his sketchy need for evidence.

He also wondered what Rosalyn was doing at the moment. Was she sleeping still, or maybe getting herself breakfast—probably oat bread toast and grapefruit juice. Maxene St. Clair had two cups of black tea, half a grapefruit, two soft-boiled eggs, and a piece of toast with jam every morning. The flavor of the jam was the only variable. He had discovered that a few months before when she had spent a week at his bungalow while he hunted down the person who assaulted her. After she left, the place was empty.

He was forty-two now, he thought, looking at some tiny varicose veins in his suntanned feet. The last time he sat out on this porch was last week with Wyoming. They had joked about their mutual bachelor status. Being oldest sons in large Polish families had been responsibility enough for a lifetime.

Still, he was tired of being single. He didn't take advantage of it; in fact, he hadn't gone out with anyone but Maxene for the last year. Wyoming hung out with artists, models, theater types; he traveled, met interesting people.

The sun turned to orange, then yellow, as it rose. A sweet smell blew off the lake, as if the rising sun were pushing the wind.

Every case had a key, a pivot that the problem turned on. Sometimes the pivot became obvious as soon as he started to poke around. But other times, the pivot wasn't obvious until events were pushed to the extremes. Grabowski was beginning to think this was that kind of case, one with a lot of strange loose ends.

Who was Rosalyn Mueller? She knew a lot about art and enough about business to turn a small gallery into a well-run operation. Art was a field Grabowski knew nothing about. He wished Syzinski were here to give him advice, not lying in that hideous white hospital bed. The sun rose higher. Grabowski yawned. He went back to bed.

At ten o'clock, rested, dressed, and reasonably clear-headed, he drove across the Dan Hoan Bridge from Bay View to talk to the caterers and continue interviewing the gallery owners or directors. To some detectives, this was the tedious part of an investigation, but Grabowski liked it best. He could suspend reality and move backward in time by tracing events in reverse. He felt no hurry, just a need to gather as much information as possible. He always took extensive notes, often finding that a small comment from an obscure individual could trigger a chain of reasoning that led in the right direction.

The catering service was in a remodeled brick warehouse in the yuppified Martin Luther King Square. The caterer looked tired.

"That gallery opening was total chaos," she said, rubbing her eyes. "Too many people, and I ran out of food. I do all Ros's functions, and usually we guess right on the numbers, but not this time. About eleven-thirty I sent a truck out to pull supplies from an event scheduled for today. Now I'm scrambling to fill orders for that one. Don't ask me what was going on there; I didn't see anything except how fast the trays were being emptied."

Grabowski left with the names of the kitchen staff and servers. The addresses were scattered all over Milwaukee and West Allis, so he would move on to those this afternoon.

A few blocks from Rhinestones he parked in front of a small gallery and showed his card to a young woman at the reception desk. She didn't seem surprised to see a detective. Either she had been expecting him, or surprises were few in the art business. She buzzed the owner by intercom and poured Grabowski a cup of coffee. "Did you know Soren Berendorf?" queried Grabowski.

To his interest, the girl flushed. "Ah, everyone knew him," she stammered. "He was famous."

"But did you know him personally?"

Her flush deepened. "He was in here a lot when his papier mâché sculptures were on display."

The arrival of the gallery owner allowed her to escape. Grabowski made a note of her name and settled back to find out the owner's opinion of Soren Berendorf. The gallery owner was a chubby, middle-aged man wearing tan chinos and a Polo shirt. He watched the young woman as she left the room.

"The man was completely unscrupulous," he promptly said, to Grabowski's question about what kind of person Soren Berendorf had been. "He had talent, sure, maybe he even had a gift. But he kept his eye on the bottom line, and if he could use someone to maximize his profits, he'd do it."

Grabowski wasn't surprised since he'd heard this before. Still, each bit of news added to the complete picture. He felt like an artist himself, re-creating a person who had vanished. "Specifically?"

"He played fast and loose with contracts. Contracts are only as binding as the signers want, and Soren's intentions changed with the wind.

"Artists need galleries—we display their work, for God's sake, along with handling all the taxes—but Soren used galleries as free space. As soon as buyers started coming, he'd yank his stuff out and sell directly to them, skipping the gallery commission."

"Why didn't you refuse to carry his work?"

The gallery owner drummed his fingers on the mahogany desk. "He's persuasive, plus he's a known name. Having his stuff in the gallery drew in people who bought other things."

Grabowski made a few notes, nothing extensive. It was old news. What came next was new.

"He met his match at Rhinestones," the man said with a satisfied smile. "She's tough, that Mueller woman, built like a greyhound, strong as a mastiff. Had to be, to survive that divorce. Her husband kicked her out with practically nothing, you know."

"I didn't."

"The settlement was the talk of the medical community, where I have a few friends. She walked out of a mansion with a check for a hundred thousand and a couple suitcases of clothes. And her jewelry, not a small item."

"Why did she leave?"

"Neglect, according to my wife, but then that's the woman's view. All women feel neglected. Men do, too; we just don't build a case around it. I think Ros got tired of playing second fiddle. She's too smart for it, and too tough."

"Sounds like she left, not that she was kicked out."

"She could have had half a million if she had fought for it. Maybe she was saving her strength for her gallery."

"Was she having an affair?"

The man shrugged.

"How is her gallery business?"

The owner smiled. "You gotta respect your enemies. She cut into my business in a way I didn't expect. I thought they would be just a group of medical wives dabbling in art to fill their time. But Ros sails close to the wind, that woman, and she cut ahead of us before we even knew what was happening. She had to, economically. You can't run an art gallery long on only a hundred thousand."

"You think she outwitted Soren Berendorf?"

He smiled again. "I'm sure of it. He came in here a couple days before the opening, trying to move his exhibition. That means she got him in a corner on the contract, and he was trying to get out before it was too late."

"Is the art at Rhinestones any good?" Grabowski asked, looking around at the gallery. Even with his limited knowledge, he recognized one Picasso, one Dali, one Chagall.

"She's got a good eye. Of course she's limited by her partners. The gallery has to display their stuff, and I bet it grates on Ros's nerves. Kitty Zelazak is strictly amateur, and Lillian Hochstedder, well, she's got a gimmick that detours her lack of talent, but then the public doesn't necessarily recognize or reward talent."

The receptionist was dusting the gallery when Grabowski left. She gave him a quick sideways glance, and he could see she had been crying.

People at the next two galleries offered no more real information. Soren Berendorf was respected as an artist and detested as a human being. Grabowski wrote down the names of people who had purchased his art and walked on toward Rhinestones. He liked walking through Milwaukee, no matter what street. Even in the poorest areas, the city had vitality, people struggling to survive and having some success. It wasn't a liberal city—the parks and social services were a result of rigid German paternalism that dictated the public good as a form of control, but the structure of city services provided a framework on which immigrants could climb upward.

Rhinestones Gallery had the "Closed" sign hanging on the front door, but it swung open at his push. The dismantled sculpture had been stacked into four piles of wood, segregated roughly by its size. Grabowski's crepe soles made no sound on the hardwood floor as he crossed to the office to look for Rosalyn Mueller.

She was sitting behind her desk, a large folder with unframed drawings lying in front of her. She was paging through them carefully, making notes on a legal pad. The circles under her eyes were gone, Grabowski noticed. Some women recovered quickly from trauma, others carried it the rest of their lives.

Today Rosalyn was wearing a black suit and some kind of soft blouse that was gray or pink, Grabowski couldn't decide. A purple handkerchief was tucked into the jacket breast pocket. He tapped lightly on the door.

Rosalyn half shrieked. She passed a hand over her face and tried to smile. "I can't believe I didn't hear you. Normally I hear everything going on in the gallery."

Grabowski eased himself into the soft white leather armchair opposite the desk and fished around for a question. He really had nothing to go on. Maybe honesty was the best policy. Sometimes it worked.

"Yesterday morning I was too tired to come up with good questions, and you had a mess to clean up, so I didn't think either of us was in a frame of mind to talk about what happened. Do you have a minute now?"

"All the time you want, Detective. I'm not making any progress here." Her red nail polish had survived the dismantling of the sculpture, Grabowski noted, or she had applied a new coat.

"You planning a new show?" he asked, pointing at the portfolio in front of her.

"Yes. It may seem callous only two days after poor Soren died," she went on, "but to tell the truth, if I sit home

I get depressed. So I came down this morning hoping work would take my mind off the situation."

"How bad is the situation?"

She leaned back in her chair. "I can't even guess whether this horrible accident has ruined my business or given me a healthy dose of publicity. The *Milwaukee Journal* photos of the sculpture crashing down are on front pages all over the country."

The phone rang, and she picked it up automatically. "Fine, that will be fine," she said into the phone, and hung up. She began drumming her long red nails on the desktop, staring at the drawing in front of her. Then she seemed to remember that Grabowski was waiting. She put her hands in her lap and smiled a thin smile.

"That was the architect for a new building in New York," she explained. "I had been negotiating the sale of one of Soren's sculptures with him for some weeks, and the architect called earlier today, wanting to know if the price was the same. I had thought he would back out of the deal, but he still wants the piece."

"So you'll make some money off the exhibit despite the tragedy."

"Maybe, it depends on Soren's estate. This afternoon I'm meeting the attorney who's handling the will. If Soren had a long line of creditors, which I suspect he did, given his life-style, the estate will have to be sold quickly to pay them off."

"So you're sitting pretty."

"If I'm chosen to handle the sales. This is a small gallery by Chicago or New York standards, and his attorney may want a big-name operation with wealthy collectors ready to buy. All I have for sure is one architect. Big galleries also have healthy publicity budgets. And then, we can't forget that I let one of Soren's own sculptures fall on him and kill him. Not terribly responsible." She laughed without humor.

Grabowski took out his notebook and glanced at some of the comments other gallery owners had made. "Now that

Soren Berendorf is dead, isn't his work more valuable? If you do get the contract, you'll make good commissions."

"Dead artists aren't necessarily more popular. Just because the supply is fixed doesn't mean the demand goes up. It depends on the artist's popularity. There has to be an existing market."

"Was there?"

"Picasso, he wasn't, but his big pieces were good enough to be bought by museums and public buildings all over the world. His fame won't help me now, though. I need contacts and money for publicity." She frowned and began drumming her nails again.

"If he's so famous, why did he have his opening here? No offense, but you yourself said you were a small gallery."

Rosalyn smiled graciously. "I am small, but I could offer him wealthy doctor connections. Years ago, I met Soren when he was a struggling unknown, and I was married to Dr. Fort Knox. I bought a couple of small things as investments. Now I'm the one who's struggling, and Soren agreed to do this for me."

"Sounds like you knew him pretty well."

She laughed. "Well enough to get good and tired of him. That's the trouble with real artists. They're eccentric as hell, and they lead such bizarre lives that it's hard to make any real connection. They travel in another time dimension, or maybe another reality."

"Another gallery owner said Berendorf only saw profit potential."

She nodded. "I had to watch him like a hawk. Even after we agreed on the contract, he tried to move money his way. It's understandable. He created the sculptures; he felt he should get all the rewards."

"Monetary and otherwise?" Grabowski asked.

She looked at him sharply. "What are you talking about?"

"I heard there were other attractions to this gallery besides financial."

"You mean Kitty, I suppose. That's been over for a while. Soren gets tired of people quickly. But Kitty wouldn't take any horrible revenge, like dumping Soren's sculpture on him. She doesn't have enough self-esteem. More likely, she'd dump it on herself."

Grabowski waited, but nothing more was forthcoming. The red nails started drumming again.

"Do doctors invest a lot of money in art?" He was glancing through his notes again.

"Oh, they invest in art like they invest in anything. Most doctors think that since they know medicine, they know everything. That means they're easily persuadable. To sell a painting to a doctor, I let him think it's his idea to buy it. Not difficult, since doctors do all the talking."

"You said 'him.'"

Rosalyn considered the thought. "I've never had any women doctors as clients, but I don't know why. Maybe they don't buy art, at least at my prices."

"Then Soren wasn't just doing this out of the kindness of his heart. You have contacts in the medical world."

"Right. In fact, since I divorced Fort Knox, my doctor business has tripled. I was still married when we started this gallery, and our husbands considered us a cute tax write-off, which we were. After I got divorced and started building up the gallery, the doctors I knew socially started realizing that maybe I knew what I was doing. And also, since doctors are essentially sexist, they think I'm dumb enough to sell them a painting for less than they could get it elsewhere."

"But you don't."

"They get what they pay for. Actually they may pay more here. Even though doctors may shop around for an investment, money is an indicator of worth for them. They work in a salary hierarchy, with surgeons at the top, and out-earning one another is part of the fun. So the more expensive an investment, the better. It shows how much they make. Sometimes I tell them, 'You're paying a little extra for this because it's so good.' And they go for it."

"You're sounding cynical."

She shrugged. "I was a spoiled rich lady for twenty years, and after my divorce, I grew up quick. Maybe that made me cynical. I admire people who strike out on their own early and get reality in small doses. I got reality all at once, and for a while, I was reeling."

"Your husband was a surgeon?"

"Cardiac. Top-dollar breadwinner."

"Didn't you come out of the marriage with lots of money?"

Rosalyn folded her hands. "Is that question related to the investigation, or can we let it go as bad taste?"

"Sorry."

She let him off with a small smile.

He flipped through his notebook hoping a question would rise from the scribblings, but none did. When he looked up Rosalyn was staring at a painting propped up against the wall.

"Why do artists think that grass and leaves and sunlight can look different from one another when they're all painted with the same stupid dabbing? Can't that lurking-in-the-grass effect happen any other way besides using matching brush strokes in different colors?"

She was speaking English, Grabowski thought, but the words had no meaning to him. He pushed back his chair. "Go back to work; prepare yourself for this afternoon. If I think of something else to ask, may I come back?"

"Any time."

Grabowski hesitated. He wanted to ask if 'anytime' meant over a cold beer in a quiet bar. He was deciding not, when she half rose.

"Why don't you come over for dinner tonight?" she asked. "I want to figure out what happened as much as you, and maybe over a glass of something in a more relaxed atmosphere, we can come up with some answers."

Moments later he pushed out into the heat waves wondering if taking her up on her invitation had been a good idea. Was he mixing pleasure with business? Or was she up to something? If she were, a relaxed dinner was a good way to find out.

The question for the moment was what to do next. What he really wanted was to see Szyinski's apartment again. There might be something there to hint at what happened. On the other hand, police headquarters was just a few blocks away. He'd check in there first. He hadn't shown his face there yet today.

CHAPTER

9

A KNOT OF detectives, including the captain, were lounging around Grabowski's desk drinking coffee. Grabowski pushed through them with a few absentminded hellos and began hunting in his drawers for the list he had made of the galleries in town. After a minute he realized everyone was watching him.

"What's up?" he asked, leaning back in his chair.

"Did you hear Koranda has disappeared?" the captain demanded.

"The Koranda who's guard at the crime lab? He's up in his cabin, fishing."

Grabowski continued searching through his drawers. Normally his desk was reasonably tidy, but he had spent too many days just shoveling papers into the top drawer. Time to sort them out. As he began piling them on top of his desk, he realized everyone was still watching him.

"He's not fishing," the captain said. "The county sheriff says nothing in his cabin looks moved, and today a meter maid found his car in the parking lot by that old tannery on Water Street."

Grabowski started paying attention. "How long had it been there?"

"Don't know. All we know is the crime lab schedule says Koranda had two days off from guard duty; then he didn't show up for work."

"Don't his friends know where he is?"

"He doesn't have friends, at least among his neighbors, and the coppers he worked with didn't socialize with him."

"I don't blame them." Grabowski didn't like Koranda much. He was an ill-tempered, scruffy man in his late fifties whose wife had died or left him decades before. Nobody knew the real story. He had been transferred to guard duty at the new crime lab when it opened, and he did the minimal amount of work. Whenever he had time off, he drove to his cabin in northern Wisconsin and fished for lunkers in the lakes and rivers.

The captain of detectives tossed a folder on his desk. "Whatever you feel about Koranda, he's a cop, and he's disappeared. You're assigned to the case. Find him."

"I'm busy," Grabowski protested.

"You're the least busy of anybody. All you've got are a couple robberies and the art gallery accident. You're spending too much time on the gallery. Close it up."

"The wire was cut. Does that sound like an accident?"

"I don't care what it sounds like. The mayor's office called this morning pissed off because the *Journal* found out about the cut wire. The mayor and his wife were at the gallery last night, and they don't like nosy reporters asking what they know about a possible homicide. The mayor's up for reelection this year, and the order is, no bad press."

"Maybe the mayor cut the wire himself. He hates art fairies, as he was once quoted in the *Journal*."

"The mayor says Close up the case."

"But I have no idea who cut the wire."

The captain sighed and sat down on the adjoining desk. "To tell you the truth, I'm on your side. The more pressure I get about closing the case, the less I like it. The mayor's PR people are publicity-shy, but now that the *Journal* knows it's no accident, it will be hard to sweep it under the rug. Tell you what, I'll tell the reporters we've got some leads and stall them for a couple of days. In the meantime, don't talk to journalists, and get busy on Koranda."

Grabowski scowled at the broad back of his captain and wondered who else besides the mayor had put out the no-bad-press order. Bad press wasn't something that bothered Grabowski. He'd spent too much time bending the elbow with reporters to worry about anticop conspiracies. But speaking of the press, the art critic's other photos would be good to look at. Art critics didn't count as journalists. He jotted the thought into his notebook, then flipped open the folder with Koranda's name on it.

Why should Koranda tell anyone where he was going? On the other hand, Wyoming had gone off for a week and got himself shot. Grabowski picked up the phone and called the hospital. Wyoming was still unconscious. He sighed, suddenly washed with fatigue. The blood donation he had given yesterday had sapped his energy. He went to the coffee machine for a cup of tepid brew. It seared his stomach.

Koranda's folder was empty except for a piece of paper with the address and phone number. He dialed the number, and after twenty rings, called Information. The number was accurate. He looked at his watch. Time for lunch. Then he'd drive out to Koranda's house and look around, maybe stop by Syzinski's apartment. As he was scribbling the address in his notebook, the phone rang. It was Maxene.

"I just got up," she said. "Want some lunch?"

"Tony's. Ten minutes."

"Make it twenty," said St. Clair. "I'm coming by cab."

Tony's was the dirtiest bar in downtown Milwaukee. It also served the crispest fish fries, the thickest corned beef sandwiches, and the cheapest good beer. For that reason it was permanently inhabited by alcoholics taking a break from the soup kitchen at St. Anthony's homeless shelter.

Grabowski had eaten at Tony's for years. One night he had walked in after midnight to discover Maxene St. Clair sharing a fly-specked linoleum table with two prostitutes

sporting bandages, all gorging themselves on corned beef
and beer.

At the time, Grabowski himself had been wearing
stitches in his arm that St. Clair had put in a few days before. At the ER, Grabowski had been impressed with St.
Clair's casual acceptance of his injury as well as the bloody
condition of the handcuffed arrestee. That night at Tony's,
it seemed natural to join the three women for a beer. Since
then Grabowski had met Maxene at Tony's after midnight
a couple of times a month.

Tony's during the day was the same as Tony's at night,
only hotter. A feeble window air conditioner blew sausage
fumes from the grill. The waitress was wearing a sleeveless
red T-shirt with cutoffs, and sweat ran down her neck, but
the mug of beer she smacked in front of Grabowski was
icy.

As he was holding the glass to his forehead, a taxi pulled
up and Maxene St. Clair got out. Grabowski watched her
pay the driver and hurry across the scorching sidewalk into
the café. She held up a hand to him in greeting, shouted for
a beer, then checked the chair seat for debris left by the
previous customer. Grabowski felt a sudden surge of affection. He reached across the table and took her hand.

"I don't know many women who can sit in Tony's and
enjoy themselves," he said.

She gave his hand a squeeze, then took her beer from the
waitress. "To be honest, Grabowski, central air-conditioning
would do a lot for this place. I may have to shower again
before work."

"What's up, or is this lunch strictly social?"

"Louie didn't do anything," St. Clair said promptly. "The
poor man has broken out in total body hives. Don't you
have someone else you can frighten?"

"If he's so innocent, why is he panicked?"

"Because that's Louie. He does nothing in moderation,
and being accused of murder is bringing his hysterics out in
full force. He can't possibly have cut a wire and dropped a

sculpture on top of someone. He doesn't have the nerve—or he's got too many."

"I can't figure out what's going on," Grabowski admitted. "I can't even concentrate on this thing, I've got my mind on Wyoming. I've got two burglaries and a disappearance—a cop, if you can believe that."

Grabowski caught the waitress's attention and pointed at the corned beef sandwiches she was carrying. He held up two fingers, and glanced at St. Clair. She nodded.

"A cop disappeared?" St. Clair asked.

"A guard at the crime lab on South Eleventh Street. Anything happens to a cop, it's priority, and my captain stuck me with it because the mayor is putting on the pressure to close the art case. The wire at the gallery was cut, for God's sake, and somebody outside the force is telling us to close the case. I don't like it."

"That means you don't think Louie did it."

"Louie could have done it easily, although I have no idea why; with Berendorf dead, he can't be his groupie. But then, his hives could come from his fear of getting caught."

"Surely you don't believe that."

"Look, Maxene, an investigation is like playing baseball in the dark. You don't know where the ball is, you can only see a vague white blur and hear a funny rushing noise. You can't even look at the ball directly; you have to look to the side or it disappears completely in the dark. All you can do is put your hands out and hope it doesn't hit you in the face."

St. Clair smiled. "I'm a sucker for your baseball analogies, but Louie isn't part of whatever happened."

Their corned beef came, and they ate in silence.

"Why do women wear perfume?" Grabowski added finally. "Do they wear it to attract men?"

St. Clair stared at him. "Some women wear it to attract men. Others wear it just to smell nice. I smell antiseptic odors all day; it's a treat to smell something else."

"So how does a man know whether a woman is wearing perfume for him, or for herself?"

Maxene shrugged. "Lots of days I don't know myself. Who's wearing perfume?"

"Rosalyn Mueller, the director at Rhinestones."

"Well, that's easy," she smiled. "She wears it to attract clients. Selling is a form of seduction, and she's using every tool she's got."

"Don't get catty."

"I'm not," she protested. "A friend who sells expensive jewelry says that in sales, the relationship between the salesperson and buyer is more important even than the beauty of the jewelry. Selling art has to be the same. Seller seduces buyer. Why? Are you going to tell me that an investigation is like smelling perfume in the dark?"

Grabowski dropped St. Clair at the St. Agnes' ER and drove west on North Avenue to North Fiftieth Street. Koranda lived in an upper flat in a bungalow off Vliet Street, in a working-class neighborhood of nearly identical two-story bungalows. Rusted Chevys were parked in narrow driveways. The maples were small by East Side standards since Dutch Elm disease had wiped out the elms planted in the twenties, and the new maples hadn't reached full size. Grabowski parked his car under a maple in front of Koranda's address and threw a plastic sheet over the windshield to keep off the sticky sap.

Nobody answered the bell to the upstairs flat. He punched the other bell and a young woman with a whining baby on her hip opened the door. Grabowski flashed his badge.

"I'm looking for Officer Koranda," he said.

"He's not home."

"When was the last time you saw him?"

"A week, maybe. I lose track of time." She glanced at the baby.

"Do you have any idea where he went?"

"Fishing, I thought." She shifted the baby to the other hip and watched Grabowski open the screen door to the upper flat and rattle the knob.

"I've got a key," she offered. "When he goes fishing I put his mail inside."

The small front hall at the bottom of the steps was littered with bills, multicolored flyers, letters addressed to Resident. Grabowski picked out the electricity and gas bills and stuffed them into his jacket pocket. The young woman carrying the baby followed him upstairs.

The front room was L-shaped with an orange couch, matching chair, and a coffee table with the TV and VCR stacked on it. Two tables covered with fishing paraphernalia filled the other half of the L. Fishing gear was also jammed into the glass-fronted, built-in china cupboards.

One of the two small bedrooms was empty, the other had a double bed and dresser. The closet held uniforms and some flannel shirts.

"The place came furnished," said the young woman, following him through the rooms. "If this is what you call furnished."

The kitchen cupboards held the minimum—one shelf of dishes, one of dry goods, the rest bare. The refrigerator had a six-pack of Old Milwaukee, some eggs, and meat. The milk had not yet soured.

Grabowski had a sudden vision of his own bungalow, with its mismatched kitchen chairs and living room full of other people's leftover furniture. He owned a few more dishes and a microwave, but his kitchen was as unmistakably solitary as Koranda's.

He took two beers out of the refrigerator and handed one to the young woman. "Did Officer Koranda have any visitors?" he asked, pouring the cold beer down his throat.

She took a sip and considered the question. "Hardly ever. He comes home, ties his fishing flies, watches TV. He mows the lawn, takes the garbage cans out to the curb. My husband works nights, so it's nice to have a cop in the house. Sometimes he brings me fish from up north."

"You never saw any visitors?"

"A lady came by once, couple of months ago. He gave

her a Styrofoam cooler out of the back of his car, like the
ones he brings his fish back in."

"Would you recognize her again?"

"She looked like anybody, blond hair, small. She was
wearing jeans. I only saw her a minute. I got busy." She
looked at the baby.

Grabowski went back into the bedroom, started looking
through the papers in the top drawer of the dresser. The
woman leaned against the doorjamb, sipping her beer.

"What happened to him?" she asked.

"Nothing, I hope. His car was found in a parking lot."
Grabowski started thinking about Maxene's car, found
abandoned in the inner city.

"He left it there?"

"Maybe."

She set the beer on the floor and shifted the baby to the
other hip, then picked up the beer. "Let me know, will you?
I gotta keep taking in his mail, and the rent's due next
week. The landlord will want to know where he is. It's
strange him not being here. Can I call you every once in a
while, to find out what you know?"

Grabowski looked up from the drawer of papers. The
woman sounded nervous, worried. He hadn't been paying
enough attention to her. He fished a card out of his wallet.
"Call whenever you want. It's scary when people don't
show up."

After she left, Grabowski sat down in the kitchen to
think. The trouble with having three or four cases on his
hands was it was hard to keep them straight in his mind. It
was also easy to lose direction. Losing direction was how
cases started to drag. Life, too.

He draped a handkerchief over the receiver to keep from
adding his fingerprints to the collection and called the fin-
gerprinting unit. They said they'd be out in an hour or so.

Grabowski wandered through the pathetically empty
apartment. The hallway echoed. There was little in the
bathroom cabinet. Where did Koranda spend his money?
Guards didn't make much, but they could afford better than

this. The apartment couldn't cost more than $400 a month plus utilities. He went back to the bedroom and started hunting through the papers in the top drawer for a bank statement.

CHAPTER

10

WARM TAR STUCK to Maxene's shoes as she hurried through the heat waves in the blacktopped parking lot at St. Agnes' and through the refrigerated lobby. In the chart room on the third floor, she leaned against the counter and peeled a chunk of tar off her shoe while she waited for the clerk to retrieve her overdue charts. Sister Rosalie had stuck a severely worded memo in her box saying that certain charts needed attention—signature, diagnosis, referral.

Aaron Simonson, the hospital pathologist, came out of the elevator and joined her at the counter. He was wearing his usual stained green surgery trousers and green V-neck surgery shirt, with a line of bare white belly the material didn't cover. He reeked of formaldehyde.

"Whew," he exclaimed, holding his nose. "Where have you been? Cleaning out cow barns?"

"I ate lunch at Tony's," St. Clair said stiffly.

"Last week I autopsied two people who ate there—one coronary, one pancreas, not totally food-related. Really, Maxene, ER patients won't care how you smell, but Shirley will."

St. Clair winced. The ER charge nurse was obsessed with keeping the decay of the inner city outside the ER doors, and she was never short on adjectives. St. Clair waved at the receptionist to take back the charts. "I'll shower and change," she muttered.

Agreed, she needed a bath, but without a car she had no time to get home and back by three o'clock. She took the stairs to the surgery floor, where she grabbed a surgery nurse's dress from the nurse's station closet, and hurried down another floor to the doctor's lounge where there was a shower.

Every hospital she had ever worked in had a doctor's lounge with showers and cots for napping. During her residency in other hospitals, she had opened her eyes more than once to a naked male emerging from the shower, the man having not noticed or cared she was there. At St. Agnes, most of the doctors had been in practice for a long time, and their pale, aging paunches were in no way alluring. After several startling experiences, she had stopped napping in the doctor's lounge, even when she was exhausted and the ER was quiet.

She was drying herself and hoping no male doctors would decide to shower, when she heard the door bang open. When she emerged clothed in the green surgery dress, Aaron Simonson was sprawled on the couch eating a candy bar. St. Clair passed a hand through her still-damp red hair.

"Stink gone," she smiled.

"I hope you're fumigating your clothes." Simonson flipped the candy wrapper toward the wastebasket.

St. Clair picked it off the floor and dropped it into the basket. "Done the autopsies yet?"

"Which?" Simonson yawned and closed his eyes.

"The black girl who died of poisoning, came into the ER couple of days ago."

"She OD'd on isoniazid. Didn't I put a note in your box? The symptoms you told me made me think of it— hallucinations; reduced blood pressure, pulse and respirations. It was an obvious conclusion anyway; half the inner city has TB, and they don't follow the drug regimen. What's happening to this country? I thought we got rid of tuberculosis years ago."

"She had TB, and she died from an overdose of her medication?" St. Clair couldn't believe it.

"OD on INH, that's what I wrote on the death certificate.

There's a TB epidemic all over the country; I'm surprised you don't wear a mask in the ER. Immune levels are down among the lowlifes you spend your time with, thanks to HIV. Police even get TB when they're coughed on by TB-toting felons."

"Her friends didn't tell me she had TB," St. Clair protested.

Simonson spoke with patience. "She was a hooker, which meant she was likely HIV positive, which meant her immune levels were bottoming out. Which meant one of her clients coughed in her face, and she got TB."

"Are you sure she had TB?"

Simonson shrugged. "I didn't test for it, or HIV, after I found the high blood levels of INH. Who's going to pay for the lab tests? Welfare? Not on your life."

"How could she overdose on INH?"

Simonson's patience was wearing thin. "Maybe she forgot and took her daily dose twice. Maybe she was drunk and took more than she thought."

"Would one extra dose kill her?" St. Clair frowned.

"Call the health department; they're the experts."

Ron Zelazak came out of the toilet at that moment, zipping his pants.

"Cute outfit," Zelazak said, looking St. Clair over, "but it doesn't suit your figure. Try something lower cut."

"Quite an accident the other night at the art gallery." St. Clair automatically switched subjects. Some women doctors and nurses kept up the banter, but she had found that sexual innuendoes in medical circles quickly led to propositions.

"What do you mean 'accident'?" Zelazak demanded. "I heard the wire was cut. Incidentally, nice CPR work that night. You were tuckered out afterward, I noticed. Big job for a little lady."

"And you were too busy to help?" St. Clair carefully held her temper.

Zelazak shrugged. "Kitty was upset, and I had to stay with her. I'm not surprised there's an autopsy. Rosalyn called Kitty this afternoon and said somebody cut the wire. Of course, Kitty barely knew Berendorf."

"She knew him well enough to help hang his sculpture," said St. Clair. Zelazak was getting on her nerves.

He looked at her coldly. "You taking a personal interest in this since you did the CPR?" he said. "Got yourself involved in something similar once, didn't you—you and Aaron?" He winked at Simonson.

Simonson winced, looked away.

Maxene gritted her teeth. As if it wasn't enough for her to put up with looking at their fat, naked bodies emerging from the showers in a doctors' lounge designed for only male occupation, she had to put up with a constant, overbearing, male condescension. She yanked a lab coat over the surgery dress, wishing she had grabbed the more comfortable surgery trousers and smock.

"What do you know about the crush accident?" demanded Zelazak.

"Nothing." She slammed the door.

With the few minutes before her shift started, she went up to Intensive Care to see Wyoming. His bed was moved closer to the nurses' station, but only one IV was hanging now.

"Doing better," the nurse said, looking at St. Clair's badge and making a note on the chart.

Rosa, the other gunshot victim, was in a room down the hall, propped up in bed with her hair wrapped in a turquoise turban. She was staring with disbelief at a tray of broth and Jell-O.

"Hi," St. Clair said, leaning on the bed rail. "I'm Maxene St. Clair. I was at your apartment when you were shot."

The woman nodded. "I remember you now; you came to see Latoya. Rolondo told me she died." Her mouth drooped.

St. Clair nodded.

"You know why?"

"They think she died of too much of the medicine she

was taking," answered Maxene. "Tell me, did she have TB—tuberculosis?"

Rosa pursed her lips. "If she did, she wouldn't go telling nobody, or Rolondo would get worried the health nurse would be coming around. Latoya lived over on Eighth and Locust. The health nurse would go there."

"The public health nurses also come when you have TB?"

"And if you're hooking, they tell you to quit and go see a social worker. Like you're actually going to do it." Rosa rolled her eyes.

Maxene smiled. "Do you remember anything about the shooting?"

Rosa shook her head emphatically. "Not a thing, honey, and don't you ask or I might have to think about it."

"Rolondo says you think they were shooting at you. Why would they do that?"

Rosa looked around the empty room and lowered her voice. "There is always somebody out there wanting to take over your life, and Rolondo, he's got a nice life. He watches all the time that don't nobody move in on his operation."

"That's it? Just business competition?"

Rosa shrugged. "What else?"

St. Clair took the elevator to the emergency room level. Today Joella was wearing black toreador pants, gold lamé pumps with four-inch heels, a red sleeveless tank top, and a lab coat.

"Help me untangle my earring," she ordered through a mouthful of chocolate. The pink feather of a dangling earring was tangled in her long black hair.

"I see you got yourself involved with the criminal element again," said Shirley, who was sitting in the chair at the entrance to the supply room, filing her nails. She had big fleshy hands with delicate fingers that could insert an IV needle into a child's arm without eliciting a murmur of pain. Shirley handed the emery board back to Joella and accepted the buffer. She buffed with energy, an eye on the ER doors and another on St. Clair.

"Which criminal element?" asked St. Clair, concentrating on untangling the earring.

"That pimp Rolondo has been calling for you. Won't leave no messages. Wants you to call him back."

Rolondo answered the phone on the tenth ring. "What about my lady who died?" he demanded. "You know what happened yet?"

"The autopsy said she overdosed on her tuberculosis medicine."

"Say what? Lady wasn't on no medicine."

"It's all I know," she said.

"How's Rosa doing?" he demanded.

"Improving, but not enough to go back to work."

"You still without no car?" he asked, after a pause.

Maxene groaned. "My insurance company said they need the police report before they'll pay. I'm going to the police station tomorrow to get a copy of the report. Or maybe I'll call Grabowski and have him pick it up."

"My advice is, don't call him," Rolondo said. "He'll get suspicious. Did you know he goes and sits in that apartment where his friend lived? Just sits there. He got the cops swarming around there like bees." The phone went dead.

She dialed the Milwaukee Health Department TB Clinic downtown and asked for the charge nurse.

"One of your patients died here at St. Agnes' of an INH overdose," she said, feeling depressed. "You'll want to close out the record."

The reaction was not what she expected. The nurse's voice became sharp. "Overdose? I don't think so. No, I have not heard of any of our clients dying within the last few days. The family or the DOT worker would have told us already. We have over ninety-nine percent compliance and no serious side effects. Name?"

St. Clair felt confused, as she always did when confronted with overcompetence. "Mine?"

"Well, all right, we'll start with yours."

The nurse got all the information, or as much as St. Clair could remember without the chart in front of her. She was starting to apologize when the woman cut in.

"No, not one of ours. I'll recheck the address, but I'm sure it's a private patient. Typical. No supervision. Thanks for calling."

St. Clair hung up feeling overwhelmed. "Do TB nurses take their patients personally?" she asked Joella.

"You betcha," Joella replied. "When my old man had TB, the health nurse came every day for six months to watch him take his pills. She about made my mother crazy. My mother would hide in the basement and make one of us kids tell the nurse nobody was home. Of course, the nurse came in anyway and gave my old man hell for drinking."

Shirley sniffed the air suddenly. "You been at Tony's with that detective of yours, haven't you?" she said. "Something smells like fried pork fat."

"I bathed upstairs." St. Clair sat down in the red plastic armchair in the supply room and propped her feet up on the third shelf. The swelling in her ankles was still pronounced.

"You getting something going again with that detective?" Shirley was watching her closely.

"I don't know." St. Clair sighed. Her emotional life was open season in the ER, but she didn't really mind. The staff was like a big family who kept tabs on one another's hearts. She watched Joella select fluorescent purple nail polish from her drawer and put a tiny drop on a nick on her nail.

"How's Grabowski's friend?" asked Joella.

"Still unconscious. Grabowski found out that he was living in the apartment across the hall from where Rolondo's girls work, and now Grabowski is giving everyone in the building the third degree. Rolondo wants him out of there."

"Is that why that pimp is calling you?" demanded Shirley.

"You watch your step, girl," said Joella, waving the nail polish brush. "That pimp is like all men. You think you're in control, then they come up behind you and you are nothing but screwed. Just like that student nurse that Dr. Zelazak was patting on the ass."

"What are you talking about?" St. Clair asked.

"First the doctor is complimenting her on her cute uniform, then on her cute hair, then on her cute suntan. Next thing he's patting her on the ass, and she's kicked out of school."

"I beg your pardon?"

"Sister Rosalie doesn't like student nurses having fun chats with married doctors on staff, and you think Sister is going to kick out the doctor? That poor girl has to find herself another school or another career. She didn't know what hit her."

"Zelazak did this?"

"And the asshole doesn't know a thing about her being kicked out, which is the worst part, in my view." Shirley picked up one of Joella's emery boards and began whisking the tips of her nails.

St. Clair closed her eyes.

"You upset about that girl of Rolondo's dying?" Shirley asked, studying her nails.

St. Clair sighed. "Yes, I am. If I'd got there earlier, even an hour, we could have saved her. Dr. Simonson said it was INH overdose, which means we could have pulled her out of it just with a life-support system."

"You're shell-shocked, is what you are," pronounced Shirley. "You saw somebody get gunned down, and it's inside you, taking away your energy. Then you saw a big sculpture fall on somebody and he died, and that's inside you. You can't be doctor to the whole city, honey. What happened to these folks happened because they were in the wrong place at the wrong time."

"Just bad luck?"

"Not bad luck, exactly. If you get born in the wrong neighborhood, that's bad luck, but you can get out. It takes work and smarts, and you can't get all the way out, but look at me, honey. I got a life I like, and it's a whole lot better than the one I started out with. Rich folks who got born with everything can end up less happy than how they started out, and that ain't bad luck either. They made their choices and got to the place they are."

"I can't believe that poor girl had anything to do with how she died," St. Clair protested.

"Wrong place, wrong time. You'll see I'm right."

CHAPTER

11

AT FOUR THAT afternoon, Grabowski drove south on
Twenty-seventh Street across the industrial valley on what
was locally known as the bridge that divided Poland from
Africa—the Polish South Side from the black inner city. He
wanted to pick up the wire that had snapped and dropped
the sculpture on Soren Berendorf. The property officer had
taken it to the new crime lab on South Eleventh street and
could have picked it up for him, but Grabowski needed to
clear his brain. The drive across the industrial valley got
him mentally away from the glitz of the art world.

At the corner of Greenfield and Twenty-seventh, where
the Casanova Gun Store created a daily parking problem,
he turned east and wound through the tree-lined Mexican
district to the quiet street where the brick crime lab stuck
out like a sore thumb among the ramshackle, tumbled-down
wooden frame houses.

Dark-skinned Mexican children were playing soccer in
the street. They stopped the ball long enough for Grabowski to pull into the parking lot surrounded by an eight-foot
chain-link fence. The new lab was built in the bunker-style
red brick architecture that had become popular in Milwaukee over the last ten years when burglary became a way of
life. The one-story, windowless building sat low to the
ground and looked exactly like the new Catholic church on
Keefe, the new public library on Center, and the Milwaukee
Enterprise Center on Fifth and Hadley which was as sus-
ceptible to being hit as any other place despite its purpose
to house minority businesses.

111

A small notice by the front steps read, "24 hour surveillance; you are on videotape." Grabowski showed his badge through the bulletproof glass door and was buzzed in. He handed over his evidence receipt and chatted with the lab technician.

"Artistic piece of work," said the tech, holding up the frayed wire. "The ends have been clipped at different lengths with something very sharp, which is most likely dull or chipped now. See this last one? Either the clippers dulled or the final job was done with something else, a file maybe."

Grabowski looked at the frayed ends and thought of the specialized tool cabinet in the kitchen at Rhinestones. He tossed the tagged evidence in the trunk and drove three blocks to the South Side Health Center. A friend of his, Felicia Martinez, was a staff nurse at the city Tuberculosis Clinic. He met her a few years before when she had helped him straighten out some confusion involving a non–English speaking Mexican family and a robbery. Afterward they had remained friends.

The two-story brick South Side Health Center had been the original Milwaukee Tuberculosis Sanitarium but the wide, shaded porches where patients used to take the air were empty now and the TB clinic only took up a corner of one floor. The rest of the building served as headquarters for the public health nurses who covered the South Side of Milwaukee. It also housed the public health dental clinic.

Grabowski pulled into the parking lot, also surrounded by an eight-foot chain-link fence topped by barbed wire, and walked around the building to the TB Clinic entrance.

Felicia was in her office with a patient, so he leaned on the counter in the waiting room. He had been here a few times to use the translation services of the Hmong and Laotian interpreters. Today a Hmong family with small children waited along with an older black man, two overweight women speaking Russian, and a black woman wearing a long robe and turban, possibly from Ethiopia.

In a few minutes, Felicia came out followed by the Laotian translator and a small Asian woman carrying a thin toddler. Grabowski waved hello to the translator and followed Felicia down the hall to her office.

"How many of your TB patients die of medicine overdose?" he asked, dropping into the visitor's chair and accepting the cold soda she pulled out of a cold pack under her desk.

"None I've ever known," she said in her strong Puerto Rican accent. "We have a chemical questionnaire that we go through with all our clients, and if they have any symptoms of toxicity, we stop the med and maybe try another one." She pulled out a chart labeled "Chemoquestionnaire" at the top. "See? 'Rash, nausea, dizziness, dry mouth, dark urine.' Very specific."

"But how often do you go through the questionnaire with each patient?"

"Reliable people we go through the questions once a month, then we count out the medication they need for the next month. Every three months they get a blood test to check the medication level. But if there's noncompliance, somebody from here goes out to evaluate the stressors at home. Then we might go see them every day for the full six months of drug therapy. Nobody I knew ever had complications we didn't catch."

"What if the client is a prostitute?"

"Prostitutes get a DOT—direct observed therapy worker. Every day the worker finds the client, hands over a pill, and watches her swallow it. Homeless people get the same, but prostitutes, we check them right away for HIV, then we tell them to stop their play-for-pay."

Grabowski smiled at the expression. "So how do the girls make a living?"

"Well, they're supposed to enroll in the Milwaukee AIDS Program so they don't have to resort to prostitution. But they don't like that too much, you know, go talk to a social worker every week. One pretty lady, she was going back and forth from Milwaukee to Chicago, and her boyfriend was HIV positive. She used to show up here with a black eye or whatever."

Felicia took a phone call, chatted a few minutes in Spanish, laughed. Grabowski watched her expressive face with a feeling that he recognized as affection, surprising himself. She had a large nose and a heavy mouth, and her eyebrows didn't seem to sit in the right place on her tall forehead, but she was beautiful. She was so at peace with herself and her life, and so unabashedly optimistic about keeping disease at bay in a city full of forces against a healthy life.

"Could somebody die from an overdose of TB medication and you wouldn't hear about it here?" he asked when she hung up.

"Maybe they went to a private doctor. What's the name?"

She copied the information from the paper where Grabowski had written Latoya's name and her home and working addresses, then shook her head.

"We got a couple clients in that district, but I don't recognize the name. I'll ask the DOT workers and also see what I can find out from Keenan Health Center on the North Side, and from the Socially Transmitted Disease Clinic downtown. TB is only one of many communicable diseases, and she may have a record for hepatitis or maybe she had a high-risk infant we followed."

"Where do you keep your meds?" he asked, making a note.

She pulled out her desk drawer. "Each nurse has some, and the medical consultant keeps some in his cabinet. All locked, of course."

"Any chance they might get stolen?"

She shook her head. "The meds are sent by the state, and we have to account for every pill. The nurse-manager tracks them all on computer. Believe me, the state can tell you the location of every isoniazid and rifampin pill they issue in the state of Wisconsin."

She gave him a quick tour of the clinic. They were just closing, finishing the last of the patients. The clinic was

T-shaped with offices for the four RN's, the translators, the DOT workers, and the medical consultant. Everything was locked and accounted for. She handed him a copy of the treatment protocol and the Chemoquestionnaire and walked him to the clinic entrance.

"Still got the same lady friend?" she smiled. "Wasn't she a doctor or something?"

He gave her arm an affectionate squeeze. She barely came up to his elbow. "Same lady friend."

"Maybe one of these days a lady like that is going to get tired of waiting, even for a nice guy like you. You got something holding you back?" .

He hesitated. "I've met someone else. She's different— elegant, lives a side of life I never knew existed."

"Beautiful, too, probably. Did she grow up in Milwaukee?"

"On the North Side. Rosalyn Mueller."

She patted his arm. "Sounds like you have some hard choices. But you'll do what's right."

It was after five. He drove the frayed wire back to headquarters, checked it in with the evidence clerk who stored it for possible courtroom use, and went to pick up his messages. Felicia had already called: No one living at either of those addresses had been a patient of the city TB Clinic. A few years before, a man in a lower apartment had been a patient, but he had moved to Chicago and the record was closed.

He stuck the message into a folder marked "Syzinski," flipped it into his desk drawer, and left for home.

The cleaning lady had left a note on the kitchen table about putting new formica on the counters if he expected her to get the kitchen clean. He shoved it in the back of the towel drawer with her other notes, grabbed a beer from the refrigerator, and went to take a shower. The cleaning lady had taped another note to the bathroom mirror about getting the bathtub tiles regrouted if he expected her to get the bathroom clean. He checked the beer can to make sure she hadn't taped a note to that, and took the beer into the shower with him.

An hour later, refreshed externally and internally, he drove over the Dan Hoan Bridge from Bay View to the East Side high rise condominium on Prospect where Rosalyn Mueller lived.

She buzzed him into an ornate, mirrored lobby stuffed with tropical plants that were surviving despite the arctic air-conditioning. As Grabowski waited for the elevator, he noticed in the mirror that his stomach bulged over his belt more than it used to. His eating habits hadn't changed; maybe he needed to run more, or swim.

In Arizona, he and Wyoming had gone running every evening in the dry, clear light that hung briefly over the cooled desert once the sun dropped. Wyoming said he lived in Arizona because of that light. Why had he left all that beauty to come back to Milwaukee? All he had said the week before he moved to his apartment off Center Street was that he needed to be with real people again. There hadn't been enough time to find out what that meant. Grabowski wanted him to move into the little bungalow in Bay View, but Wyoming said the ceilings were too low, that he needed space, space, space.

The brass elevator doors slid open without a sound, and Grabowski stepped into its carpeted, mirrored confines. When the doors opened onto a .tiny green-carpeted hall on the eighth floor, Rosalyn was standing in the doorway of her apartment waiting for him.

She was wearing a white V-necked sweater and loose white pants that seemed to float around her long legs. Her only concession to color were bright blue sandals and iridescent blue earrings. They caught the light from the fading sky through the French doors to the balcony. Grabowski followed the white pants into the whiteness of her home.

Rosalyn Mueller's apartment was as far from Wyoming's flat as an interior decorator could get. Everything was white: white walls, white carpet, white chair, white shawl thrown over the back of the white couch. Even the lamps were white, one china, the other wood.

"I'm genuinely glad you came by, Detective." She smiled, moving toward the kitchen.

"Call me Grabowski; everybody else does."

The kitchen walls were white tile, with white cupboards, white linoleum, and space enough for one person. The window looked out over Lake Michigan where tiny sailboats blew across the whitecaps, their colored sails tipped crazily. Closer, a pigeon stood on the windowsill, its feathers ruffled with the breeze, its coo silent beyond the tight seal of the window and the faint whir of the air-conditioning. Grabowski lounged against the doorjamb and watched Roslyn put together a gin and tonic for both of them.

"You have something against color?" he inquired.

She smiled. "I'm surrounded by color at the gallery—crazy colors and insane shapes. All day, I try to choose art for the gallery that is good, or at least marketable. Then I hang it in a way that will control the way people react to it, so that they'll buy it. By evening I want to come back to a plain room where I don't have to control anything."

"But by having no color, you're still controlling things," Grabowski commented.

"A person is influenced by what she sees or hears the last thing before she sleeps, and nothing here will influence me about what I'll be looking at tomorrow. I don't have a television and I don't listen to anything but classical music. Every evening I wash away whatever happened during the day, and in the morning I can start fresh."

"Like a canvas before a painter starts painting."

She dropped a slice of lime and a sprig of mint into the two glasses of gin and tonic, handed him the finished products, then took a Mexican tile tray already laden with hors d'oeuvres from the refrigerator and led the way through the white living room and out onto a curved balcony with big white enamel planters filled with pink geraniums.

The air was cool on the eighth floor. The curve of the balcony wall protected them, but even so the lake breeze ruffled her smooth black hair. Grabowski leaned back in his cushioned deck chair and put his feet up on the balcony railing, then took them down again.

Rosalyn Mueller smiled slightly. "Now tell me," she started, settling back into her lounge chair and crossing her feet under her. "What's your preference? Interrogation first or dinner? The food is ready in half an hour."

Grabowski took a meditative sip of his gin and tonic. She had put in a lime instead of a lemon, the tonic was crisper than what he bought, and the Tanqueray gin, well, there just wasn't any better. The appetizers were good, too, spiced ham skewered on small sticks between slices of melon. He ate two skewers' worth before answering.

"I've been traded to a different league," he began. "Artists, sculptors, gallery directors, you people play the ball game by different rules. But I've come up against you, and we're going all the way to the play-offs."

Rosalyn studied him. "Are you talking about the accident at my gallery? Or are we speaking different languages and I missed the translation?"

Grabowski smiled. "I'm talking about the gallery. And it wasn't an accident, remember? The wire was cut."

"So you said." She seemed to have recovered from the news. "You're telling me that we're in early innings, and you and I play on opposite teams."

"You got it."

"Can't we play on the same team? It appeals to my sense of innocence."

Grabowski smiled and took another skewer of ham and melon. The gin was beginning to hit him. It had been a long day. Koranda's apartment had taken longer to fingerprint than they thought, mainly because the squad had been overthorough, in the process finishing off all the beer in the refrigerator. There had been an unspoken consensus that either Koranda would come back and they'd replace the beer at a happy reunion, or he wouldn't. The woman who lived downstairs from Koranda had come up without the baby and renewed the beer supply. Here on the balcony was the first time he had sat down for more than the fifteen minutes since lunch with Maxene.

He looked over Rosalyn's white silk slacks and sheer blouse that showed her lace underwear. He thought about Maxene sitting at the cracked linoleum table at Tony's Café eating corned beef sandwiches. Maxene rarely wore white. She said it was too hard to keep clean.

Grabowski drank off his gin. "Let's assume that the wire was cut by someone who wanted to either destroy the sculpture or destroy the man who made it."

"Or destroy me," Rosalyn said promptly. "My gallery is doing very well, and in this town there's only one pie. Other galleries now have a smaller slice."

Grabowski emptied a few more skewers of ham and melon into his mouth. "Okay, let's start there. You got a few threatening letters about torching the exhibition. Could they have cut that wire?"

She shook her head slowly. "I'm beginning to think they were the other gallery owners trying to scare me off."

"Unsophisticated method for art dealers."

She laughed, easy and relaxed. "Milwaukee isn't the most sophisticated place in the world. That's part of its charm."

The phone rang. Rosalyn picked up his empty glass and went inside. When she came out with a full one, her pleasant look was gone. She dropped into the lounge chair, took a deep breath, and kicked off her sandals. Her toenails were painted bright red to match her fingernails. The breeze brought a drift of her perfume.

"Trouble?" he asked.

She frowned. "That was Kitty. She gets agitated over unnecessary things. The trouble with a partnership is that not every link is as strong as the others." She took a sip of her drink.

"I saw her draped over the sculptor when he was at the piano," Grabowski said. "As a matter of fact, I caught them in a clinch in the kitchen just before the evening opened. Was there something going on between them?"

"Soren liked to have everything—art, life, money, people. Kitty was one of them. I think he made a play for her that night for old time's sake. Of course she fell for it."

"Did her husband know?"

"Maybe. He's a surgeon, hardly ever home. Frankly, I don't think he'd care, beyond the ego crunch."

"And Lillian Hochstedder," Grabowski pressed on. "What was her relationship with Berendorf?"

Rosalyn paused, thinking. "They didn't really have a relationship," she answered finally. "Lillian didn't like Berendorf because he said her sculptures were strictly amateur, which they are, of course. That's why the insult hurt so much."

Grabowski started again. "I understand your premise for starting the gallery initially was to sell the artwork that your group of friends had produced. My problem is, it seems like too much work just for that. What was it that you really wanted?"

Rosalyn was watching a sailboat cross the path of a freighter. "You know what I wanted?" she said. "My own life—no one else's. A small beautiful apartment, lots of flowers, nice clothes, interesting work I could control. And a few people who like me enough to call me up to ask how I'm doing."

"And opening an art gallery gave you all that?"

"The gallery and the divorce. I couldn't have done one without the other. I had lived a life controlled by other people for twenty-five years without even knowing it. I think a lot of doctors' wives take up art as a release from that control. They feel compelled to dress a certain way, send their children to the right schools, live in the right neighborhoods, ski at the right resorts. I left all that. Now I'm learning how to take control."

"But everybody is controlled somewhat by outside forces," Grabowski said. "For example, my job is to control what falls outside the law."

Rosalyn nodded. "My problem was that I mixed up control with security. I thought security meant an ordered, safe, lined-up life. Actually, that's control. I married a man who was a controlling person, by profession. Doctors control disease, symptoms, people's treatments. The trouble with living with a controlling person is that eventually people around him become passive and dependent, and that's what happened to me. I needed him totally, and I resented it. I was always charging him with being complacent and self-satisfied, when what I hated was his control."

"And now you control everything."

"Of course running this gallery to make a living is a whole lot different than running it as a second income to six figures. I spend more time working and I travel less to New York, but when I do go, I make the trip pay; in fact, it's more fun because things are real."

"But scary, too," Grabowski offered.

She nodded. "Right after my divorce I used to have panic attacks that literally took my breath away. In a second, I'd be covered with sweat. Now I get nervous before a show, or tense when I write out a big check, but the panic is gone, thank God. I never want to go through that again."

The sky had darkened. A faint pink ribbon drifted across the horizon, a trail of clouds stained by the sunset. She stopped talking and sat quietly. Grabowski watched the first star appear.

"The interesting thing," she said suddenly, her voice gaining life in the dark, "was that the three of us—Kitty, Lillian, and me—we painted to unload our minds. Then we opened this gallery to unload the paintings; and then we discovered that running the gallery unloaded our minds in a bigger way. We started needing each other—the way I used to need my husband—to talk to, to work out problems."

"And when you discovered you didn't need your husband for security, you got rid of his control, too," Grabowski hazarded.

"I'm still learning how to make my own security," she conceded, "but what's even harder is learning how to give my life meaning. When I was married, my husband's life had the only meaning. Every phone call was more important than me. We never had a conversation that wasn't interrupted by a phone call. I used to get angry; then I'd feel guilty about being angry at sick people. Finally I stopped investing effort into conversations because it was too wrenching to be cut off mid-sentence."

"I know someone who hates the phone as much as you do," said Grabowski, thinking of Maxene. She hates them, but she answers them, he thought. What would it be like to live with that?

Rosalyn wasn't listening. "What killed the marriage was that the phone controlled the sex," she said, her voice unsteady. "We would be right in the middle of making love, the phone would ring, and my husband would roll over and pick it up. I would lie looking at the ceiling, listening to him tell a nurse how to handle somebody who fell out of bed or whose medications needed changing. To him, any phone call was more important than the most intense, intimate moment between two people."

"I'd rip the phone out of the wall," said Grabowski, not certain if he were giving comfort or making the memories worse.

She smiled at him. "I used to laugh it off; then I got angry. But after a few years, all I felt was humiliation. It is a form of abuse to make love to a woman, then turn away from her when the phone rings, as casually as putting down a book."

Grabowski didn't know what else to say. He felt like she

was questioning the whole male experience and he was being exposed as a fraud.

"Will you ever trust a man again?" he asked, staring into his empty glass.

"That kind of trust is naïveté, anyway," she said. "To give yourself physically and emotionally is simply setting yourself up to be shot down."

CHAPTER

12

AT ELEVEN-THIRTY, ST. Clair took a call from Grabowski who said he would pick her up when her shift ended. At midnight she went outside the ER doors to wait in the warm, humid night. The street noises had quieted, and she could hear rock music from a house across the street. The green Plymouth pulled up just as the hands of her watch joined.

"This is nice, Grabowski," she said, climbing into the car and closing her eyes. "Security, that's the secret to long life." She opened her eyes with a jerk, however, when the car stopped and she heard Grabowski mutter under his breath.

All the lights were on in her flat, as well as in Louie's flat downstairs. "Want to come in and find out who's visiting?" she asked.

"Just what I was waiting for." He pulled out his gun and led the way up her stairs.

At the top, St. Clair turned off the TV and stereo and followed Grabowski slowly from room to room looking for a visitor. She found the visitor asleep in her bed.

"Louie," Grabowski said. "I should have known." He put his gun away and stomped into the kitchen. A beer cap rattled onto the counter.

Louie was curled up in the fetal position around one of Maxene's flowered chintz pillows. He was snoring softly. St. Clair shook his foot.

"Time to go home, Louie."

Louie jerked awake, then groaned. "Don't make me go

downstairs, Max," he begged. "I'm afraid to be alone. The police will come get me while I'm sleeping."

"Don't be crazy, Louie. They only do that on drug busts. And before you panic, Grabowski is in the kitchen."

Louie clutched his hair. "He's here to get me!"

"Relax. What do you have to hide?"

Louie shifted nervously on the bed, drew his legs up under him. "Actually, that was what I was going to talk to you about. How much of my business do you know about?"

St. Clair took her nightshirt from the closet door. She yawned. "Well, I've been to your shop, and I know you do restoration at home, at least that's what you said the last time I complained about the smell. Can't this wait until morning?"

"It's on my conscience, Max. I never intended to be a criminal; it sort of grew on me."

Grabowski had come to stand in the doorway, sipping a beer. "Does this have anything to do with faking antiques, Louie?"

Louie stood up quickly. "I don't fake antiques, Detective, I restore them. That takes more work than you might think." He edged past Grabowski. The back door slammed.

St. Clair laughed, then realized she was standing holding her nightshirt. Grabowski was watching her. He started to say something, then he tossed off his beer and put his arms around her.

"Can I stay, Max?"

The moon was making squares of bluish light on the carpet by her bed, and the muscles in Grabowski's shoulders seemed carved out of moonlight and shadows when St. Clair opened her eyes. Her fingers disappeared into his dark hair as he lay in her arms. A light film of perspiration on her shoulders caught the cool breeze from the window. She felt Grabowski shiver and stir.

"Max, are you awake?" he whispered.

She pulled the sheet over his back. "How could I sleep lying here watching you and the moonlight?"

He settled his head on her shoulder. "Does Louie seem more nervous than usual?" he murmured.

She smiled. "Don't you ever stop working? But yes, I agree, Louie seems more than usually hyper."

"He's had a fake antique operation going for quite some time that the bunko squad knows all about," said Grabowski. "It's not enough of a consumer fraud problem to do anything about, but sometimes I drop in on him, just to keep him from going too far. Yesterday, he seemed more bothered than usual by my presence."

St. Clair was starting to doze off. "He's freaked out by the sculpture falling."

"Maybe." His nose rubbed her neck. "Find out what you can about private doctors who handle TB patients, will you? A friend who works in the city TB Clinic told me that the girl who died of INH overdose wasn't being treated at the clinic. I'm trying to find who her doctor was, and there's no way I can do it, given the privacy laws."

"I'll ask around," she said. "By the way, do you know whether the wire was cut?"

"Definitely," murmured Grabowski. "And whatever instrument did it is either chipped or dull."

CHAPTER

13

MAXENE ST. CLAIR woke up at eleven A.M. feeling more rested than she had in a week. Grabowski had left while she was sleeping; she hadn't even heard him go. An empty beer bottle sat on the floor beside the bed.

She lay in bed thinking over the past three days. Everything blurred together. Someone had told her once that things become clear if a person can get far enough away to see them as a whole. The entire planet can be seen from space. Surely the events of a mere three days would become clear given time and distance.

But was there time? She felt an urgency, not the urgency of simple need to find the answer to a problem, but the urgency of needing to stop something before it got worse. When patients came into the ER, the first thing that staff did was "triage," assessing the severity of the illness or injury, and deciding how much time they had to deal with it: a minute, an hour? After nearly a year in the ER, St. Clair knew right away how quickly she must act. It wasn't just intellectual assessment; it was also gut instinct.

And gut instinct was saying this situation was urgent. What did she need to know before she could move on to the next step? She clipped off the thoughts in her mind like listing problems on a patient's chart.

First, she didn't understand why the sculptor had died. He had left the ER in fair condition, despite the serious head injury and the need to resuscitate. Logically, he shouldn't have died, and clearly Grabowski thought so, too, or he wouldn't have ordered an autopsy. Also, why had the man just sat there at the piano? He had only seconds to act, but it was long enough to duck under the piano. Maybe he had been drinking heavily. Alcohol was a stronger drug than people realized.

And why, said a sneaky little voice, hadn't Grabowski told her about ordering the autopsy? The detective was naturally close-mouthed about his work, but she was directly involved in the case. Not that her medical treatment was faulty; her actions had been textbook.

Second, she didn't understand why Latoya had died so quickly after she arrived at the hospital.

Third, Rolondo appeared convinced that the shooting of Rosa and Syzinski was not random violence, a strange reaction for someone whose life was one criminal activity after another. Rolondo must have some reason behind his belief, St. Clair decided, although he was as close-mouthed about his activities as Grabowski. There was no hope he would let her in on his thinking.

St. Clair felt uneasy, as if there were something she should be doing. Maybe the unease rose from the psychological effect of being a witness to violence. Or possibly it came from being without a car, she decided on a more practical level. Automobile-dependency was a need she had always fought by using her bicycle for exercise, errands, and grocery shopping, but now that she was having to stand behind her philosophy, it was anxiety-provoking.

In the kitchen, she poured herself a glass of iced tea, then stood at the window looking down at her neighbor's flower beds. She had moved into this flat after her divorce the year before. Even though her ex-husband had moved to Iowa with the chemistry student, Maxene had wanted to get away from the memories in their old apartment. Her furniture had been in storage anyway, since her faded Oriental rug, Chinese lamps, and chintz sofa hadn't gone well with the modern motif of her ex-husband's flat.

It had been nice to collect her belongings again and find an older flat with gracious rooms and built-in china cabinets. Even nicer was to be alone again, to deal only with her own laundry and dishes. But now, for some reason, she felt lonely. This flat was pleasant, but still anonymously similar to all the other apartments she had lived in through medical school and residency.

And here she was at age forty-one, an acceptable savings account, some modest investments, and a history of rented apartments to which she returned each evening alone. Grabowski's charming, uncivilized bungalow on the South Side of Milwaukee had neglected flower beds and porch steps that tilted at a crazy angle, but the cottage looked across the road to a beach on Lake Michigan, and Grabowski owned it.

Grabowski belonged somewhere. That was it, she realized. She was drifting in a single-occupant boat. What did she want, double occupancy or simply a place to call home? Flower beds were hard to weed from an upper flat.

As she was standing there thinking, the phone rang. Louie was calling from his antique shop.

"Maxene, dear," he began breathlessly, "tell me the truth about last night. What did that detective of yours want to know about me? Did he ask about my antiques?"

Maxene decided that avoiding the question was the only route. Telling Louie that his fake antiques were no secret would send him into hysterics.

"What's the problem, Louie?"

"Come down here to the shop. I have to talk to you, and not on the phone. Just come."

Maxene looked at her watch. It was three hours before her shift started at St. Agnes', and she wanted to get to the hospital early to say hello to Rosa and check on Wyoming. Syzinski kept nagging at the back of her mind. As of last night, he was still unconscious. Yesterday, she had gone up to sit with him where the quiet of the ICU was only broken by the hum of the cardiac monitor. It was a restful place to ease the stress of the emergency room, and she had found herself talking about the patients she had seen, how she felt about them, and about the perfection required of her. She could go to Louie's shop and still have time to drop in on Wyoming before work.

"I'm coming, Louie. Give me half an hour."

She threw on a pair of loose khaki bermudas and a white tank top, dragged her aging green Raleigh out of the damp basement, and headed for the East Side of downtown. The thick leaves of the big maples along Prospect cooled the light breeze, and the sweet green smell overpowered the exhaust. She pedaled through the dappled shadows, weaving in and out of parked cars, then left the trees behind as she moved into the blocks of ritzy boutiques and galleries just north of Wisconsin Avenue.

When she turned the corner onto Louie's street, she squeezed the brakes and stopped. Grabowski's dusty green Plymouth was parked in front of the gallery. Was Grabowski in there frightening Louie again?

She was moving her bicycle forward when the door next to Louie's opened and Grabowski came out of Rhinestones. St. Clair was about to call out his name, in fact, had her hand half-raised to wave, when she saw him turn and hold the heavy glass door open for someone behind him. The person who emerged was wearing black tights, a billowy white skirt, and a broad-brimmed scarlet hat with a purple scarf tied around it. It was Rosalyn Mueller, the gallery director. At the curb, Grabowski took her elbow to cross the street.

St. Clair felt drained of energy. Her feet were made of lead, glued to the pavement as she straddled her ten-speed. Her khaki shorts and tank top felt clumsy and provincial, and her sturdy brown sandals the depth of fashion. Sweat trickled through her hair and dripped down the back of her neck.

She watched the pair cross the street and enter the china and crystal shop. Presumably, they were headed for the tearoom upstairs, a restaurant that Grabowski had said once was an overpriced haven for people with more money than taste.

St. Clair rode her bicycle slowly down the sidewalk, studiously avoiding looking up at the tearoom's blue-gingham-curtained windows. She ran the bicycle chain through the legs of the heavy wooden planter under Louie's window and padlocked it.

Inside, Louie was nowhere to be seen. St. Clair let the air-conditioning cool the sweat on her neck and peered through Louie's picture window at the tearoom. Two people took their seats at a window table, but because of the curtains, St. Clair couldn't tell who they were. She turned her back firmly on the scene and let her eyes adjust to the muted light so she could hunt for Louie.

Louie's front room was lighted by only a few low-wattage lamps scattered among the crowded furniture, Louie having said once that antiques, like women over forty, looked best in dim light. St. Clair threaded through the maze of rocking chairs, overstuffed settees, and round oak tables to the kitchen in the back. Louie was neither there nor in the adjoining bathroom.

The door to the basement storage area opened off the kitchen. St. Clair looked around for the basement light but couldn't find it.

"Louie?" she shouted into the basement gloom. Often Louie could be found at Rhinestones, and since Rosalyn had left for the tearoom, Louie was probably watching the gallery for her. After a minute's hesitation, she crept down the dark, steep steps, leaving the door open to give some light. She intended to cross the basement and go up the other side into the gallery.

A chest and two partly refinished tables were positioned on layers of newspapers on Louie's side of the basement. St. Clair stepped through the shadows around them, holding her breath at the heavy smell of turpentine and refinishing chemicals. The deep shadows on the gallery side of the basement held nothing but empty wooden packing crates. She felt for the railing and climbed the steps to the gallery.

The door on the gallery side opened into Rosalyn Mueller's office, St. Clair remembered from the day of the accident. No one was there, nor in the main floor gallery.

The space was larger than Louie's and appeared even larger because of the two-story space in the center of the gallery. All the debris of the sculpture had been piled into open crates and pushed against the wall under the balcony. Someone was walking around upstairs.

"Louie?" St. Clair called, and mounted the open spiraling stairs to the upper galleries.

Kitty Zelazak came out of one of the display rooms carrying several cans of paint. Her blond hair was pulled to the top of her head with a purple ribbon, and she was wearing loose, faded denim jeans and an oversized T-shirt. Her face was flushed. She caught sight of Maxene at the top of the stairs and shrieked.

"I didn't hear the chimes from the front door," she gasped, staggering backward.

St. Clair grabbed her arm to steady her. "I was looking for Louie, and I saw Rosalyn going into the tearoom across the street, so I thought Louie might be watching the gallery."

"Rosalyn's talking to that detective, and Louie isn't here. At least I don't think he is." She rested her box on the railing.

"Actually," St. Clair added, remembering her vow to tell Kitty that her husband was drugging her cocoa, "I wanted to talk to you, too."

"Little old me? Well, come into my parlor." She giggled.

St. Clair frowned as she followed her unsteady gait into the room. Was the woman drunk? Kitty put the box on the floor and wiped her hands on her jeans.

"This room is my studio, when Rosalyn doesn't have a show scheduled," she explained.

The windows that looked over the alley were bare now, and the floor was covered with a heavy gray canvas tarp. An easel stood in the center of the room with pots of paint stacked near it, and a few paintings were leaned against the wall. The top one looked like one in the exhibition.

Kitty noticed where Maxene was looking. "Those will go back into storage unless Ros agrees to hang them downstairs. I can't stand to look at my own stuff when I'm working. Actually, I'm considering painting over them."

She looked depressed, St. Clair thought, taking in the dark shadows under her eyes and the way her hands shook as she poured out two plastic cups of what looked like ice water from a thermos. Maxene took a hefty swig and coughed. It was white wine.

Kitty sat down on the floor and crossed her legs under her. "I'm tired all the time since that awful evening. It takes time to recover from watching somebody be crushed to death, at least that's what Ronnie says, and doctors always know. Now what was it you were going to tell me?"

Maxene drew a breath. The actual telling was awkward, and this woman had clearly been drinking. To delay, she began looking through the stack of canvases leaning against the wall. They were typical Wisconsin scenes—green meadows and red barns—realistic with a dose of Impressionism, as far as St. Clair could tell from her limited knowledge of art. Nice, but nothing she would buy.

"Have you been painting long?" she asked, stalling for time.

Kitty took another swig of wine. "After Ronnie was out of medical school, I took a lot of art classes. I never improved much, but I liked it, so years later, when Rosalyn and Lillian wanted to open this gallery, I put in my ante, too. Hardly any of my stuff sells. One day maybe I'll produce real art instead of looking like somebody just trying hard."

She was right, Maxene realized, staring at the paintings against the wall. Her paintings lacked the spark that would make someone stop to take a longer look.

"So you keep working, just on hope?" she asked. At a dinner party once, someone had asked her the same question about her research when they found out she had gone two years without results.

"Oh, sometimes I paint to make order out of things, like the colors in my flower garden. And sometimes I paint to understand something, like the shapes in a sunset. And

sometimes I paint just to prove I'm here. But a lot of the
time I paint because I feel free then, and I can breathe more
deeply and sometimes I hear a faint, sweet singing like the
last notes of a symphony."

Her voice trailed off, and she drained her white wine.
"Sounds like the meanderings of an innocent."

Maxene took a small sip of wine. "What's wrong with
being innocent?"

"Because when reality hits innocent people, it hits harder
because they don't see it coming. They're sitting ducks. I'm
tired of being innocent. I want to be a relaxed wise person
who makes good choices."

"Everybody has to go through an innocent stage," offered St. Clair.

"But for some women it lasts forever," said Kitty. "Being taken care of is so seductive that breaking the habit can
be impossible." She polished off her wine and poured herself another glass. "Now what were you going to tell me?"

"Did you know," St. Clair plunged in, "that sometimes
your husband puts Valium in your hot cocoa at night?"

Kitty looked at her.

St. Clair fumbled on. "I'm only telling you in case you
decide to drive somewhere. You might fall asleep at the
wheel."

Kitty propped her chin on her fists. "I wondered why cocoa puts me right to sleep," she said. "At least it isn't
strychnine. Ronnie does it because he's a doctor. He's
afraid of women, starting with his mother, and he's got this
control problem that makes me even more dependent than
I am naturally. Really, I should leave him, like Rosalyn left
her husband."

"Why don't you?"

"I have my weaknesses. I like the big house and the lack
of need to worry about money. I can paint here whenever
I want and go home to a housekeeper-cooked dinner and a
spotless house. If I'm sweaty, I take a swim in our pool before dinner. How is that so different from artists who lived

off patrons? A lot of men artists were supported by wives, lovers, sisters.

"You know what I need right now?" Kitty concluded. "A nap. I wonder if Ronnie put Valium into this thermos." She curled up under the easel in the fetal position and closed her eyes.

St. Clair poured the remains of her cup back into the thermos and left Kitty breathing heavily curled up on the canvas. Louie was still not in the kitchen or any other part of the gallery, so she went back through the office into the basement. The lights for the basement weren't at the top of the stairs at Rhinestones either, so she held tight to the banister and groped down the steps, leaving the basement door open.

The gloom was still deep. She was moving by the carved antique chest that nearly blocked the stairs on Louie's side when a sudden intuition made her stop and look at the chest. Was there a funny smell that persisted above the paint thinner smell? On impulse she opened the lid.

In the shadows inside the chest lay a man curled up on his back, his arms folded across his chest and his legs bent and crossed. He was wearing dirty jeans and a work shirt. A dark smear covered his forehead, and he was definitely dead.

St. Clair stepped back with a jerk, backing into the sticky table next to the chest and letting the lid to the chest fall with a bang. The noise made her shriek, but the shock cleared her head. She steadied herself against the table, then stepped forward and carefully opened the lid on the grisly sight. He was still there. She took a couple of deep breaths, then sat down on Louie's basement steps. She saw a lot of violence done to the human body every day, but nothing prepared her for finding a dead person curled up inside a makeshift coffin. After a minute or two, her knees stopped quivering and her thoughts cleared.

Where was Louie? Could he have killed this man and put him in this trunk? Was this the cause of Louie's hives and the hypersensitive behavior? Or had Louie just found this body, called in a panic this morning, then run away to hide somewhere? Either way, was the man the reason why Louie wanted her to come this morning?

Whatever was going on with Louie, this was a situation for the police. And one of them was nearby, consuming a quiet lunch in the tearoom across the street.

Louie still hadn't returned to his shop, St. Clair noted, hurrying through Louie's kitchen and the silent antiques. The street, however, was busier, and the china shop was bustling. Upstairs, at the entrance to the tea room, her progress was stopped by the mâitre d', who held up his hand like a traffic cop.

"Sorry, madam. We ask our patrons to dress appropriately for the tearoom."

"I don't want to eat," St. Clair protested. "I'm looking for someone."

"Perhaps you could come back after you've changed clothing."

"This is an emergency," St. Clair insisted. "I need to talk to a policeman who is eating here."

"A policeman is eating in this establishment?" The man winced.

"You do serve policemen, if they're dressed appropriately? This one is a detective in plain clothes."

The man winced again.

"Could I just take a quick look around?" St. Clair pleaded. "He's with the woman who owns the art gallery across the street."

"Ms. Mueller! Why didn't you say so?" The man looked relieved. "If you'll wait at the bottom of the stairs, I'll tell her you're here."

St. Clair descended to the china shop with as much dignity as she could pull together, feeling the man's eyes on her back. She leaned against a china cabinet and stared at an overdressed porcelain shepherdess waving her ribboned staff at a too-white sheep. I'm reasonably calm, she thought, considering I know there's a dead body in a trunk across the street. She looked around the room wondering if any of the appropriately dressed, white-haired ladies at the silver flatware counter had knocked the man into the trunk and then followed her across the street.

Grabowski appeared, carrying a linen napkin and interrupting her scrutiny of a middle-age man buying a lace tablecloth. Mustard was smudged at the corner of his mouth. "How did you know I was here?" he demanded.

"Excuse me for interrupting your luncheon, but there's a dead man in a trunk across the street," St. Clair answered, deciding not to mention the mustard.

"A dead man? Where?" His irritability vanished.

"In the basement between Louie's antique shop and the art gallery." St. Clair took the napkin from his hand and scrubbed away the mustard.

"Wait here. I'll be right back." He took the stairs two at a time.

St. Clair looked around the shop and realized that she herself had become the object of scrutiny. Had any of these people heard her being ordered to wait? She decided to wait anyway, especially since Grabowski was already coming down the stairs with Rosalyn hot on his heels.

Rhinestones was still deserted as they burst in the front door and hurried through the office. Rosalyn opened a fuse box behind her desk and flipped a switch. Lights flooded the basement steps. St. Clair hurried down the steps and pointed silently at the trunk, then waited as Grabowski opened the lid.

He and Rosalyn stood looking down into the trunk, the raised lid hiding its grisly contents from St. Clair. Finally he carefully lowered the lid and looked at St. Clair.

"Is this some kind of joke, Maxene? There's no body here."

"But there is, Grabowski." She hurried to the box and peered inside.

All that was there was a pile of crumpled gunny sacks supporting one of Lillian Hochstedder's clay sculptures that had stood on a pedestal in the upstairs gallery the night before.

St. Clair sat down on the cement steps and put her head in her hands. "There was a dead person inside that trunk, Grabowski. I saw him."

"What did he look like?"

"Small, lying on his back. Darkish hair. His eyes were open." She shuddered.

"What was he wearing?"

"Jeans, I think. It was dark."

"You didn't turn on the light?" This was from Rosalyn.

Suddenly, the electric outside door of the basement opened and bright sunshine flooded the room. Louie walked in through the open doors and hit the switch by the door. The electric door slammed shut.

"What's going on?" he demanded, staring at them in surprise.

"There was a dead man in your trunk," answered St. Clair. "I found him and went to get Grabowski."

Louie's jaw dropped. "That trunk? Impossible. I just brought it in today to work on it."

Rosalyn crossed her arms. "Dr. St. Clair says there was, and Detective Grabowski actually may believe her."

"There was a body," insisted St. Clair. "Why should I make up something so stupid?"

Louie sat down next to St. Clair on the steps and put his arm around her. "Come on upstairs, Max. I'll get you some water, or maybe some of my iced cappuccino. Can you make it?" He put a hand under her elbow.

St. Clair scowled at him. "Where were you, Louie? I looked all over your shop and the art gallery. Why did you call me to come down here? Was it because of something you found in a trunk in your basement?"

Louie raised his eyebrows dramatically. "Certainly not, my dear. I called you for an entirely different reason, and I was outside waiting for you. I thought you'd park in the back." He stomped up the stairs.

St. Clair followed more slowly, thinking over the situation. First, there had been a dead body, even if no one believed her. Second, Grabowski was acting in a bizarre manner. He didn't seem to believe that she had seen a body; he seemed to think she had made it up for some reason; and he was more irritated than he should be at having his little luncheon disturbed with Ms. Gallery Owner. And third, Louie had started using eyebrow pencil.

She sat on a tall stool in Louie's chintz-draped kitchen and watched his penciled eyebrows raise and lower as he carefully concocted two iced cappuccinos. She accepted hers less than graciously and drank off half of it.

"What's up, Louie?" she demanded, coldly. "Why did you call me down here? And what do you know about the body in that trunk? There was one, you know."

Louie pursed his lips and stared at her intently. "I don't know anything about a body. And the reason I called you has to do with a social disease."

"Oh God, Louie, not HIV."

"No, no," He waved away the thought. "The problem is one of the women who owns Rosalyn's gallery with her. She drinks."

"Kitty. I know. But I thought Rosalyn owned the gallery."

"All three of them put in money. Rosalyn wrote them in as part owners so she could accept the money as noninterest loans, tax write-offs, you know."

St. Clair didn't, but she decided it didn't matter. "So Kitty drinks. Why are you telling me?"

"Because you're a doctor and you know her husband personally, and they would listen to you if you counseled her to go for a cure."

St. Clair shook her head, disbelieving. "You brought me all the way down here to discuss an alcoholic I barely know? Why couldn't you tell me on the phone?"

"Because Kitty is here now and you could speak to her."

St. Clair narrowed her eyes. "What are you hiding from me, Louie?"

"Nothing!" The eyebrows raised again.

St. Clair slid off the stool. "I already chatted with Kitty Zelazak today. At the moment she's taking a nap, and even if she weren't asleep, I wouldn't impose any counseling on her. Now if you don't mind, I'm going to look around your store."

She left Louie sitting in the kitchen and began searching among the crowded furniture for other chests large enough to hold a person.

CHAPTER

14

GRABOWSKI WAITED UNTIL Maxene and Louie had climbed the steps to Louie's shop, then he followed Rosalyn up the opposite steps to her office, irritation with her mounting with each step. What the hell was going on? A possible body in a trunk in her own basement and she was simply annoyed?

Despite his aggravation, Grabowski couldn't help watching the motion of her well-muscled ass in the black tights under the long white sweater. What man was she keeping herself in shape for, he wondered, then caught himself. Maybe she just enjoyed exercise. Maxene St. Clair rode her bicycle to feel better physically, not for male approval, a point she had made clear at a bar one night to a man who had admired the muscles in her arms.

Grabowski leaned against the doorjamb as Rosalyn seated herself at her desk and began to look through a portfolio of drawings.

"Why do I get the feeling that you spirited me over to that tearoom so that Louie could dispose of a body in your basement?" he demanded. "You and Louie are the only two who know the combination to that outer door."

Rosalyn flushed and glared at Grabowski. "There was no body in the basement, and I have no reason to be in cahoots with Louie. Your friend the doctor invented the whole thing."

Grabowski was astounded. "Maxene invent something? Why on earth would she do that?"

"Because you and she had something going at one time, possibly still do."

"What does that have to do with anything?"

"Jealousy, Detective."

Grabowski's jaw dropped. "What?"

Rosalyn Mueller flipped through more drawings on her desk, then drew a long breath. "Okay, she didn't make it up. But she did make a mistake. The lights were off, and it was practically total darkness. She saw the blanket wadded up around Lillian's bust, and she thought it was a body."

"I'm looking over your place," Grabowski said coldly, "unless you're rather I get a warrant."

"Look anywhere you want." She began staring at a lithograph, making notes on a pad.

Grabowski went out the front door and turned left down the sidewalk past Louie's antique shop. St. Clair's green Raleigh was chained to the planter outside Louie's. The sight depressed him. That meant she was still inside with Louie, probably fuming. And with justification. Maxene St. Clair was not a person who would invent bodies in chests. Clearly the body had been removed while she was running to the tearoom. Grabowski felt guilty being at the tearoom when he should have been giving Rhinestones another thorough search.

At the street corner he turned west and walked down the block to the alley entrance, then down the alley to the back entrance of Rhinestones and Louie's antique shop. What had Louie been doing out in the alley? Either he was helping move a body, or he saw it happen; there were no other alternatives.

Parked in front of the electric door were a blue Ford, a red Jaguar, and a steel blue Mercedes. He assumed the Ford was Louie's. He walked quickly back around to the front of the building to his car, moved it to block the three cars in the lot, then radioed for backup. When the two squad cars arrived, he told two of the officers to watch the three cars and went with the other two around to the front of the building and into Louie's shop.

Louie and Maxene were sitting in the kitchen sipping iced cappucino. Louie put down his cup when he saw Grabowski and the two uniformed policemen in the doorway. Grabowski didn't give him a chance to stand up.

"I want to look around your basement. Do I need a warrant?"

Louie shook his head and silently pointed to the basement door. The uniforms disappeared down the stairs.

"What were you doing outside in the parking lot when Maxene, Rosalyn, and I were looking at the crates in your basement?" Grabowski demanded.

"Getting something out of my car."

"Show me."

Louie dumped a screwdriver and tacks out of a small sack on the counter. "I bought these at the hardware store this morning, and I forgot them in the trunk."

Grabowski looked at the sales slip. The computer receipt read today's date at nine A.M.

"When you were outside, who did you see?"

"No one. A couple of drunks."

Grabowski turned and went down the basement stairs. St. Clair and Louie followed more slowly. The cops were poking through empty crates on the gallery side of the basement. One pointed at the padlocks on the storage lockers.

"Who has the key to those locks?" Grabowski demanded of Louie.

"Rosalyn."

Grabowski took the stairs two at a time and returned with a tight-lipped Rosalyn. She began unlocking the lockers.

"I want to see inside the trunk of your car," Grabowski said to Louie, who was standing, hands clasped. "You can show me now or wait with an officer until I come back with a warrant."

Without a word, Louie reached into the pocket of his jacket and held out his car keys. Grabowski pointed to the code pad by the electric door and watched Louie punch in the code. The electric door raised; sunlight flooded the room. Grabowski waved everyone outside.

"The blue Ford is yours and the Jag belongs to Ms. Mueller?"

Louie nodded.

"And who owns the Mercedes?"

"Kitty Zelazak. She's upstairs in the gallery."

Grabowski beckoned to Rosalyn. They hurried up the basement steps and through the gallery to the upper level rooms. In one, Kitty Zelazak was curled up asleep under an easel. Rosalyn sighed and picked a set of car keys out of the purse next to the sleeping woman.

"This whole mess has been hard on her," she said quietly. "She's not a strong person, and she copes by retreating."

"On the floor?" He picked up the thermos and sniffed the contents.

Back outside, one cop was leaning against the squad car, arms crossed, looking steadily at Louie. Sweat was running down Louie's face, and he was scratching the backs of his hands.

"Open the trunk," Grabowski ordered.

It was empty. So was Rosalyn Mueller's and so was Kitty Zelazak's.

Rosalyn was tapping her foot. Her arms were crossed. "Satisfied, Detective?"

Grabowski scowled at Louie. "Tell me again: at the precise moment that Maxene was running across the street to tell me about this body, you decided to go outside for your screwdriver."

"I never saw Maxene. How should I know she was running across the street?"

Grabowski raised his eyebrows. "She walked through your shop, through your kitchen, into your basement, and back through your shop and you never saw her?"

"I wasn't in my shop. When I saw Ros going to the tearoom with you, I went over to Rhinestones to cover for her. Then I went outside."

"Leaving your own shop empty."

One of the cops chuckled. Grabowski let a minute drag by. "You need to come down to headquarters and go over this story again."

Louie's flushed face drained of all color.

Rosalyn stepped forward. "Louie's story makes absolute sense, Detective. We cover for each other all the time."

"I can see that."

Rosalyn Mueller glared at him. "Kitty is self-engrossed when she works and doesn't watch the shop as carefully as Louie. I depend on him."

Grabowski put his face very close to Louie's sweaty one. "I'm watching you, Louie," he said, distinctly. "You already run a funny operation, and it's getting stranger. Watch your ass, because I'm right behind you."

Rosalyn glared at Grabowski, then turned on her heel and stomped off, Louie trailing in her wake. The loading door slammed. St. Clair remained leaning against Louie's car.

Grabowski grimaced at the cops. "Keep an eye on this place, visibly. Park the squad car back here and in front a couple times a day. Pressure that joker."

"Him and the woman," said one cop. "I wouldn't trust that one with my breakfast coffee." Their wheels spun on the gravel.

Grabowski walked over to St. Clair and leaned against Louie's car. "Are you positive about that body? You're sure it wasn't the blankets and the skull?"

"I'm sure."

He sighed. "Why did you bicycle down here, what were you doing prowling around his basement, and why did you happen to open that trunk?"

St. Clair drew a deep breath. "Louie called me and said he had to talk right away. When I got here, I couldn't find him, so I went down through the basement to the gallery to look for him. I didn't find him, but I chatted briefly with

Kitty Zelazak; then I came back through the basement again. The reason I looked in the case was because something smelled funny."

"You looked in both galleries and didn't find Louie?"

"He must have been outside, like he said. I don't understand it either."

"Why did Louie call you down here?"

"I think he was nervous about how much you knew about his antique operation, and he wanted to pump me for information."

"Why couldn't he ask you on the phone?"

She shrugged.

"When you found Kitty Zelazak upstairs, was she awake?"

"She had been drinking. We talked about art. She's depressed." She paused. "Grabowski, I did see a body in that trunk."

Grabowski lips tightened. "It's beginning to feel like there was a plan at one time, but it fell apart. I don't know what the plan was, but this is all very strange."

Grabowski gave St. Clair a lift to the front of the building and watched her unlock her bicycle. The heat in his car was oppressive and inhibited the conversation, even if he had felt inclined to talk. It was two o'clock now. He had planned to talk to Lillian Hochstedder and Kitty Zelazak, as the two other owners of the gallery, but one of them was in a drunken stupor. At the stoplight he checked in his notebook for the address of the other, and drove slowly north.

Lillian Hochstedder lived in the East Side suburb of Whitefish Bay, popularly known as White Folks Bay. As he drove along the Lake Shore Drive neighborhoods, the houses got larger and the yards became actual grounds with curved brick driveways, statuary, and fountains. Grabowski rarely drove through these north shore suburbs since he lived on the South Side and his work took him more into the heart of Milwaukee, but the ritzy suburbs never changed. It's hard to improve on perfection, he decided, looking at the carefully manicured lawns. The air was softened by greenery and pumping sprinklers. The children cycling along the street wore helmets, rich kids having the luxury of worrying about their skulls.

Lillian Hochstedder's house was Elizabethan with ivy trailing around the leaded-glass windows and wide flower beds lining the brick driveway. Grabowski parked in the shade of an oak between a white Mercedes and a fountain with a bronze boy pissing. Goldfish swam around the boy's feet. He put his hand on the hood of the Mercedes. It was hotter than the top or trunk.

The heavy carved wood front door was rounded at the top and had a brass knocker shaped like a hand knocking. A Korean maid wearing a gray dress with white apron answered his bang and took Grabowski's card. In a few minutes she returned and mutely gestured for Grabowski to follow her around the outside of the house to an enclosed gazebo whose leaded windows and half timbers matched the main house. Lillian Hochstedder was standing in the doorway.

Grabowski walked slowly toward the gazebo, trying to place Lillian Hochstedder in his mind. She had been at the gallery opening, of course, since her sculptures were displayed in one of the upper galleries, although he couldn't remember how she or they looked. The woman standing in the doorway had short dark hair and was wearing cut-off jeans and a T-shirt with the picture of Shakespeare on it. She had thick shoulders and the muscles in her arms and legs were pronounced.

The heat was beginning to get to Grabowski. He had missed most of his lunch thanks to St. Clair's summons, and he was thirsty from standing outside in the hot sun looking fruitlessly into car trunks. He longed for a beer. During a previous investigation involving doctors' wives, he had been offered only mint iced tea. He wondered if doctor's wives who were artists were different.

"Beer?" offered Lillian Hochstedder. An open bottle of Miller stood on a workbench.

Grabowski declined. "Water," he said, with regret.

Lillian's hands trembled as she poured a tumbler full of ice water from a carafe in a small refrigerator. Grabowski gulped down the liquid and let her refill the glass. Despite the cool breeze through the room, she was perspiring, small beads of sweat along her hairline.

Glass in hand, he wandered around the studio. The gazebo had screened windows on all sides, except for a narrow stretch of wall with sink and storage cabinets. Several venetian blinds were closed against the sun, but others were open to the green trees and shaded lawn.

In the middle of the room stood a pedestal with something on it covered by a damp cloth. Grabowski lifted the cloth. Underneath was a partially finished sculpture of the head of a man. Eyeballs had just been inserted, glass orbs like doll's eyes protruding from the clay. Lips were pulled back over what looked like human teeth. Grabowski drew back at the grotesqueness of the sculpture and at how real the teeth looked; then he peered closer. The teeth were carefully molded from clay, detailed even to tiny vertical ridges.

"I'm into realism. It's popular," Lillian Hochstedder said, taking the cloth from his hand and replacing it over the bust. She gestured at two sealed crates on the floor, labeled and ready for sending.

He wandered farther, opening the storage cabinets to find blocks of clay wrapped in plastic, boxes of tools, cleaning supplies, insect spray.

In the center of the room near the pedestal was a movable storage cabinet with drawers and cupboard space. Next to it was a tall stool. Grabowski sat on the stool and sipped his water.

"I suppose you know why I'm here," he began.

"You want to know about the accident at the gallery when Soren was killed."

"It wasn't an accident," Grabowski said. "The wire was cut. Someone tried to drop that sculpture, possibly while the man was sitting there." He lifted the cloth to look at the sculpture again. It had strong cheekbones and a heavy jaw. The jawbone was hard and cold to the touch.

"That's what Rosalyn said. The wire was cut." Lillian Hochstedder settled the cloth over the art again and remained standing beside it, hand on the cloth. "It was an awful thing, that sculpture falling. Kitty was right there, talking to him only a few minutes before it fell. She could have been killed!" Her voice trembled.

Grabowski watched her. "How about you? Did you talk to him just before it fell?"

"No." She took a big gulp of beer. "I hadn't seen him all evening. We had a drink together—Kitty, Ros, Soren, Louie, and me—just before the caterers arrived. Soren was excited about something, I don't know what."

Grabowski pulled out his notebook and made a note. "How well did you know Soren Berendorf?"

"Not too well. He was quite famous, and I'm just beginning my career. I've had a few successes, but I've got a long ways to go."

"I heard he said your work was amateurish. Was he trying to give you direction? Sometimes well-known figures take on, well, disciples."

"I wasn't his disciple," Lillian said sharply. "I do my own work, without copying anyone. Too many artists are just prostitutes for somebody else's style, or for money. I have enough money to do exactly what I want, and I'm old enough not to be influenced by other people's style."

Grabowski leaned an elbow on the pedestal, bringing him even closer to Lillian Hochstedder. Close proximity to a cop, he had found, made people nervous. They blabbed information they would normally contain.

"But you're hard at work here on your sculpture, even though two days ago you were having a drink with a murdered man shortly before he died."

Lillian shuddered. "What do you want me to do, mope around? Art has always been therapy for me. Is that a crime?"

"You talked to Rosalyn just before I got here, didn't you?" he demanded, switching subjects.

Lillian drew a deep breath. "Yes, I did. She said you had been in the basement looking for some body that Maxene St. Clair said she found."

"Maxene found one." Grabowski said. "But by the time we got there, there was only the head left. Your head."

He lifted the drape over the skull again and stared at the deep eye sockets filled with doll's eyes. Maxene said the eyes in the body in the antique chest had eyes that glittered. In the dark, they would have looked like human eyes.

Lillian replaced the drape. "I really don't know what you're talking about," she said.

She was still standing by the bust with her hand on it when Grabowski left.

CHAPTER

15

ST. CLAIR ARRIVED at work that afternoon irritable. Finding the body in Louie's antique trunk had shocked her already-stressed system and put her nerves on edge. Then the bus down Prospect to North Avenue and Brady Street took longer than she expected so she missed her transfer. It was hot on the street corner; the hamburger odor from the McDonald's made her nauseous; and the traffic noise gave her a headache. She finally grabbed a taxi for the short ride down North Avenue instead of waiting for the next bus.

Louie had been exasperating beyond belief. He was sticking to his story that he had been outside or in Rhinestones the whole time she was looking for him. On top of that, Louie didn't believe she had seen anything except three gunny sacks and a clay bust in the chest. She had shouted at him.

The sick and injured at St. Agnes' were coming in slow waves. St. Clair had just finished explaining to an anxious young woman how to put antibiotic ointment on her six-year-old's firecracker burn and was scrubbing her hands at the sink when Joella came over with a note.

"ICU called," Joella said, examining her teeth in the mirror over the sink. "Your friend Wyoming woke up. The nurse said he's in possession of all his faculties. I hope that's the truth about all of his body, if he's as good-looking as I hear."

St. Clair looked at her sharply. Hospital gossip spread like cholera, and her late-night chats with an unresponsive

ICU patient may have become hospital speculation. "What else have you heard?"

"I heard the head nurse in ICU has the hots for Detective Grabowski."

"Who doesn't?" St. Clair grabbed a paper towel out of the dispenser and began scrubbing her hands viciously.

Joella raised her eyebrows. "Man trouble?"

Shirley joined them at the soap dispenser. "How is it those two words always go together?"

St. Clair looked at her watch. "I'll be in ICU for fifteen minutes unless you page me first," she said, ducking the discussion. "And will you tell Grabowski about his friend? The police switchboard knows where he is." She hurried out the double doors.

In Intensive Care, St. Clair glanced over the chart and spoke briefly with the nurse. Syzinski was lying on his back with his head turned toward the nurse's station. St. Clair moved into his line of vision.

"I'm Maxene St. Clair," she said quietly, not sure he was awake.

"Grabowski's Maxene St. Clair?" The words were fumbled and slow. His voice was deeper than she expected, and his eyes brighter blue.

St. Clair let the possessive pass without comment. "How are you feeling?"

He frowned. "Alive, barely. It was dark, and it happened so fast."

"I know. I was there, upstairs. Did you see the person who shot you?"

"No," he sighed. "Maybe when I'm more awake I could remember. I wish I had my sketchbook. I could think on paper."

"We'll get your art things," she promised, patting his hand. "Now rest and get better."

His fingers tightened around hers briefly; then he closed his eyes.

She took the stairs down to Rosa's room. Rosa was sitting up in bed wearing a hot pink nightgown with matching bed jacket trimmed with feathers, watching a soap opera on television and applying green fingernail polish to long curved nails. "What's happening, Doc?" she said cheerfully.

"Wyoming just woke up. He seems okay."

"Isn't that nice! I'll get over to visit real quick."

"Are you feeling good enough to go home?"

Rosa blew on her nails. "Feeling better, yes. But go home? Honey, I never had such a vacation. I read my magazines; they bring me food. I am getting used to this."

"Wyoming says he might be able to remember something about the people who shot you two," St. Clair said tentatively. "If he drew a picture, would it help you remember?"

"Sometimes it ain't healthy to have a good memory."

Back in the ER, St. Clair phoned the police switchboard. Grabowski hadn't picked up his message that Wyoming was conscious.

"Can't you beep him?" St. Clair demanded.

"He's off duty," the operator said, and hung up.

St. Clair dialed Grabowski's home. The phone rang fifteen times without answer. A vision of the man lounging in a cool bar with that stringy-legged art dealer rose before her, and she slammed down the phone.

As far as getting Wyoming's art supplies, there were two alternatives: she could wait until tomorrow morning, call Grabowski, and go with him to Wyoming's flat to pick up the supplies. Or, she could go to Wyoming's flat tonight and bring the art supplies back to the hospital so Syzinski would have them when he woke up in the morning.

She hunted through her address book and dialed Rolondo's number. "Wyoming is awake," she announced, after the tenth ring. "I need to get into his flat after work to pick up a few things. Is that possible?"

"What am I, your chauffeur?"

St. Clair forced herself to stay polite. "Wyoming is an artist. He says he might be able to draw a picture of the man who shot him. For this he needs his art paper and pencils."

She could hear Rolondo talking to someone. He came back on the line. "I'll pick you up at midnight."

She hung up thinking she should leave a message with the police switchboard telling Grabowski she was going to Wyoming's, then decided not to. Grabowski would want to know how she got there and how she got inside the flat. He hated the pimp and now that Wyoming had been shot in the company of Rolondo's employee, Rosa, Grabowski's antipathy had escalated.

Rolondo's white Caddy rolled up at midnight, and St. Clair climbed into the front seat. Joella clicked her tongue disapprovingly but waved a cheerful good-bye. As they wound through the streets, Barry White blasting on the CD player, St. Clair decided not to think about the intelligence of visiting an empty flat accompanied only by a pimp. One had to have a certain faith in other people, she reasoned; one couldn't go through life anticipating the worst.

The approach that had served her the best in the past was to determine a person's motivations as accurately as she could, then predict the actions that would follow those motivations. Most people were astonishingly predictable, once motivation became clear.

Rolondo's motivations were obvious. His operation was high-risk but with predictable expenses: he bailed out his girls whenever the vice squad picked them up, and he paid hospital bills whenever welfare wouldn't cover. But now he was faced with an unpredictable expense: two of his girls from the same flat were out of commission—one was dead—and not because of vice squad or normal work-related abuse. Rolondo didn't think this was regular business risk, or he wouldn't be placing himself and his white Caddy on call for St. Clair. He must have reason to believe that she could help.

He had more confidence in her than she did, St. Clair realized. She wondered why she didn't feel more anxious about the assignment, then realized that really this was like figuring out what's wrong with a person. I list the problems, see if they fit into any pattern of disease or injury that I'm familiar with, then try a treatment, she told herself. If it doesn't work, I try something else.

"Any luck finding who was in the car that shot Rosa and Wyoming?" she asked Rolondo.

Rolondo shook his head. "Illinois plates, old blue Chevy, dudes wearing masks."

"Masks? Isn't that unusual for random violence?"

Rolondo frowned. "You white folks are always talking about random violence. Where I live, there ain't no random violence. Everything got a cause. Something happens to a dude; he does something to get rid of it. Maybe he doesn't even know what happened to him; maybe it happened when he was a kid, but he can't get it out of him. Or maybe he knows what happened, but what he does to get rid of it don't look related. Maybe it's related only in his head. There ain't nothin' random about what goes down, not in my district, not in yours. There's patterns."

"But that means we can change the patterns and stop the violence," St. Clair reasoned.

Rolondo shrugged. "Maybe, maybe not. Got some heavy patterns going down."

"But that's what you're trying to do right now, isn't it? Find out what happened to Rosa so you can change the pattern?"

Rolondo didn't answer.

Half-inhabited lodgings are not pleasant to visit in the middle of the night, St. Clair decided, watching Rolondo open Syzinski's door with burglar tools. He pushed the door open, then disappeared back into his own apartment. Alone, she walked into the dark room and flicked on the lights.

The bare bulb in the apartment foyer gave the boxes and crates a lonely feeling. The police had been very thorough in their search. All the seals on the boxes had been broken and the contents were spilling out. She wondered how she would ever find Wyoming's pencils and sketch pad among the chaos, then decided to go through the smaller boxes first and work up. The crates looked like they held larger objects than she wanted, possibly paintings or sculpture equipment.

The seals. Suddenly St. Clair remembered Grabowski's threat about staying out of the apartment until the investigation was over. But the seals were already broken. What possible harm could come from bringing Wyoming art therapy that might hasten his recovery?

Still, she thought, it wouldn't hurt to find the art supplies soon and leave before a squad car cruised by and the officers remembered that these lights were in Wyoming's flat. As she was digging through a box of art paper, she heard a noise from one of the bedrooms.

"Hello?" she called, standing up abruptly. She was a woman alone in a deserted apartment in the inner city, a setup for disaster.

There was no response. She stood there, wanting to immediately run across the hall to Rolondo's flat, but she forced herself to think logically. The door had been locked, and the lights were off when she arrived. No one could be in the apartment. She sat back down on the crate in the hall and pulled a box toward her.

She was starting to rip the strapping tape off one box when she heard a footstep behind her. Panic caught her by the throat. She jumped to her feet, but it was too late. Something very hard hit her over the head, and she fell forward among the boxes. When she awoke, one of the girls from Rolondo's apartment across the hall was putting a cold cloth on her head. It didn't help the ache.

"What happened?" she groaned.

"I could ask you the same thing," said Rolondo. He was sitting on a packing crate, smoking a cigarette.

The woman from Rolondo's apartment across the hall

took the cloth away from St. Clair's head and sat back on her heels.

St. Clair slowly sat up. "Something hit me."

"Some person hit you," corrected Rolondo. "Likely the same person who made the mess in here. I assume that wasn't you."

The girl went into the kitchen and came back with a glass of water, then returned to the kitchen to make a cup of coffee. Rolondo lit another cigarette.

"I came back here to see how you was doing and here you were stretched out on the floor like a corpse."

"Who would want to hit me?" St. Clair asked, putting the cold cloth to her head again.

"Somebody who didn't want you here," answered Rolondo, pulling a box toward himself and yanking out the contents.

The caffeine cleared her head, and with Rolondo's help, she didn't take long to find what she wanted. Inside the third box were pencils, brushes, sculptor's knives. She scooped a handful of pencils into her purse, then dug underneath for the sketch pad.

Rolondo pulled a sketch out of another box and held it up to the light. "The dude can really draw. This guy is always standing around Tenth and North."

He began leafing through a stack of drawings. Some were sheets of just mouths, eyes, or ears. Under the stack was an FBI manual with pages of mug shots.

"This must be how artists learn to draw people," said St. Clair, taking the sketches from him and placing them on top of the art supplies. She took her cup to the kitchen sink.

The kitchen was stuffy and hot. The police had locked the window. She rinsed out her cup and put it on the drainboard to dry. A sour smell was coming from the refrigerator, an old model that couldn't handle the heat of the flat. She opened the refrigerator, sniffed the milk carton, and poured it down the drain.

Rolondo waited at the St. Agnes ER entrance while she gave the art supplies to an orderly to take up to Syzinski's room; then he drove her to her bungalow.

"Your cop friend sitting up for you," he said, pulling up behind the green Plymouth. "Don't tell him where you went. He got a problem with my part of town."

St. Clair felt like she should come to Grabowski's moral defense but decided to wait until she found out what Grabowski himself had been doing that evening. She nodded good night to Rolondo and walked slowly through the darkness to the silent figure rocking on the porch swing.

"Don't tell me that being taxied around by pimps is safe," Grabowski said.

"It's safer than driving alone at night," she said, getting out her key. Her head hurt horribly when she spoke.

"Where were you?" He followed her up the stairs.

"At Wyoming's apartment. He woke up and wanted his drawing pencils."

"I know he woke up. I pick up my messages. You could have waited for me to come with you. Technically, the flat is sealed, but not against people who think laws and seals are made to be broken. And what's wrong with your head? There's blood on your hair."

"Somebody hit me in Wyoming's apartment," she muttered, waiting for the explosion. She got it.

"Maxene," Grabowski threw up his hands, "the apartment is sealed because the person who lived there got shot. Go there and expect to get hurt, regardless of your motivations. Let me look at your head."

St. Clair sat down at the kitchen table and put her aching head on the cool surface while he probed until he found the lump.

"It looks all right," he said, doubtfully, "but I'm taking you to the ER."

She shook her head. The motion made her feel sick.

"Then I'll get you some ice to put on it, and you'll go to bed. Promise not to go there anymore without me?"

St. Clair took the beer he handed her, then held the chunk of ice onto the painful lump. "There's something in Wyoming's apartment that somebody doesn't want us to find," she said.

"If you're right, it's probably gone now." He sighed. "You walked in on someone and trapped them in the back. Frankly, though, I think it was a burglar. You're lucky you're alive."

"What could Wyoming possibly have in his apartment that someone would want?" she persisted.

"I'll ask him tomorrow. Now go to bed. I'll sleep on the couch here tonight to make sure you don't have more of a head injury than you think."

"Where were you earlier?" she murmured, pulling on her nightshirt and stretching out on the cool sheets. "Even the switchboard couldn't find you."

"I was having dinner," he said, after a pause. "Do you want to know who with?"

"Rosalyn Mueller?"

He sat on the edge of the bed, sipping his beer. "I can't figure her out. She's either a complete innocent or one of the most convoluted people I ever met."

"You planning on seeing her regularly?" St. Clair closed her eyes. She heard Grabowski sigh.

"I wish I knew what was going on," he said. "In a baseball game, there's a pattern to where the players move. If you watch the players, instead of the ball, you can tell how the game is really being played. You can predict what will happen."

"Are you picking up any patterns?"

"No. Everything is disconnected, too carefully separate, like there are three or four baseball games in the same ballpark. Even Louie isn't giving me straight answers, and Louie cracks if you look at him sideways. He says that while you were looking for him this morning, he was either in the bathroom, in Rhinestones, or outside. How you two kept missing each other, I can't figure."

"And what about the shooting? Any clues?"

Grabowski shook his head. "Not a thing. Now go to sleep. I'll be on the couch if you need me."

CHAPTER

16

THE NEXT MORNING, the headache was gone. St. Clair gingerly felt the lump and decided it had functionally disappeared. Grabowski had disappeared, too, leaving a cereal bowl and coffee mug drying on the drainboard. She made a cup of tea and hunted through her address book for the phone number of Ivan Petrovich, a friend who had gotten his Ph.D. in chemistry at the same time she was getting her M.D. Ph.D. in Immunology. Ivan worked in the State Lab of Hygiene in Madison where he and Maxene had done independent study projects together fifteen years before. He owed her a favor—a couple of them, in fact—for one she did for him involving his citizenship.

"Maxene St. Clair, from your past," St. Clair announced, after she had been transferred five times and put on hold for ten minutes. "I need a favor. I have some food samples that may be contaminated. Any chance I can bring them over and have you take a look?"

"Of course you can bring them over, and you'll stay the night."

"Absolutely not, Ivan. Don't start this again."

"Then have Marquette send them to Madison when they send their usual samples. Why make the trip if you don't want to see me?"

St. Clair felt a flash of remorse. "I do want to see you, Ivan. The problem is I don't work at Marquette anymore—I took a leave of absence—and this is for my own information. I need it today. Can you help me out?"

She could hear bubbling noises in the background.

"You're divorced now, aren't you?" Petrovich demanded.

"Yes, and I'm still not going to sleep with you."

He laughed. "Will you at least have lunch?"

St. Clair hung up the phone, smiling. Ivan had been overweight and balding in his twenties, and the last time she saw him, a few years before, he had gone totally bald. He imagined himself the world's biggest lover and never gave up trying to prove it. The question now was how to get to Madison. She took a deep breath and dialed Rolondo's number. To her amazement, the pimp was awake.

"You still want help finding out who did that drive-by shooting?" she asked.

"I told you once. That isn't enough?"

"Absolutely," she said hastily. "My problem is, I need to go to Madison today to find something out, and I don't have a car. Could one of your people give me a ride?"

She watched her cat, Ruby, climb up on the kitchen counter and rip at a pound of bacon while she waited for Rolondo to make up his mind.

"What you need is a car," Rolondo said.

"Agreed, but I don't have time to look for one, especially if I'm spending my free time hunting down information about the drive-by shooting."

Another long silence. "When do you want to go?"

"Now. And come back at one o'clock." She held her breath.

"Be outside in half an hour." The phone went dead.

A red Pontiac convertible with the top down and the stereo blasting rolled up half an hour later. The driver leaned on the horn. St. Clair looked out the window long enough to see her neighbor drop the hose he was washing his car with and run indoors. Assuming he was dialing the police, St. Clair hurried out and got in quickly with Rolondo's employee. The man was wearing three earrings in his right ear and one in his left, and the silver buttons on his lavender silk shirt glinted in the sunlight. She smiled a greeting, unwilling to compete with the stereo noise, and belted herself in tightly.

The ride to Madison took half the time she normally took. Rolondo's employee dropped her at the end of State Street across from the University of Wisconsin Bookstore. The stereo music was too loud to permit communication, so she pointed at her watch and held up one finger, hoping he would understand she meant one o'clock. It took the nearly fifteen minute walk over Bascom Hill on campus to Henry Mall and the State Lab of Hygiene before her hearing fully returned.

The Wisconsin State Lab of Hygiene hadn't changed in the nearly fifteen years since she had done an independent research project there as part of her Ph.D. Ivan had been in the midst of his own research project, but he had managed to make his hours coincide with Maxene's. He was good company during the long hours of hanging over microscopes, once he got the idea she was not interested in sex.

The student receptionist called Ivan's lab, and in a few minutes he charged through the door.

"Maxene, my sweet!"

She disentangled herself from the bear hug. "Ivan, your stomach has moved upward."

"Weight lifting, weight training. The girls love it; I can't keep them out of my bed."

St. Clair followed his now trim hips up the stairway of the old building and down a crowded hallway that needed repainting. Refrigerators and cabinets blocked the passageway. In the less-crowded chemistry lab, Ivan pulled a tall stool inches from hers. St. Clair moved her own stool back.

"Here's the contaminated food," she said, pulling the box of chocolates out of her shoulder bag. "Autopsy says the girl died of isoniazid overdose, but I can't figure out why. As far as I know, this is the only thing she ate that day. This is all very unofficial."

"Are you saying there's INH in these chocolates?"

"No. The opposite. I think the pathologist found a high level of INH in her blood, decided that was the cause of death, and didn't do any further autopsy tests. She was a welfare patient."

"So look for botulism or salmonella?"

"Or rat poison. The candy was sitting on the floor."

Ivan shouted at one of the student lab techs, shoved the chocolates at the aide with a list of commands, and dragged Maxene off her stool and across campus to the Rathskeller in the Student Union. He ordered hamburgers and beer, then carried them out to the shady terrace overlooking Lake Mendota. Sailboats glided by, birds chirped, and the soft summer air warmed Maxene's legs. She felt the tension ease out of her shoulders.

"You still going out with that cop?" Ivan demanded.

St. Clair raised her eyebrows. "How do you know about him?"

"I keep track of your every move, my sweet. One day you will come to Ivan's bed."

"Can't we just be friends, Ivan?"

He waved away the idea. "Now tell Ivan. What is this candy poison all about?"

St. Clair outlined Latoya's death and her desire to find out what happened. "There's so much violence in Milwaukee, and I see the results of it every day. I like knowing there's purpose in my job, but sometimes it seems like a hopeless fight."

He was watching her carefully. "So you're trying to create meaning in an event that seems meaningless, to make your own life have meaning again."

Tears came to Maxene's eyes. Embarrassed, she fumbled for her dark glasses. Ivan passed over his handkerchief.

"You love this Polish detective person, don't you?" Ivan asked.

"I don't know. How does a person know?"

He nodded and sipped his beer. "You will know. Or, you can come sleep with Ivan and settle for good sex."

Rolondo's employee drove St. Clair back to Milwaukee well before her shift started so she had time to visit Wyoming Syzinski. He had been moved out of ICU into a room across the hall, and he was propped up in bed. His blond curly hair was damp and combed, and a nurse with a razor had just finished perking up his face.

"You're looking human," said St. Clair, shoving a bunch of violets into his water glass.

"Grabowski said the same thing this morning."

Wyoming had opened his sketch pad on his lap, but the hand holding the drawing pencil lay limp upon the bedspread.

"You'll be strong enough to start drawing soon," said St. Clair, glancing at the still-blank page. She removed the box of art supplies from the visitor's chair and sat down.

His fingers twitched at the bedclothes. "I keep getting flashes of the car coming at us and the man leaning out the window, but I can't get a grip on the image." His voice trailed off, and he looked anxious.

"Would it help if Rosa came up and told you what she saw?"

His frown cleared. "A lot. That's what I do to help make a living—draw portraits from other people's descriptions for various law enforcement agencies."

"The mug shots in the post office?"

"The ones that are drawings. It's called composite drawing—someone tells me what kind of ears a bank robber had, and so on."

St. Clair lifted the sketches out of the box and began leafing through them. "You're good," she said. And then she stopped. Sitting in front of her was a sketch of Kitty Zelazak.

"I know this woman," she said, astounded.

Wyoming wasn't surprised. "She's the wife of a doctor in this hospital. I heard him being paged."

"But how do you know her? I went to an opening at her art gallery the night you were shot. Grabowski was there doing security."

"He wanted me to go, too. I knew Kitty because she took a class I was teaching at the Scottsdale Artists School.

She was at a tennis ranch with some friends, and she took a break from the courts."

"How did she know you were coming back to Milwaukee?"

Grabowski walked in at this moment, cutting off his answer. St. Clair held up the sketch.

"Wyoming knows Kitty from Arizona. Isn't that a coincidence?"

Grabowski glanced at the sketch. "I'm not surprised," he said. "Another one of your women, Wyoming?"

Wyoming grinned. "They think the instructor comes with the course."

Grabowski sat down and put his feet up on the bed rail. "Why don't you move into my place? It needs remodeling anyway, and I called a carpenter. He said he can rip the ceiling out of the living room in a week. That should be enough space for you. He'll make a loft out of the rest of the upstairs for your bedroom, and I'll take the kitchen and the back bedroom."

"Nice thought, but I've lived alone too long to share quarters." Wyoming glanced at St. Clair.

St. Clair felt it was a good moment to leave. She promised to be back later, and left for Rosa's room where Rosa was busy painting her toenails purple. A large poster of a tall basketball player was taped to the wall under the crucifix.

"Wyoming is sitting up," St. Clair. "Why don't you go visit?"

"Soon as my toenails are dry. I'm going home tomorrow. Got to work." She sighed.

St. Clair sat on the end of the bed. "Why don't you do something besides hooking?"

"Like what, wait tables? Honey, what I need is a man to take care of me."

St. Clair debated discussing the wisdom of this route and decided not to. Rosa knew the odds of finding a decent male better than she did.

By five o'clock the ER had cleared out. St. Clair went up

to Syzinski's room and found him sitting cozy in bed with Rosa, who was wearing her red, feathered bed jacket. They were working on a sketch of the masked gunman. Syzinski put down his pencil with a sigh.

"This is the best we can do," he confessed. "It was dark and both of us were terrified. Just thinking about it makes me afraid. Say," he said suddenly, "how's Latoya? She was sick the afternoon before I was shot. I was planning to drop by."

Rosa looked away. "She died. OD'd on her TB pills."

"She died?" Syzinski looked shocked. "She was in my apartment just that morning. She wasn't sick at all." He pursed his lips and concentrated on shading the drawing, as if he were coping with the news by removing himself mentally.

St. Clair watched the sketch get fuller and more alive. Finally, Syzinski dropped the pencil. His face was pale and a film of perspiration shone on his forehead. Maxene and Rosa lowered the head of the bed and plumped up his pillows.

"Milwaukee is a tough place to live," he murmured, eyes closed. "But that's what makes it real. The Southwest is slow and predictable. I came back here for a reality check."

"You're right," St. Clair agreed. "Living here isn't easy, but it's real. You have to know the ropes and keep your eyes open." An idea occurred to her. "If I told you what a man looked like, could you draw a picture of him?"

Wyoming's eyes remained closed. "Come back after my nap."

Out in the hallway, St. Clair ran into Lillian Hochstedder who was looking confused. "I'm supposed to meet my husband in the doctor's lounge," she said.

"Next floor." St. Clair punched the elevator button.

Back in the ER, St. Clair lounged in the red plastic armchair and listed mentally everything she didn't know. She didn't know why Latoya died, why Syzinski and Rosa were shot, why the sculpture dropped on Soren Berendorf.

"None of the pieces of this mess are even within

reach," she said to Shirley, who was doing inventory. "Maybe if I could figure out the motivations of different people involved, I could get a grip on it. If I knew why these events happened, I could know who was doing it. I'm in the 'helping' profession, and I should know enough about human nature to attach motivations to personalities."

Shirley sat down and put her feet up on the rungs of Maxene's chair. She crossed her arms and looked at St. Clair hard. "Once I read a novel about a woman psychologist who thought she could predict anyone's behavior because she was an expert in psychology. Unfortunately, she second-guessed everyone totally wrong because her ego got in the way and she didn't notice how people around her had changed."

"Are you saying my ego is getting in the way?"

"I'm saying that happens to people in the 'helping' professions," said Shirley, "After a while, we think we've seen all there is to see, and we begin to feel power over people—the power that comes with position plus insider knowledge. We even think it's moral power because we're 'helpers'."

St. Clair thought this over. "Possible," she admitted. She thought about Kitty and Lillian. "Do artists fall into that trap?"

"Some fall," Shirley said, "but not into the same trap. Some artists I know are too busy watching what's around them, or looking in their heads and putting it on paper to get ego problems. Other artists have big ego problems, but that's because they start thinking they can create like God. They cross the vanity border."

St. Clair put her head back and closed her eyes. Her head ached again.

"You're tired," Shirley said. "You've seen a lot happen in three days and you're trying to react to new stress like you haven't already had all the stress you can take. Give yourself time to recover."

Two hours later, the ER quieted down and she went up

to Wyoming's room. His color was better, or maybe she was deceived by the soft light of the single bedside lamp. His sketch pad sat on a pillow on his lap, and he was drinking steadily from his water carafe.

"I wonder how long before I'll be able to work again." He sounded depressed. "When I teach forensic sculpture, I have to stand for hours. I get tired even when I'm healthy."

"What's forensic sculpture?"

"Reconstructing a skull by adding clay all around the bones to flesh out the face and make it recognizable. We do it when a skull is found and the police want to identify it."

St. Clair noticed a red and blue flowered scarf lying under the bed. She draped it over the chair. "Company?" she asked, surprised to feel a mild attack of jealousy.

"Kitty Zelazak. Remember I told you she took my drawing class in Arizona? Her husband stopped in, too."

"Is she any good as an artist?"

He moved his head restlessly. "She doesn't see clearly, and it shows in her watercolors."

"You mean she has trouble with her eyes?" St. Clair couldn't get out of the medical model.

He smiled. "Look at it this way: every new experience changes you. You have some choice over how much you change, or what you do with the changed you. But even if you do nothing, you can't escape being changed. An artist has to paint or sculpt that personal change or the art isn't genuine. You know how certain paintings hit you in the soul? That's because the artist is painting a change in his or her own soul. The trouble with Kitty is that looking honestly at a change requires suffering."

"And rich women don't have to suffer?"

"A real artist has to have the courage to take off the rose-colored glasses and the chintz curtains and look at life. Clear vision is like a full suitcase. In order to put in something new, you have to take out something old."

"What did you take out?"

He sighed. "I used to think it was innocence that people had to lose to become real artists, but now I think it's security. In fact, I think artists have to stay innocent to see life in an unbiased way; they just have to gain the courage to look."

"And you can't do that and be rich at the same time?" St. Clair thought of her three-room upstairs flat.

"Money cushions reality. Appearances become more important than reality, and artists who only look at appearances produce superficial art that doesn't reach real human emotions."

He picked up his pencil and drew a flock of butterflies swooping over the paper. Then he accented the wings and drew two of them kissing.

"Bathroom wallpaper." St. Clair smiled.

"Kitsch. Kitty Zelazak. Her life is so sheltered that she'll never see life's real shape. She paints sugar-coated images from her imagination so she'll never leap from gifted amateur to artist. Believe me, I meet all these women in the art classes I teach."

"They don't have anything to say?" St. Clair asked.

"They can't focus it sharply enough to turn it into the human experience. For example, many well-educated women can write a beautiful sentence, but they'll never get anything published. Truth doesn't always have happy endings, and the morality of a literary piece can contradict itself when it's all written."

"And that's why Kitty can't paint." St. Clair stared at the sketch of Kitty Zelazak.

"It can happen to anyone," said Syzinski, watching her. "Doctors who just treat a patient's symptoms aren't looking deep enough to see the real person."

The paging system blurted out St. Clair's name and cut off her response. She picked up Syzinski's phone.

"Rolondo called," said Shirley. "So did Dr. Hochstedder. You coming back to work? We got people here who claim they need a doctor."

Syzinski was fiddling with the drawing pad. "Grabowski wants me to move into that little house of his," he said. "I think he feels responsible for me getting shot."

"He's a cop. He has a need to look after people."

"Like doctors?"

"I guess so." A wave of depression hit. Did she only look at patients' symptoms? Was she afraid of the reality surrounding the wounds and illnesses?

"Grabowski's lonely," Szyinski went on, "but he's afraid to do what he must do to stop being lonely. He's afraid to commit himself to a woman he loves, so he's asking me to move in. He's filling up space to fill up time."

"It's a cute little bungalow," she said evasively.

"Not your style?"

"So far I don't have a style."

He picked up his pencil. "Let's get off this depressing relationship stuff and get into even more depressing stuff—dead people. Grabowski said you saw a person in a trunk in the gallery basement. You want to describe him?"

St. Clair leaned over the bed rail. "It was dark," she admitted. "But it wasn't so dark that I couldn't make out a man lying on his back. It looked like someone had tucked in his feet and crossed his hands over his chest. And closed the lid."

"Could you see his face?"

"His head was propped on the end of the chest so I could see his hair and his eyes and nose but not his mouth so much. Gray hair, lots of it, and eyes that glittered." She shuddered.

He started the sketch, a bare outline of a curled up torso, then a thatch of hair etched with pencil lines.

"Long nose," she instructed. "Big hair. Oh, and ears that stuck out through the hair. Broad face."

The man's face took shape under the pencil. It was vague and indistinct but as the lines grew stronger, it reminded St. Clair of someone. It felt creepy looking at a drawing of a person who was dead.

"I know who that is," she realized with a start. "I mean I know where I saw him. He was at Rhinestones the night you got shot. I saw this man looking at Lillian Hochstedder's heads."

"Heads?" Syzinski asked.

St. Clair explained. "Lillian has a new technique with clay, very popular. She makes modernistic busts with glass eyes and realistic teeth. This man was standing in the gallery looking at them. I noticed him because his ears stuck out."

"Lillian Hochstedder? The wife of the doctor I hear getting paged?"

Grabowski walked in then. "Up and drawing!" he exclaimed. "I just talked to the carpenters, and they say the living room will have a tall ceiling in just under two weeks." His voice trailed off as he saw the sketches spread across the bed.

"That's the gunman?"

"The best we could do." Wyoming tossed it over, revealing the sketch of the body in the trunk that was on his lap.

Grabowski grabbed at the sketch of the body, and his face went pale. "Where did you get that?"

"I drew it. This is the man Maxene saw in the antique chest in Louie's basement."

"He was also at the gallery opening the night Wyoming was shot," Maxene added.

Grabowski sat down in the visitor's chair. "That's Koranda, the police officer I'm trying to find," he said, almost inaudibly. "This means he's dead."

St. Clair and Syzinski watched Grabowski's jaw bulge as he clenched his teeth.

"But where is he?" St. Clair asked faintly.

"I sure as hell am going to find out." Grabowski snatched the pile of sketches off the bed and walked out of the room.

Syzinski looked at Maxene. "Tell me about Lillian Hochstedder's busts."

St. Clair dragged her attention back from Grabowski and concentrated on the evening at Rhinestones. "I heard all of this from various sources," she explained. "Lillian started doing sculptures only recently but came up with a technique that's striking. Many of the statues at the show had 'Sold' stickers on them. Frankly, I didn't like them much. They reminded me of anatomy lab."

The page cut off the rest of her explanation. Shirley was calling her to the ER.

"I'll be back," she said to Syzinski.

St. Clair made it just to the double swinging doors of the ER, but she didn't go through. Instead, she turned back quickly and headed for the stairs. By the time she got to Syzinski's room on the third floor, she was completely out of breath. She burst into the door of his room, still gulping air.

Leo Hochstedder was sitting in the visitor's chair. They both looked up in surprise when she burst into the room.

"I forgot to ask you something," she said to Wyoming, but, spotting Hochstedder, she picked up the box of art supplies and sketches and rummaged through it until she found what she wanted.

Hochstedder rose. "We were through, anyway," he said. "I saw on the chart that Mr. Syzinski was from Arizona. I'm thinking of retiring out there."

St. Clair followed him into the elevator.

"What do you know about INH overdose?" she asked. "You're a pulmonary specialist, you must run into it from time to time."

"Rarely," he said. "It usually happens when someone takes someone else's meds without realizing it. The person is usually not paying attention—in the middle of the night, or some similar circumstance."

"Do people ever use the drug to commit suicide?"

"I suppose—you can suicide on just about any drug—but I've never seen it."

When St. Clair got to the ER, Shirley was scowling. She shoved a chart at her. "We're stacking up here," she said. "Clear 'em out."

St. Clair nodded, but first she scribbled the name of the

Arizona Artists School on the message pad. "Can you get me this number?" she asked Joella. "And then get them on the phone."

CHAPTER

17

GRABOWSKI STALKED OUT of the hospital carrying Wyoming's drawings in his hand, forming a plan as he walked. First, he drove downtown to his office and made copies. Then he drove north on Seventh Street. The intersection at the freeway entrance was six inches deep in broken car window glass, as usual. When the intersection light turned red, children who lived in the row houses along Seventh Street would run out carrying bricks and smash the passenger windows of women driving alone. Then they'd grab the purse sitting on the passenger seat.

He turned west onto North Avenue. The heavy afternoon heat had cleared the treeless sidewalks of pedestrians except for a few people straggling into the storefront churches for an after-work prayer. Rolondo's headquarters was upstairs from an abandoned grocery store across from Luigi's Italian Restaurant. Grabowski climbed the dirty stairs that were vibrating with rap music. At the top, he didn't bother to knock.

Rolondo was sitting in a lounge chair talking to two other men. They took one look at Grabowski and melted out the door. Rolondo turned down the music.

"Know anything yet about the drive-by shooting in front of your apartment at Fifth and Center?" Grabowski asked, pulling up a chair and holding the drawings rolled up in his hands.

Rolondo's pleasant expression didn't alter. "Two black dudes wearing masks, blue Chevy, Illinois plates."

Grabowski unrolled the drawings. "Here's a drawing of the man doing the shooting. He's wearing a mask, but maybe you could ask around, see if anybody recognizes him."

Rolondo reached for the drawing. "Mask covers most of his face."

Grabowski nodded. "How about this next drawing? You know him?" He passed over the sketch of Koranda.

Rolondo looked at it long and carefully. He reminded Grabowski of Rosalyn, looking through her lithographs. "I seen the man." Rolondo waited.

"He was a guard in the crime lab."

Rolondo nodded. "Wasn't he transferred to that job because of being too rough on folks he got inside the police van?"

Grabowski shrugged. "He was found dead in the art gallery basement. You heard anything about that?"

Rolondo shook his head. He stacked the two drawings neatly and reached for the drawing of Kitty Zelazak. He looked at it carefully.

"Never seen this one," he said, handing it back. "But right now, we have another problem. My lady didn't have TB, so she couldn't have been taking any TB medicine. If she had TB, the health nurses would make her stop working because she might also have AIDS, and those nurses track girls down and pester them until they do what the health nurse wants. Plus I don't want no AIDS in my houses."

"So where did she get the isoniazid?"

"Somewhere else. Maybe your friend the sculptor."

"Syzinski didn't have TB." Grabowski shook his head.

Rolondo turned up his palms. "I think you got some big blind spots in your vision," he said. "The problem is, something's missing. Time I found out what."

Grabowski drove next to the apartment at Fifth and Center. He went through the building, apartment by apartment, showing the drawings of the masked gunman and of Koranda. The hallway smelled of fried chitlins and cabbage. Televisions blared from every doorway. No one recognized either drawing.

At Rolondo's apartment, Rosa and several other women were sitting in the red carpeted living room, smoking. He stood in the doorway while they looked at the drawings. No one knew either face. On impulse, he passed around the drawing of Kitty Zelazak. No one recognized her either.

"That Wyoming is quite a looker, ain't he," said Rosa, handing back the drawing. "When's he going to be back?"

"Never," said Grabowski.

He let himself into Syzinski's apartment and stood scowling at the mess. Maxene had cut through all the police seals and left the contents of the boxes spread over the floor. He spent half an hour tidying the boxes, looking through them as he did. Wyoming hadn't brought everything from Arizona. The garden sculptures weren't here, and neither were the piles of Navaho blankets. Or possibly the burgler that struck Maxene had stolen them.

Next he drove west on North Avenue to Fiftieth Street and Koranda's house. The woman from downstairs answered her door, baby on her hip, beer in hand.

"You know what happened to my neighbor?" she asked.

"We think he's dead."

She nodded sadly. "He was never away this long. Besides, he's a cop; things happen to cops." She sipped the beer and jerked her head toward inside. He waited in the living room while she got him a beer from the refrigerator; then she sat on the couch and looked at the blank TV. The baby played with her earring and put his head on her shoulder. Finally she nodded to herself.

"I never talked to him much, but still, I feel bad. He was a person, and now he isn't."

"Did anyone ever visit him?"

"The lady who came for the fish."

"If I gave you a drawing, do you think you might recognize her?" He handed over the drawing of Kitty, carefully concealing the one of the man in the trunk.

She looked at it carefully. "Hard to say, you know? I'd

hate to get somebody in trouble by mistake. But I think she's the one. Who is she?"

"An artist." Grabowski rolled up the drawings. She followed him outside to the porch.

"What shall I tell the landlord?" she asked.

"Look for another tenant."

He drove down the block then stopped the car under a tree to think. Shade-cooled breeze blew through the hot car.

It was starting to pull together, he could feel it. The problem was that the person who organized all this was still part of the game, playing out a role, and as such knew what he was doing. But who was the person? There were three or four good possibilities. He had found a connection to Koranda, but still couldn't figure out why Koranda was dead. There just wasn't any reason.

CHAPTER

18

AT EIGHT, ACTION slowed in the ER. St. Clair called Pathology hoping Aaron Simonson was working late.

"I'm coming down," St. Clair told him. "Unlock your doors."

Dr. Simonson was slouched in his desk chair eating from a Styrofoam container while a corpse lay on the autopsy table covered by a sheet. The pathology lab reeked of garlic and formaldehyde.

"Want some?" Simonson waved a plastic fork at the substance in front of him. His eyes were bloodshot, and his beard had at least two days' growth.

St. Clair averted her eyes and sat a safe distance from corpse and dinner.

"Remember the sculptor who died a few days ago when his sculpture fell on him?" she asked. "I want to see his autopsy report."

Simonson pointed his fork at a filing cabinet. St. Clair began hunting through the files. As she was pulling a folder out of the drawer, the Pathology doors swung open and Leo Hochstedder hurried in.

"They told me you were working all night again," he said to Simonson, not noticing St. Clair standing by the files. "I need an autopsy report."

Simonson again gestured with his fork at the files and Hochstedder found himself face-to-face with St. Clair.

"Good evening," she said cheerfully, resuming her appraisal of the report. She found the information she wanted and carefully replaced it.

Hochstedder hesitated. "I'll come back in the morning," he said to Simonson, and followed St. Clair out the door.

"You're working late," she commented.

"It's summer, and all the asthmatics have crises during the high-pollution periods," he said. "Can you stop in the cafeteria for a coffee? I want to talk to you."

The main cafeteria was closed and the ceiling lights were off except for two over the coffee and sandwich bar. The darkness made the orange carpet almost tolerable. St. Clair poured herself a glass of ice water. Hochstedder was drinking coffee.

"A Polish police detective came around to see my wife again about the Berendorf accident," Hochstedder said, stirring in multiple teaspoons of sugar. "I understand you somehow actually know this detective person."

"I met him last year."

"What do you know about this art gallery accident? Is he close to finding out what happened?"

St. Clair thought hard. It was logical for Hochstedder to ask. His wife was co-owner of the gallery, and as such was up to her neck in trouble. Hochstedder had a source of information in St. Clair. She was part of the medical community, a group tightly knit by their common defense against malpractice suits and cost-containment measures. Doctors shared information from who messed up a surgery to what were high-season condo rates at Aspen. Hochstedder was assuming she would tell all she knew.

"They think Berendorf's death may not be an accident," she began with caution.

"I know, I know." He was impatient. "What about a body you supposedly found in the basement? What about that?"

"The police think they might have identified the man."

"How?" the doctor demanded. "Rosalyn told Lillian it was one of Lillian's sculptures, damn the things. I wish I had a nickel for every time I walked into her studio and thought a person was standing there."

"The man I saw was definitely identified," St. Clair snapped, instantly regretting it.

"How?" Hochstedder was onto it like a terrier.

"A forensic artist drew a picture from my description and a police officer identified it."

Hochstedder thought that over. "Where is the body now?" he demanded.

"They don't know."

"See?" He held up his hands triumphantly. "You never really saw a body. Your imagination took over. Imaginations are powerful things, especially in women."

St. Clair set her teeth.

"Kitty Zelazak is a loose cannon," he said abruptly. "She had quite an affair going with that fairy."

"Are you referring to Berendorf?"

"Who else? The man slept in all kinds of beds; anybody could tell that. He dumped her like a load of bricks when she started putting on the pressure to make a commitment. She'd bail out of that fancy house in a second if she had a place to go."

The hospital PA system blaring St. Clair's name interrupted Hochstedder's next question.

"Keep me posted," Hochstedder said.

It sounded like a warning.

CHAPTER

19

GRABOWSKI DROVE DOWN Locust from Rolondo's headquarters to the East Side, then north on Prospect past Rosalyn Mueller's condo, and up North Lake Drive to Kitty Zelazak's house in Whitefish Bay. It was nearly eight in the evening, and the soft summer dusk was dissolving into Lake Michigan as he drove past the sweet-smelling lawns. The Zelazak home was at the turnaround of a quiet cul-de-sac, a gracious white-frame colonial with pillared portico and green shutters.

He hadn't spoken to Mrs. Zelazak since the day in the gallery when she had talked about her relationship with Berendorf. He thought he had her pegged that day—a woman who had made all the right social choices and couldn't figure out what had gone wrong. Lights were on at one end of the ground floor of the Zelazak home, and someone was moving from the screened sun room to the kitchen. The doorbell chimes played the first few bars of "America."

Kitty Zelazak came to the door wearing jeans and a man's shirt unbuttoned to where he could see she wore no bra. The circles under her eyes were dark and defined, and she looked thinner. She was carrying a glass of something that clinked.

He followed her through a darkened dining room and a kitchen gleaming with brass cookware to the sun room where a large-screen TV flickered silently. She turned off the picture with a remote control and sank into a green leather armchair softly lit by low table lamps. Grabowski sat on the matching green corduroy couch.

"I met someone today who knows you," he said.

She concentrated on pouring him a glass of something thick and pink from a clinking pitcher. He tasted it—a margarita, heavy with tequila.

"I suppose it has to do with this nasty accident." Her tongue was thick with liquor.

"The woman who knows you lives in a little apartment on the other side of town." On the other side of the planet, he thought, catching the glimmering green light from the swimming pool.

She didn't answer.

"In case you're deciding whether to deny it, don't. It's too easily proved," Grabowski warned.

"Shall I call my lawyer?" Her cheeks wore two red spots.

"If you want."

"All right," she sighed, "I went to that awful little apartment. I can deny this later. It's your word against mine."

A surge of anger flooded him at the arrogance of her assumption that her word would be believed over his. He controlled the anger. "What were you doing there?" he asked.

"Picking up art supplies for Lillian." She laughed and tossed off her drink. She filled it up again from the pitcher.

"Art supplies?"

"I can't think what else to call them. Hideous things. Some even had patches of hair on them. Lillian had to boil them for hours with bleach."

Grabowski suddenly remembered one of the crime lab guard's tasks: he picked up and stored unidentified human bones found in Milwaukee. Koranda had found an income source. "They were skulls," he guessed, "models for her sculptures."

She smiled crookedly, the alcohol showing on her face. "You're not a detective for nothing, Detective."

"So what's the big secret?" Grabowski forced himself to

go slowly with the questions, move carefully to why the crime lab guard was found tucked into a trunk in Rhinestones' basement.

"Lillian is a scaredy-cat." Kitty giggled. "She thinks if people knew she was using the skulls of societal rejects for inspiration, they might not buy her sculptures. People want to pay big prices for an artist's imagination, not for copies of drunks who died on the street."

Grabowski tried to think over the legality of a crime lab guard providing skulls as models. It wasn't illegal; cadavers of the dregs of society found their way onto the dissecting tables of medical schools over the country. These skulls probably had turned up in obscure locations, and their identities had never been traced. Normally, they were stored until their identities were determined. After that, they were buried in paupers' graves with the derelicts. "Did he charge for the skulls?" he guessed.

Kitty thought this over. Choosing her words, Grabowski wondered, or trying to remember? People who drank heavily had trouble dividing truth from wishful thinking.

"He charged for the inconvenience, is what Lillian told me. It wasn't really wrong, he said; it was just inconvenient to be transporting police property."

Grabowski nodded. It fit Koranda's secretive nature. He was saving up money for something, maybe a new cabin up north. "Sergeant Koranda disappeared last week," he said.

Her face seemed to pale in the dim light, although he couldn't be sure. He continued.

"Then he turned up again, strangely enough, at Rhinestones, curled up inside one of Louie's trunks."

She sucked in air.

"Do you know how that could have happened?"

She didn't answer.

"Did he ever come to Rhinestones?" Grabowski persisted. He leaned forward. "Maybe to deliver some skulls himself?"

She shook her head, looking at him wide-eyed. She was probably one of those intuitive types who went through life on instinct, Grabowski decided. Some people trusted their sixth sense more than the other five. Many criminals were intuitive types, using their instincts to get around basic human conventions. Grabowski was not unintuitive himself.

"You know what happened, don't you," he said sharply.

"No! Do you?" Her voice quavered.

"We have a very good idea." He, too, could skirt the convention of honesty.

"What are you going to do?"

"That depends on you."

Her breath was coming in short gasps now, and her hands were clenching the glass so hard he was afraid it would break. He pried her fingers off the glass and set it on the tray.

"Why did you pick up the skulls from Koranda? Why didn't Lillian?" he asked, sharply.

She jumped, startled. "Lillian asked me to," she said instantly, her eyes wide. "I didn't actually know what was inside the Styrofoam cooler until I watched Lillian open it at her house. I screamed. Then, later, when she asked me to drive over to his house and get some more, I wouldn't. Too creepy."

"How many skulls were in the box?"

"Six or seven, maybe. I didn't count. She shut the lid as soon as I saw them."

"Was that the only time you saw Koranda?"

She hesitated a split second. "Yes. Like I said, I told Lillian I wouldn't pick them up anymore."

Grabowski felt he had made a mistake somewhere. He watched her take a deep breath—a self-calming measure or real relief?

"Lillian Hochstedder lives only a short distance from here, doesn't she?" he said.

He was telling her he was going there and warning her not to call Lillian as soon as he left, or at least warning her that he would know if Lillian were prepared for him when he arrived. It was the best he could do.

He borrowed her phone to call Louie's apartment to

make sure Louie got the news about the identity of the body in the trunk from him first. There was no answer at Louie's house or at his shop.

The moon was above the trees when he walked out to his car. Maybe it was better if Kitty did call Lillian; at least he wouldn't have to stand long under that grim medieval overhang waiting for the maid to answer the door. The Zelazaks didn't appear to have a maid, or maybe she went home at night. Mrs. Zelazak was alone in the house, with only the screens of the porch to protect her. Maybe the house was wired for burglars; she wasn't surprised to see him when he came to the door.

The porch light was on at the Hochstedders when Grabowski drove up the curving driveway. The light was a lantern affair, suitable for a medieval castle. Lillian opened the door almost as soon as he raised the brass knocker and stepped back to let him into the broad hallway. A thick Persian carpet with long fringes covered the flagstones and a tapestry hung on the back wall. Brass candlesticks on a heavy bureau gleamed from a concealed light source. He was half-curious to see the wealth in the living room, but he shook his head when she started in that direction.

"Can we chat in your studio?" he asked. "Bring your husband if you'd like," he added, noticing her hesitation.

"Not home." She moved past him to the outside, closing the door firmly behind her.

The silence around her house was even deeper than around Kitty Zelazak's. Even the swish of cars on North Lake Drive disappeared in the leafy solitude. A star appeared through the foliage, then vanished. She stumbled on the gravel, and he caught her elbow. The glass windows of the round gazebo gleamed in the moonlight.

When she flicked on the lights, he could see that the packing crates were gone and so was the work in progress that had been sitting on the pedestal. She opened the tiny refrigerator and offered him a beer, which he accepted without a word.

Carrying it in his hand, he wandered around the studio,

opening cupboards, looking under the worktables. The only clay present was in new, plastic-wrapped gray packages. There were no busts and no skulls. He leaned against the worktable.

"Kitty called, didn't she? Where are the skulls?"

"I gave them back to Mr. Koranda. They were police property."

"How did you do that? Koranda is dead."

"I gave them to him before he died."

It was a lie, and they both knew it. The sculpture in progress had been there only yesterday. Lillian must have been using a skull for a model, but Grabowski couldn't prove it. He had never even seen any of the skulls. He began to pace the studio again. The skulls weren't the issue, anyway; Koranda was.

"Where were you yesterday just before I came here?" he demanded. "That was about the time Koranda's body was found in the trunk and about the time it also disappeared."

She stared at the worktable for a long moment, digesting this information. "I was shopping for a baby present."

"You have the receipt, I assume."

"I never found the right gift."

Another dead end. Grabowski perched on the stool by the pedestal, intrigued. What did this rich woman have to do with a debauched police officer, except to use him as a procurer for her models? "How did you know that you could get skulls from Sergeant Koranda?" he demanded.

"My husband told me. At one time Koranda provided a few cadavers for the medical school. Strictly legal. He was happy enough to help me out, too."

"How often did you do this happy thing?"

Her lips tightened at his sarcasm. "A few times. Kitty picked up one box; I picked up the others at a mutually agreed-upon spot."

She was more confident now. Why? Grabowski sipped his beer and considered how he might have got off the track.

"Strange coincidence," he said, "you buying skulls from

him, then his body turning up in a trunk at your gallery. Did he ever come to the gallery?"

"I can't imagine why he would."

"You have a limited imagination for an artist." Grabowski was losing his temper. These frail-looking women had nerves of steel. And the motivation was still a complete mystery. Why would either Lillian or Kitty kill a crime lab guard when the man was providing the very source material Lillian needed? Grabowski had had it. He needed sleep. "Expect to hear from me tomorrow," he said abruptly, and found his way out.

CHAPTER

20

ROLONDO APPEARED AT the ER at midnight, responding to a call from St. Clair. She needed to talk to his employees at the apartment at Fifth and Center.

Work in the ER had been steady since she got back from Syzinski's room, and she hadn't had a chance to call the charge nurse, as she intended, to find out if Syzinski's recovery was continuing. He had looked pale after doing the drawings. She hadn't realized that drawing required such power of concentration. The intensity of the effort had sapped his energy.

At midnight she turned over the charts of the two remaining patients to Dr. Malech, and she and Shirley followed Rolondo outside into the steamy night air. Shirley was scowling.

"You're not going to that apartment on Center Street at night," she said, climbing into the backseat of the Cadillac. "You got beat on there once. It's not safe to go back."

"Don't be silly," said St. Clair. "I'm with Rolondo. The women at his apartment will make a quick identification, then Rolondo will take me home. I have to go now—night is when everyone is there, working."

As the car started to pull away from the curb, Joella came running up and banged on the window. "Some guy named Ivan just called," she said. "Wants you to call him right away, either at the lab or at home. He also asked me out. Who is this guy?"

Shirley gave up arguing with St. Clair as the Caddy

pulled out of the parking lot. "Take me home," she muttered and fell asleep. She barely woke up long enough to walk from the car to her darkened house.

There were no lights visible from the apartment on Fifth and Center, but St. Clair knew that wasn't because everyone there was asleep. The shades were down to hide the muted light.

As Rolondo promised, Rosa and the other girls were waiting for her in the living room, their heavily made-up faces theatrical in the red light from the lamp shades. St. Clair held out the sketch of Kitty Zelazak and the second sketch—the one of Lillian Hochstedder she had taken from Syzinski's room earlier that evening. The women looked at them steadily, passed them from hand to hand. They all shook their heads.

"Neither woman visited Wyoming across the hall?" St. Clair demanded. "You're sure? Wait," she thought suddenly. "Here's a photograph of them on the gallery brochure. Maybe you'll recognize them better."

She dug the opening night brochure from her purse and held it out.

The reaction was quick. "She's the one," Rosa said, handing back the brochure. "Hard to miss that shiny black hair. It looks waxed. And those cheekbones sticking out like knives. What does she live on, carrots?"

St. Clair tucked the brochure back into her shoulder bag.

"We also figured out where Latoya got that chocolate candy," said Rosa. "She got it across the hall."

St. Clair didn't speak all the way home. Rolondo drove silently, not even turning on his stereo, letting her think in peace. They crossed the river and turned north on Prospect. The Cadillac floated up the nearly deserted street where the few parked cars didn't slow their progress.

"Say," said Rolondo suddenly. "Isn't that the car of your friend the cop?"

St. Clair twisted in her seat. A dusty green Plymouth was parked in front of a tall condominium building. "What's he doing there at this hour?" she blurted.

Rolondo looked steadily ahead.

At her apartment, she nodded good night to Rolondo, then crossed the silent lawn and climbed the dark stairs. The night light Grabowski had installed at the top landing was on, showing there was no one standing there to mug her, as had happened six months before. The living room was empty, and so were the kitchen and bedroom. Normally, she felt a wave of comfort walking into the soft yellow light of the Oriental lamps, but tonight she barely noticed. She went straight to the phone and dialed Ivan's lab. When there was no answer, she dialed his home. A woman answered the phone.

"Just a minute, he's tied up." The woman laughed.

St. Clair pictured the scene. Ivan favored red satin sheets, but bondage? In a few minutes he came to the phone, out of breath.

"Maxene, my sweet, we couldn't find any of the normal toxins so I looked for INH. You were wrong. There was INH in that candy."

"Impossible."

"Nothing's impossible, sweet; ask my friend here. Listen, a Milwaukee doctor was at the lab today, wearing a white coat like he still worked there. I can't think of his name, but he was doing research the same year you were. Remember him?"

"Lots of people did research there with me." She hung up. Why was INH in the candy? Did the girl really have TB and pushed the capsule in the candy to help it go down easier? Aaron Simonson said he hadn't tested for TB, but in the autopsy report, he noted that he had frozen some lung samples and stored them in his freezer. He could do a tissue smear and test for TB. She dialed the hospital, but the switchboard said he had gone home.

She hung up the phone, puzzled. She paced uneasily from kitchen to bedroom to living room, sipping a beer, then eating a container of yogurt. Maybe Louie knew something that would pull this together. Louie might even tell her where he was when she was finding Koranda's body in the trunk.

She stomped down the back steps and banged on Louie's kitchen door. After a few seconds, she tried the knob. Unlocked. The light was on in the bathroom.

"Louie?" she called, tapping on the bathroom door.

It swung open. Louie was curled up on the bathroom floor in the fetal position. The room smelled like vomit. She shook his arm hard, then felt for a pulse on his limp wrist. Slow and difficult to find. She knelt beside him and tried to count his respirations, but they were slow and his chest moved too slightly for her to be certain she was counting right.

"Louie!" She lifted his head and pushed him to a seated position, but his body slid back to the floor, limp. She hurried to the phone. The ambulance arrived in less than ten minutes.

Grabowski wasn't home yet, she discovered, letting his phone ring twenty times as she watched the medics start the respirator and the IVs. She left a message at the police switchboard to beep him, then grabbed her purse and followed the stretcher out to the ambulance.

"Take him to St. Agnes," she said, climbing into the back after the stretcher.

"No need to come, Dr. St. Clair," said one of the medics, strapping Louie's stretcher into place.

St. Clair sat firmly on the empty stretcher opposite. "You fellows are doing a super job," she said, "but I made the mistake twice in the last week of not following through, and I'm not making it again. Besides, I have something to do at St. Agnes."

The ER was empty when the medics wheeled Louie into the bright white room. Dr. Malech took one look at St. Clair's grim face and pulled her aside to ask what happened.

"Louie isn't a stable person," she explained, "and someone he was close to died recently. I think he overdosed on something, no telling what."

She picked up the phone and dialed Grabowski at home. Still no answer. She called his switchboard and left another message for him to call the hospital.

The elevator was held up on another floor, so St. Clair took the stairs to Wyoming's room, surprised to find herself running. Wyoming was sleeping, his breathing barely audible even in the intensely quiet room. At the nurse's station St. Clair flipped through the chart to see what time the last vital signs were taken. "Ten o'clock vitals?" she asked. She must have spoken sharply because the nurse stood up and reached for a slip of paper in her uniform pocket.

"Midnight, actually," she corrected. "The nurse's aide took the vitals, and I haven't recorded her notes yet." She read the piece of paper and her eyes widened. She dropped the paper on the desk and hurried down the hall to his room.

St. Clair read over the numbers on the paper, then flipped to the medication chart, and then to the progress notes where the visitors' names were noted. With rising alarm, she hurried into Syzinski's room.

He was sleeping too heavily. The pulse under her fingers had dropped to half the normal level, and his respirations were barely readable. She pried back an eyelid. Unresponsive.

"Get a respirator in here," St. Clair snapped. "Call Code Red."

In less than two minutes, the crash cart was wheeling out of ICU, the resident was inserting the respirator tube, and the nurse was injecting medication to raise the blood pressure into the IV tubing.

St. Clair watched until she felt confident that Syzinski's condition was under control; then she called the ER. Louie was doing better, too; he was on his way upstairs to the ICU. She followed the nurses wheeling Wyoming back to ICU where the staff were preparing a bed for Louie.

"Call a pulmonary consultant?" the ICU nurse asked.

"No, the chief resident and I will handle this. In fact, leave orders that no one else is to see either of these patients except by my express orders. That includes specialists, other residents, interns, and medical students. Tell the chief resident to call me if he wants to do anything. Put the two patients next to each other and in full view of the ICU staff at all times. And if Detective Grabowski calls, let him know the status of both patients."

She wrote out Grabowski's name and home phone number, then went down to Aaron Simonson's lab.

The double doors were locked, but a quick call to security let her in. She flipped on all the lights and turned down the guard's offer to stay with her.

Aaron Simonson's freezer was as tidy as the pathologist was slovenly. She found the plastic box labeled Latoya Thompson, and inside it the baggies containing body organs. The baggie with lung tissue samples was labeled in red. She put the rest of the box contents back and stood looking at the baggie with the pink lung sample in her hand. Fifteen years ago she had done gram stains, and as far as she knew, the laboratory method hadn't changed. She put on a pair of latex gloves and settled down to work.

Half an hour later, she sat back in the chair. There, in front of her, was proof plain as day. The red stain she had added had settled deeply into the tissues and stayed even when she tried to rinse it out. Latoya Thompson definitely had died with tuberculosis growing in her lungs.

She cleaned up the mess and went upstairs to ICU. Louie was barely awake and groggy.

"Can he talk?" she asked the ICU nurse.

"He's weak as a kitten, but I suppose so."

"Listen to me, Louie," St. Clair said. "This is critical. Where did you go after you called me to come to your shop the day I found the policeman's body in the trunk?"

Louie's voice was hoarse. "Don't tell Grabowski or I'm ruined."

St. Clair made no promises. "The facts, Louie."

"South Milwaukee. A carpenter there makes antiques— old-world workmanship, fabulous stuff, looks hundreds of years old. After I called you, Rosalyn took a call from them. They told her there was an emergency."

"What emergency?"

"Ros thought the bunko squad had caught up with me, but when I got there, it was a false alarm."

"Louie," she said, taking his hand. "What pills did you take tonight?"

"Allergy pills, my usual. Ros and Kitty and I went out for coffee at the tearoom; then I came home," he whispered.

St. Clair called a taxi to take her home. As it pulled up to the lobby entrance, the receptionist came out with a message slip.

"Call some guy named Ivan," the receptionist panted. "Here's his home number. He asked me out. Who is this person?"

Back at her apartment, she phoned ICU. The nurse said both Louie and Wyoming were better; their vital signs were improving, and Louie had stopped vomiting. According to the chart, Grabowski had called in and been given the news. St. Clair had given her home phone number and crawled into bed. She sat propped against the pillows with the light on, blue sheet pulled over her legs. A moth fluttered against the lamp shade.

The house felt lonely without Louie downstairs. A few things were making some sense, but not enough to make anything fit. The phone rang.

"I thought of the person's name," Ivan said, yawning into the receiver. "It struck me, right in the middle of, well, doing something else. Hochstedder. Remember him? He was losing hair before I was."

St. Clair sat thinking. "Tell me," she said. "What color do you use to label your tissue samples?"

"Red."

St. Clair hung up. Now she knew why Latoya had died of an overdose of isoniazid, why she didn't have TB, and why Wyoming was gunned down. She also knew what was wrong with Wyoming and why he had been gunned down on the street. But why would someone resort to such violence? She wanted desperately to talk to Grabowski, but Grabowski was busy somewhere on Prospect, his police car immune from the ban against parking on the street from two A.M. to six A.M.

The green digits on her clock clicked away the minutes—three minutes, four minutes. The phone rang.

"Grabowski!" she shouted, but the caller was Rosalyn Mueller. Her voice was clear and assertive, but worried.

"I heard Louie was in the hospital," she said, after identifying herself. "Is he all right?"

"He's fine. News travels fast. How did you know?"

"Detective Grabowski called in for his messages while he was here, and that was one of them."

So that's where Grabowski had been while his car was parked on Prospect. Was he actually involved with her? St. Clair forced her voice to remain friendly.

"Did Grabowski tell you what happened?" she asked Rosalyn.

"He said Louie overdosed on something. Is that right?"

St. Clair debated whether to say. She didn't have actual proof and besides, she wasn't sure it was advisable to spread hunches. "I'm not sure," she said. "I found him nearly unconscious. We pumped out his stomach, and we're treating him with basic life support until his body handles whatever he ingested."

Rosalyn let a few seconds go by to digest the news. "He overdosed on Valium last year when he and Soren had a falling-out," said Rosalyn. "Did he do it again, because of Soren's death?"

St. Clair pretended to be surprised. "I knew Louie was involved with someone, but I didn't know it was Soren."

"Soren liked to keep his liaisons quiet, so he could have more than one at a time. Since I knew Soren and Louie both, I saw what was happening. Soren led Louie along, made him think he was a special friend, even led him on as a lover. Then he dumped him, and Louie went under. I tried to warn Louie, but he was completely infatuated."

"I found Louie that night," St. Clair remembered, "just like I found him tonight."

Rosalyn's voice became more urgent. "Keep a watch on Louie. He's out of control. He cut the wire that dropped the sculpture onto Soren."

"What!" St. Clair shouted.

"Soren had started working his nasty magic again, and Louie was completely sucked in. Louie worshipped the rat; he would do anything for him. He was in heaven when Soren let him help hang the exhibit. Then just before the opening, Louie saw Soren and Kitty in the back making love. Soren is very imaginative in that area."

"But Kitty told me her affair with Soren was over."

"Nothing was ever over, for Soren. For him, the reconquest was as fun as the conquest. He got Kitty alone before the show, the poor, naive woman. I think he did it then to torment Louie. It worked."

"But Louie wouldn't kill anybody," St. Clair protested.

"Louie was betrayed twice by Soren, and nothing is more devastating than being betrayed. Louie trusted Soren with his emotions; then Soren made a fool of him. For that, anyone would let a sculpture do the dirty work. Poetic justice."

"It can't be," St. Clair said, "I have to think." She hung up.

It was all laid out before her; all the players, all the performances. The sculpture fell, Wyoming was shot, and Latoya was poisoned—all on the same night. Wyoming knew Latoya and Rosa. Wyoming knew Lillian and Kitty. Was Wyoming somehow connected to Soren Berendorf? There was only one thing left to prove.

CHAPTER

21

ST. CLAIR CHANGED into jeans and a T-shirt and hurried down the back stairs and into Louie's kitchen. Car keys hung neatly on the hook behind the door, and a hammer and sharp clippers were lined up in a kitchen tool drawer. She tucked them into her purse and hurried out to Louie's red Karmann Ghia.

Louie's Certified Antiques & Watercolours was faintly lit from within. St. Clair hesitated on the sidewalk, wondering if she should have called Grabowski first, then decided not. He had been impossible to reach all evening anyway, having spent his time at Rosalyn's, and now he was probably at the hospital with Wyoming. She didn't want to pull him away from there. The front door unlocked easily, the door chimes tinkled, and she was inside.

A faint scent of lavender potpourri brought a pleasant sense of well-being despite the weird hour. St. Clair turned on a pink-shaded table lamp and moved through the aging furniture to Louie's kitchen. This time she kept searching through the fuse box behind the basement door until she found the light to the basement.

The trunks at the bottom of the stairs were still there, although the odor of varnish and wood restorative chemicals had faded. She stopped in their midst and compulsively opened each of the six lids, one after the other. Empty.

The door at the top of the Rhinestones Gallery stairs was unlocked. St. Clair had hoped it would be, but couldn't actually believe it, now that she stood there with her hand on the knob. She eased the door open and stepped into the darkness of Rosalyn Mueller's office.

The room was completely dark. St. Clair closed the door behind her, cutting off all the light from the basement steps, and waited to let her eyes adjust. A faint white blur from the streetlights gradually turned the blackness into furniture shapes.

Out in the main hall, the streetlights reflecting against the white walls made it possible to almost see clearly. Clinging to the railing, St. Clair climbed the winding stairs to the upstairs galleries.

The lights to the room where Lillian Hochstedder's sculptures were exhibited were just inside the door. St. Clair flipped on all of them and moved to stand amid the sculptures.

The busts surrounding her seemed like a family that resembled each other closely, a united group, calm and serene. She walked among them, studying their pointed cheekbones, sharp noses, flat ears. Their glass eyes glittered in the light and followed her as she walked. A siren floated by in the distance.

She finally picked one of the sculptures, the woman with the American Indian features. She took the shears out of her bag and raised them toward the eye socket. A repair tag tied to the handle of the sheers caught her attention. "Unable to completely remove nicks in blade," the tag read.

St. Clair stared at it. The date of the repair job was the day after the gallery opening. Had Louie's shears cut the wire that dropped the sculpture on Soren? Did Louie actually cut the wire? Her lips felt numb. Was that why he tried to commit suicide, as Rosalyn said? But if Louie had used the clippers to cut the wire, he would have destroyed them, not sent them for repairs.

Suddenly St. Clair knew what happened. It fit. She raised the clippers again to the eye socket and inserted the tips of the clippers into the clay at the base of the nostril. It was rock hard. She tapped on the bust with the shears and got a solid pottery sound. She banged harder, cracking the shiny finish. There was only one solution. She put the shears down, picked up the bust, and held it high over her head. Taking a deep breath, she smashed the clay sculpture on the wooden parquet floor.

Lines of cracks appeared all over the bust. St. Clair knelt down and peeled off a chunk. A glass eye dropped out and rolled across the floor. She shuddered but forced herself to crack off another big chunk. All of a sudden the clay broke apart and in front of her lay a human skull.

"Stop!" A voice behind her spun her around. Standing in the doorway was Lillian Hochstedder, holding a small silver gun. Her face was dead white and her hand was shaking. She braced herself against the doorjamb.

"Got it all figured out, didn't you?" said Lillian.

St. Clair rose. "Part of it," she said, cautiously. "I just wanted to make sure."

"That's what you doctors do, isn't it? Just want to make sure. Try one test, try another; then tell the person there's no hope, after a year of just wanting to make sure."

"You're talking about your eyes, aren't you?" St. Clair asked, moving slightly to get the pedestal between her and that small shaking gun barrel.

"Eye, singular. One eye. But that's all it takes, Doctor. Lose one eye, lose depth perception, lose visual perspective. One career, down the tubes. And all the damn doctors can say is, "One more test, just to make sure.""

"I thought you had a vision problem the night I saw you at the gallery. From your walk, you didn't look like you had been drinking but you fumbled the glass onto the tray and set your plate too close to the edge of the table. What happened, optical hemorrhage?"

"You're perceptive, Doctor. Most doctors don't notice anything about another person unless she is sitting in an exam room. One day I woke up and couldn't see anything but light out of one eye, and thousands of dollars later, the specialists still hadn't stopped the hemorrhage or the damage it caused to my vision. Then one day the bleeding stopped by itself, and all the specialists could say was, 'One more test, just to make sure.' I told them they were no better than witch doctors, although that's insulting the ancients."

St. Clair picked up the skull and placed it back on the pedestal. It made a small clatter. "I won't tell your secret," she promised. "But why did you do sculptures of human heads, instead of doing abstract art? Your lack of depth perception wouldn't matter with abstract art, would it?"

"That just shows how much you doctors know about art. It takes as much depth perception to create an abstract shape from an idea in the imagination as it does to create a human shape. Besides, I wanted human heads because I wanted to prove I could mold humanity into any shape I wanted, just the way doctors mold people's illnesses into any shape they want. My husband makes a diagnosis, and that becomes the truth. I make human heads, and that's my artistic truth." She drew a shaky breath, almost panting. The gun wavered.

The connection to Soren still wasn't clear to St. Clair. "Soren Berendorf didn't consider your skulls to be artistic truth, was that the problem?" she guessed.

"The bastard showed up one day at my studio and figured out I wasn't just using the skulls as models. At first he laughed. Then he called it a triumph of art over nature. The bastard was going to show my technique to the world in a wild, theatrical event—his words. He knew it would kill any chance for recognition as a real artist."

"And that's what you wanted—to be a real artist."

Lillian smiled bitterly. "I wanted to be somebody besides a doctor's wife who dabbled in art. I don't know why I was surprised when Soren decided to destroy me. That's what all powerful men do when their wives or lovers become more successful than they are."

"Is that when you decided to drop the sculpture on him?"

To St. Clair's surprise, Lillian Hochstedder laughed.

"Oh, I didn't drop it on him; he did that himself. It was part of his show—another wild theatrical event that would put him on every front page in the country. Louie got to the gallery early the morning of the opening and saw him snip that wire until it hung just by one strand. Soren probably planned to give the wire a tweak during the show and watch it drop. He didn't care that Rosalyn's insurance would be canceled, or that major sculptors might think twice about hanging their work here. So Louie told Rosalyn."

St. Clair frowned. "But Rosalyn told me that Louie cut the final wire," she said. "These clippers were in Louie's kitchen drawer with a repair tag saying that Louie dropped them off for sharpening the day of the accident."

She waited for Lillian's reaction. It was even stronger than she anticipated.

"Louie cut it?" Lillian's eyes widened. "But I thought Kitty . . ." Her voice trailed off.

St. Clair continued. "According to Rosalyn, Louie saw Kitty and Soren together before the opening, and Louie went crazy with anger that Soren had used him again."

Lillian lowered the gun. She nodded. "Soren used everyone. He used this gallery because it had a high enough ceiling to drop the sculpture and smash it flat. Maybe he even did it to get the insurance. Whatever the reason, he got himself crushed."

"But Louie is in the hospital now because somebody tried to poison him. Did one of you decide Louie was too much of a security risk?"

Lillian shook her head. "I didn't know Louie was in the hospital, but it has to be suicide. He can't stand living with himself knowing he caused that accident."

St. Clair shook her head. "I think Rosalyn isn't telling the truth. She's protecting someone. There are too many co-incidences. Wyoming is back in Intensive Care. No, Lillian, Rosalyn is protecting you. You poisoned Wyoming tonight. You didn't need to. You didn't even need to do it the first time. Wyoming isn't like Soren. Wyoming wouldn't have told anyone about your sculptures."

"He would have made me stop," said Lillian. "Men always do that. Just when women get to the edge of something great, men make us stop."

A clock downstairs chimed, three clear tones.

"You stole isoniazid from your husband's clinic and put it into a box of candy for Wyoming to eat," said St. Clair. "The trouble is, you missed your target and hurt another woman. The girl across the hall ate the candy, and she died."

"She had TB," Lillian said, "and she died of an overdose of her medication. My husband told me about the autopsy report."

"It wasn't on the autopsy report because no one tested for TB until I did," St. Clair corrected. "You told your husband how you tried to poison Wyoming, and he had to start covering for you. He had to account for the isoniazid pills by juggling his books, since the state keeps track of all the pills it hands out. Then he had to make sure the autopsy report of the girl fit the autopsy findings. So he stole a lung tissue sample infected with TB from the State Lab in Madison and swapped it for the nondiseased sample from Latoya's autopsy."

"Not guilty, Doctor," snapped Lillian. "You think I'm just another medical missus who follows her husband's career so closely that she could prescribe drugs. I know what INH is, sure, but I couldn't use it."

"That's right," St. Clair said. "You put too much in the candy. Instead of just making Latoya sick, you killed her."

She started past her toward the door, but a figure stepped out from behind Lillian.

"She knows too much," Kitty said. Her face was flushed and her eyes were wide and intense. She took the gun from Lillian's hand and pointed it at Maxene. "She's a meddler, a busybody, and she's going to keep poking around until she finds out the truth."

"You've been drinking again," Lillian said. "Give me the gun. She has no proof."

"Proof of what?" St. Clair blurted, then bit her tongue.

Kitty smiled. "You know the answer, don't you, Doctor?

You know that wire couldn't possibly have just snapped by accident, even if there was only one strand left. You know who really cut it, because you were there."

"Kitty!" Lillian snapped. "She's completely on the wrong track. You've been drinking, and you can't control your mouth."

"Ronnie told me she went up to that prostitute's room, and Ronnie said she spends her free time talking to Wyoming. We all know what that means, don't we?" said Kitty. "It means she knows there was a plan. Not only that, she's dating the detective on the case. You should be more worried, Lillian."

Lillian sat cross-legged on the floor and put her head in her hands. "One of these days Ros is going to put an end to all this, Kitty. She's warned you before."

"But Louie didn't cut the wire," St. Clair protested. "The wire was deliberately frayed, and I believe that Soren Berendorf did it, but I was the one who broke it. It snapped when I tripped over it."

Kitty burst out laughing, a high shriek. "You actually think it was an accident?"

"Yes. But it was no accident that Soren was sitting at the piano when his sculpture fell. Somebody who knew the wire was frayed handed him a drink loaded with a sedative drug, like Valium—somebody who hated him enough to enjoy the poetic justice of having him crushed by his own sculpture."

Kitty turned on Lillian and pointed the gun at her. "Like you, bitch. You thought you could become a famous sculptor until the day he laughed at how you use real skulls because you couldn't shape one if you spent the rest of your life trying. At the gallery opening he was going to smash all these skulls to let everyone know what a visual cripple you are. I think you even cut the final wire."

Lillian stood up, her face flushed. "I've seen you swimming naked in his pool like his other groupies. You thought you could become a real artist, too, if you hung around him enough. I told you all he cared about was playing with rich men's wives, but you wouldn't believe me until he said he was going to tell your husband. You were the one who cut the final wire."

Kitty raised the gun to arm's length.

"Put it away, Kitty."

It was a new voice this time, a clear, confident, no-nonsense voice from the hall. Rosalyn Mueller stepped into the light. She took the gun out of Kitty's hand with a swift gesture and tucked it into her handbag.

"Soren Berendorf is dead," she said. "His own sculpture fell on him by accident. Let's leave it at that and go home."

"But who drugged him?" Lillian quavered.

"Whether he was drugged at all is pure supposition," said Rosalyn firmly. "Even if he were, the issue is moot. He frayed the wire, it broke by accident, and he's dead." She turned on the lights in the hall and stepped back to let them leave.

CHAPTER

22

ST. CLAIR FOLLOWED Lillian and Kitty down the winding stairs, acutely aware of Rosalyn behind her. At the front door, she turned. "Could we speak just for a moment?" she asked.

Rosalyn nodded, locked the door behind the two women, and led the way to her office. St. Clair sat down in the soft leather armchair.

"You're a formidable woman," St. Clair began. "Grabowski is completely bewitched by you, and he's not easily sidetracked. You left a luxurious life to start over on your own at an age when most women are thinking about becoming grandmothers. Nothing gets past you—you're in too vulnerable a position to allow it. So I'm not surprised you knew what Soren Berendorf was planning. You must have seen him clipping the wires."

Rosalyn leaned back in her chair behind the big desk. The lamplight made sharp shadows out of her angular cheekbones.

"Louie told me," she said. "Soren didn't understand the strength of loyalty. He thought he had Louie wrapped around his finger, but Louie was burned by Soren before, and Louie was having a tough time choosing between loyalty to a past lover and loyalty to his present life. Louie's sense of wrong was also shaken. Louie was worried other people would get hurt when the sculpture fell, himself included. As soon as I saw Louie acting hyper about the sculpture just before the show, I made him tell me what he knew. It's my gallery. I should know what's going to happen."

"And that's when you drugged Berendorf."

Rosalyn looked at her for a long minute. "What makes you so sure I did?"

St. Clair forced herself to relax in the chair. "I knew your husband slightly, when he admitted patients to St. Agnes. He was a hard man when crossed, and I know what kind of obstacles he would throw in your way during your divorce. I went through a divorce myself. It took real strength for you to leave a life where you had everything you wanted, and start over on your own. But from what I have seen, you don't allow obstacles to stand in your way, and that's what Soren Berendorf tried to do."

Rosalyn smiled. "Soren was a fool. He thought his charm could get him anywhere. He liked money, and he thought I had a lot of it. I don't, but he wouldn't believe it. So he decided to punish me for holding him to his contract and cutting into his profits. He was punishing Lillian, too, for achieving some measure of success. He actually did plan to destroy her sculptures right at her own gallery opening. And poor Kitty—tormenting her was one of his favorite pastimes. The man deserved what he got."

"Did he deserve to die?"

"Ask Louie."

St. Clair shook her head. "Louie didn't clip that wire. If anyone caused the sculpture to fall, it was me when I tripped over it, but you made sure Soren Berendorf was sitting there waiting for the sculpture to fall. I couldn't understand why he didn't move, and I couldn't understand why his vital signs were so low. He wouldn't have died of his injuries if his body systems had been operating properly. Louie is in the hospital now, poisoned, because he figured out that you drugged Berendorf. Louie is all right, but I want to make sure it doesn't happen again."

"And how do you plan to do that?"

St. Clair looked at her hard. "Despite Detective

Grabowski's infatuation with you, I think he'll find his way
to the bottom of this, given some direction."

She moved toward the door.

"Hold it." Rosalyn pulled the little silver gun out of her
purse and stood up. She waved Maxene back to her chair.

"You're the wild card in this game," she said, coldly. "I
knew you were trouble the minute I saw you on opening
night hunting up dear Grabowski. Then you found the body
of that stupid crime lab policeman; then you figured out the
connection between the skulls and Lillian's vision. You're
bad luck."

St. Clair thought about what Shirley said about how luck
had nothing to do with what happened to people, that their
fate was simply accumulated choices. "Did you drug Soren
Berendorf?" she asked again.

Rosalyn smiled. "No. Someone did it for me, someone
who didn't want it known among his medical associates
that his wife was putting actual skulls of derelicts under her
sculptures. Like I said to Grabowski once, selling to a doctor is easy, whether it's art or ideas. To doctors, appearances
are reality, and doctors like to control reality, even if they
have to use drugs."

A noise in the doorway startled them both. Lillian and
Kitty were back.

"You're lying," Lillian said with hatred. "My husband
didn't drug Soren. You did."

"I didn't," Rosalyn said. "Leo did it." She smiled at
Lillian's expression. "Didn't you know, dear? Or is this one
more thing your husband kept from you, like the truth
about your eye, until even the specialists refused to do one
more test."

Lillian's face went white.

Kitty laughed. "And I suppose Lillian's dumb husband
also pushed that policeman down the basement stairs so he
broke his neck."

"No," said Rosalyn, smoothly. "He had too much to
drink and fell down the stairs."

"Then why did you shove him into a trunk if it was an accident?" St. Clair asked.

Rosalyn raised her eyebrows. "I didn't put him into the trunk. Leo Hochstedder did. I wanted to let the police handle it as an accident, but Leo was worried they might ask why a stupid police guard was at an art gallery opening. Leo saw his life as a solid, middle-aged, wealthy doctor evaporating before his eyes, so he bundled that horrid policeman into the trunk and slammed the lid."

Lillian shook her head. "You know what I think?" she said to Rosalyn. "I think you drugged Soren, and you told Leo that I did it. Leo is stodgy and lacks imagination, and he is completely devoted to his wealthy life-style. Those three things make him easily manipulated by somebody smarter than him, like you. I also think that you drugged Koranda and pushed him down the stairs. When Koranda found out how much my sculptures were selling for, he told me he was charging me more—that it would be embarrassing if my rich friends knew they were buying human skulls—and I think he did the same to you. So you killed him and made Leo help you hide the body. Poor Leo." Lillian's nerves snapped. "You killed Soren!" she shrieked at Rosalyn. "You drugged him and you cut the wire."

Rosalyn smiled. "Not me," she said. "Leo drugged him, but Kitty cut the wire." She pointed the gun at Kitty. "I saw you and so did Louie!"

"You liar!" Kitty shrieked and went for her throat.

A gun went off, but it didn't hit anybody. Grabowski had grabbed the gun out of Rosalyn's hand.

"I went to your apartment," he said to Rosalyn, "but you weren't there. Fortunately Rolondo has been keeping tabs on you all day, and he called to tell me you had come down here. Your name came up twice today—once from the Health Department TB records, and once from some women over on Fifth and Center, which Rolondo called to tell me."

Grabowski's eyes slid sideways to Maxene. He went on. "You delivered the candy meant for Wyoming, you drugged

Soren Berendorf and cut the wire, and you hit Maxene over the head in Wyoming's apartment when you were there looking for the candy box. I wouldn't be surprised if we find Koranda's body in your ex-husband's flower bed."

"You won't," Rosalyn said, smiling a smug smile. "He's under the geraniums lining the Hochstedder driveway."

CHAPTER

23

IT WAS EIGHT o'clock at night, and Maxene and Wyoming were sitting on Joseph Grabowski's front porch watching him inspect St. Clair's new car, a used Ford Taurus Sho. Grabowski opened the door, checked under the hood. He scratched his head and crunched across the desiccated lawn toward them.

"This car looks exactly like my car that was stolen," he said. "It's not the same color, and the registration number is different, but I could swear this is my car. It has the same little nick on the bumper where I hit the garbage can."

"Oh, I don't think so," Maxene stated. "Rolondo's brother gave me a good deal. He said it's a nice car for a lady, and it has hardly any miles on it."

"Rolondo's brother? That's where you bought it? My God, I paid a fortune for that car!" Grabowski slammed his drained beer bottle into the box of empties and stomped inside for more beer.

Maxene opened the pizza box with the anchovy and green pepper pizza and tore off a slice.

"I wish he weren't so paranoid about Rolondo," she said.

Syzinski changed the subject. "He's switched from beer cans to bottles," he commented. "According to him, you claim aluminum mines damage the environment. When Grabowski changes his beer-drinking habits, something serious is happening."

"I think he wants to get married," said St. Clair, staring out over the lake. The haze over Lake Michigan made the scene in front of her like a fairy tale—hazy blue sky, hazy blue water, faint cries of children on the beach.

"What do you have against being a wife? Just because you had one bad experience doesn't mean you'll have another."

"It's because the word 'wife' traditionally meant 'dependent'—it even says that on the IRS form—and I don't like being dependent. The trouble is, I'm not sure what the opposite of dependent is. Is it 'independent'? Or maybe 'undependent', as the codependents say? As far as I can tell, humans are interdependent. Anyway, I don't think a woman can feel independent when she's married, and I like being self-reliant."

Syzinski picked up a piece of pizza. "Your problem is you're afraid of a relationship. You doctors have so many pseudo-intimate relationships with so many people that you don't have energy or room for an honest connection with someone else's heart."

St. Clair scowled at him. "Look who's talking," she retorted. "Mr. Uncommitted. From what I hear, your bed is a turnstile. Why don't you mind your own business? I liked you better when you were unconscious."

Wyoming grinned. "Take it easy, redhead. It just looks to me like you and Grabowski are avoiding something that could make you both very happy."

St. Clair watched the sailboats sliding by. "Maybe you're right," she admitted. "But I hate those mood swings, the ups when he calls, the downs when he doesn't. I want a relaxed, casual relationship, where we love each other but my moods aren't so dependent on his physical proximity."

"Boring. Comfortable as an old shoe."

"And what makes you such an expert?" St. Clair flared up again. "I don't see you forging any long-term relationships."

"Guilty," Wyoming smiled. "But I avoid them because loneliness is good for artists. It makes us live on the edge and look at reality straight in the eye."

"A mere excuse for avoiding commitment," said

St. Clair. "But I know what you're talking about—that quality of being genuine. That's why you felt so strongly that Lillian had to stop putting real skulls inside her sculptures. It wasn't the illegality of her method that bothered you; it was the artistic immorality."

"Anything fake that passes for real must stop," Syzinski pronounced. "Pretending something is something it isn't destroys the art, as well as the integrity of the artist and the person looking at it."

"I suppose you gave Lillian that same speech," said Grabowski, nudging open the screen door with his toe and carrying out an armload of Labatt's Blue. He lined the bottles up in the cooler.

"No," said Syzinski, "I gave that speech to Rosalyn when she brought her present of poisoned candy to my apartment and lectured me about why I should let Lillian pretend her sculptures were all her own creation. Lillian already knew my philosophy on the subject when she took my drawing class in Arizona. I phoned Lillian when I got to Milwaukee, and she promptly told Rosalyn that I would expose her method for coping with her vision problem."

"Explain Lillian's vision problem," said Grabowski to St. Clair. He took two pieces of pizza, folded them over, and shoved half of it into his mouth.

St. Clair watched the process with awe. "She had a retinal hemorrhage, meaning a blood vessel broke inside one eye, and the bleeding in the nerve fiber took away her vision in that eye. Sometimes vision returns as the bleeding subsides and the blood is absorbed, but hers didn't. The point is, with vision in only one eye, she had no depth perception, and sculpting from a model became impossible. She could have trained herself to calculate depth by other means, like comparing larger and smaller objects, but she remembered enough about the forensic sculpture class you taught in Arizona to figure out a different method—one that worked in such a spectacular way that she built her career on it."

Grabowski looked at Syzinski. "I have a feeling she had

some personal instruction when she was in Arizona, maybe saw the clay models of skulls that are sitting around your house?"

Wyoming smiled.

St. Clair decided not to comment. "I thought of the possibility after you told me about your class one night in the hospital. I called the school in Arizona and got the name of one of your students. He explained the process."

"You two spent a lot of time chatting in the hospital, didn't you?" said Grabowski, looking at Wyoming and Maxene.

Syzinski cuffed him on the shoulder. "Relax, pal. If we hadn't, Maxene wouldn't have figured out to ask the girls at the apartment to look at the sketches of Lillian and Kitty, and she wouldn't have called the school in Arizona to find out that both Kitty and Lillian were students."

"The picture they recognized was on the gallery brochure," said St. Clair. "It was Rosalyn."

Grabowski nodded. "I knew what had happened when a friend from the Health Department Tuberculosis Clinic called and said Rosalyn had TB as a teenager, diagnosed during a routine school skin test. Rosalyn was treated by a private doctor, but she must have learned all there was to know about INH, including what an overdose does to people. She helped Lillian put the plan together. She took back her maiden name when she was divorced, and Felicia at the TB Clinic recognized the name."

"So who exactly dropped the sculpture on Soren Berendorf?" Syzinski demanded.

Grabowski threw up his hands. "It was a coalition," he said. "Berendorf frayed the wire himself, for various purposes. Louie saw him and told Rosalyn."

"Who told Lillian," added St. Clair. "They deliberately didn't tell Kitty because she was unstable, especially regarding Berendorf. But Kitty figured it out herself, listening to Berendorf brag about the big sensation he was planning for the exhibition."

Grabowski nodded. "Then Rosalyn dumped Valium into Berendorf's Sailor's Delight punch."

"Leo didn't do it?" St. Clair asked.

"Not at all, although the poor slob did help Rosalyn put Koranda's body into the trunk because she told him his wife clipped the wire."

"But who really clipped the wire?" Wyoming demanded again.

Grabowski frowned. "So far, no one has admitted doing it. Louie thought he saw Kitty cutting the wire, but she could have been just examining it, like she said."

"And Lillian?" Syzinski asked.

St. Clair answered. "I don't think Lillian cut the wire. Lillian was too expert at getting other people to take risks for her. For example, instead of learning how to deal with her failed visual perception, she put clay over real skulls. Instead of picking up the skulls from Koranda, she got Kitty to do it. Instead of going herself to Wyoming's apartment with the candy, she got Rosalyn to do it. Then she got her husband to start covering up for her."

Grabowski asked her, "How did you figure this out?"

"I got a call from an old friend in Madison, who said he saw Leo Hochstedder in the State Board of Health lab. Leo was wearing a white lab coat. As soon as I heard that, I remembered the lung tissue sample I had found in the pathology freezer that I thought came from the autopsy that Aaron Simonson did on Latoya at his pathology lab at St. Agnes'. The lung sample was bright pink."

"And?"

"Latoya practically lived on cigarettes; there would be gray patches on her lung samples. When I was doing research at the State Board of Health we joked about how easy it would be to swap samples from the freezers there. As soon as Ivan told me he saw Leo Hochstedder on the premises, I knew that Leo was swapping samples."

"Who is Ivan?" said Syzinski, raising his eyebrows.

"I'll introduce you," answered St. Clair. "You'll hit it off immediately."

"But how did this all get started?" Wyoming asked.

Grabowski answered. "It was a chain of events: you arrived in town, Koranda demanded more money for the skulls or he'd spill the beans, and Berendorf decided to make an event out of cracking open the sculptures. Lillian freaked out and told her husband what was inside her clay busts. A lot of Leo's medical cohorts had bought her sculptures, and Leo couldn't face them, knowing they had bought an actual skull. Then he found out Lillian had doctored the chocolates to keep Wyoming from coming to the gallery opening. Leo thought that was a great idea, but when they discovered that Wyoming hadn't eaten the chocolates, Leo hired somebody to mug Wyoming. He had no idea the criminal he hired would shoot him, and when he found out from you at the gallery how serious the injuries were, he freaked. He was already in a state of shock from helping Rosalyn bundle Koranda into the chest."

"I hadn't even planned to come to the opening," said Wyoming, putting his feet up on the railing. "They should have asked; I would have saved them a lot of trouble."

St. Clair watched the last traces of light rinse out of the sky. "So my tripping over the wire really did drop that sculpture," she said quietly.

Grabowski put his hand on her shoulder. "I think Kitty Zelazak did it," he said. "The problem is, I can't prove it. She plain hated the man. She knew he clipped the wire himself, and she knew Rosalyn had drugged him. She tried to talk to him at the piano, but he was half-asleep. As far as I can reconstruct the time, she left him at the piano and within three minutes the wire snapped. All it took was a nail file behind her back while she leaned against the wall."

St. Clair sighed, a weight lifting off her shoulders. She accepted the beer Grabowski held out. He tightened his fingers over hers.

"Did you ever find out what Louie was up to, while you were finding the body of the crime lab guard?" he asked.

St. Clair laughed. "The sap was led astray by Rosalyn, like a few other people. Rosalyn called Leo Hochstedder to bring his van to pick up Koranda's body, but she couldn't get rid of Louie long enough to transfer the body. Louie's nerves were on edge, and he was afraid to leave her for a minute, worried about what else she might do. To get rid of Louie, she said the carpenters in South Milwaukee who make Louie's fake antiques wanted him immediately. Louie left, completely forgetting I was coming. He wouldn't tell us where he went, because he still thinks Grabowski doesn't know he fakes his antiques." She reached over and gave Grabowski's hand a squeeze.

Syzinski promptly stood up. "Bedtime for invalids," he said. "I'm going to sleep." He stomped noisily to the back bedroom and slammed the door.

Two crazed frogs were croaking back and forth from the small fishpond in the neighbor's yard, louder and louder.

"What do you suppose those frogs are saying?" St. Clair yawned, stretching.

Grabowski put his arms around her and held her tight. "I want you, I want you, I want you," he said into her hair.

Maxene St. Clair smiled.

The doctor's wife may have been playing
at prostitution, but she wasn't playing dead.

Read all about it in

EMERGENCY MURDER
by
Janet McGiffin.

❖≫∞≪❖

Published by Fawcett Books.